Praise for

An Act

"Debut author Angela introduces a charming amateur sleuth, fun and well read. She so lovingly describes the town of Copper Bluff that readers can feel the breeze and smell the autumn leaves. Cozy enthusiasts who like Joanne Dobson and Sarah R. Shaber will dive into this new series."
—Viccy Kemp, *Library Journal*, Sept. 1, 2016

4 Stars: "The most unexpected solution proves to be the right one in this cozy debut by Angela. Set in Copper Bluff, S.D., this novel portrays small-town college life to a tee. Her suspects are varied, but apparent motives are slim as she teases the reader. Em is a force all her own and bodes well for this new series."
—Donna M. Brown, *RT Magazine*

4.5 Stars (Voted Book of the Month by LASR Readers): "The plot is believable and the supporting characters are fun and have quirky traits all their own. The mystery itself, which provides the core of the plot, constantly keeps the reader guessing [….] A fantastic read and a lot of fun!"
—Stargazer for *Long and Short Reviews*

"In this deftly executed, literate, and *literary* novel—the first in the Professor Prather mystery series—author Mary Angela introduces us to her delightfully quirky, fiercely intelligent, and immensely *likable* protagonist, English professor Emmeline Prather, along with an eclectic roster of colorful characters populating the small college town of Copper Bluff, South Dakota. With the help of her charmingly laid-back colleague,

Professor Lenny Jenkins, Emmeline applies her keen and rigorous eye for comma splices and split infinitives to a series of clues in the troubling death of her student, Austin Oliver—taking us on a madcap and rivetingly engaging series of plot twists as Emmeline discovers that not only does she have a knack for literature, she also has a knack for solving murders."
—Lee Ann Roripaugh, South Dakota State Poet Laureate

"*An Act of Murder* offers a loving description of a quiet, rural campus set amidst natural beauty, gentle, satiric gibes at faculty members who richly deserve it, and the puzzling death of a student. Professor Emmeline Prather is an unlikely detective: young and attractive, a chocoholic and a bit of a klutz, she tries to maintain a relatively low profile. But when she suspects her student has been murdered, she becomes a veritable bulldog, fiercely determined to uncover the perpetrator. Mary Angela's debut novel maintains the suspense until the last few pages and creates a delightful new character for a series that is certain to entertain. I look forward to accompanying Professor Prather on her next adventure."
—Susan Wolfe, Professor Emerita of English

"A deftly crafted novel of unexpected twists and surprising turns, *An Act of Murder* clearly establishes author Mary Angela as an impressively skilled and original storyteller. Certain to be an enduringly popular addition to community library Mystery/Suspense collections, *An Act of Murder* will leave dedicated mystery buffs looking eagerly toward the next Professor Emmeline Prather adventure!"
—Margaret Lane for *The Midwest Book Review*

"The idea that I would distinctly remember characters that make one brief appearance speaks to Angela's ability to bring the people of *An Act of Murder* to life. Angela does a fabulous job of creating a college campus that feels so real. The

descriptions of buildings, students, off-campus spots are just so perfect...they'll take every college graduate back to their days on campus [....] This is a fun book and ideal for autumn reading."
—Jodi Webb, *Building Bookshelves Blog*

5 Stars: "A well-written and imaginative tale of a teacher whose determination to get to the truth and see justice done for one of her students is right on the money. Mary Angela's debut novel in this intriguing whodunit series had me glued to every single page, determined to spot any clues to try to solve the mystery of the killer's identity before the end. With so many people to choose from, I was shocked when all of the evidence pointed to somebody I had not considered a real contender, and I applaud Mary Angela's technique in presenting such a complex tale. Each of the characters was realistic and engaging, making *An Act of Murder* a real joy to read."
—Rosie Malezer for *Readers' Favorite Book Reviews*

"What a treat it was to read a cozy mystery with such vivid descriptions that place you in the center of the story. There were times I felt like I was sitting in the student hangout and listened in on their conversations. I loved everything about Emmeline, from her directness, attention to details and a never give up attitude[....] The author really knows how to write with twists that shake up the story with surprise and excellent snippets of intrigue. [....] The ending was explosive with secrets that will leave you hanging on the edge of your seat ."
—*Texas Book-aholic*

"An enjoyable cast of cozy characters in a delightful setting. Emmeline (Em) Prather is an English professor in Copper Bluff, South Dakota. I absolutely adore Emmeline. She is a perfect cozy sleuth. The setting is just wonderful."
—*Brooke Blogs*

“There are numerous interesting angles and twists and turns in *An Act of Murder* that make it a most enjoyable read.”
—*Back Porchervations*

“Prather is a sympathetic and entertaining protagonist, and the little college town of Copper Bluff, South Dakota, is beautifully drawn. Mary Angela does a wonderful job at portraying small-town academia, and I am looking forward to Emmeline Prather’s next adventure.”
—*Island Confidential*

“Author Mary Angela paints beautiful word pictures of Copper Bluff—the town and the campus. I can clearly picture both of them in my mind.... [She] has created a cast of memorable characters, headed up by the quirky Emmeline Prather the Instigator, and her stalwart sidekick Lenny Jenkins. I love their witty repartee.”
—*Jane Reads*

“Mary Angela has begun her new mystery series with a home run. *An Act of Murder* is a cozy tale with a fun and well-read heroine, English professor Emmeline Prather. Set in a college town, the swiftly paced plot takes readers through several twists and turns. Professor Prather collects a handful of clues as she pieces together the motive, means, and opportunity to solve a puzzling murder. Her colleague and sidekick Lenny Jenkins is a charming character who may become a love interest in future installments. I look forward to adding Angela’s future books to my list of must-read murder mysteries.”
—Colleen J. Shogan, author of the Washington Whodunit mysteries

“There were so many times I could almost feel the chill of the wind or picture the breeze in the trees against the brick of the old buildings and I love when authors can create that setting

for their reader. Author Mary Angela does this beautifully and with the mystery element added to this quaint little town I found myself enjoying every part of this story. Quill says: A wonderful first mystery novel that has me wanting to read more."
—Kristi Benedict for *Feathered Quill Book Reviews*

"This series is off to a great start. The mystery is complicated and believable. The characters are real with plenty of room to evolve. The setting is intriguing with a huge pool of people to draw into future stories. Mary Angela is an author to watch. I am excited about upcoming installments to this story."
—*Escape with Dollycas*

"Emmeline is this character that you love because she just seems like a real person. I found her quirks and passions to be similar to mine (Hello, France anyone?) which made me feel a friendship with her. In fact, all the characters are this way. You just love many of the professors. The mystery was great, and set up nicely. I found that the book just flowed into the mystery. It held great clues, but twists that kept you guessing."
—Bree Herron, for *Bibliophile Reviews*

"The story is well written, full of twists and very addictive. [...] This was a great read that left me turning the pages, eager to know what was going to happen next."
—*LibriAmoriMiei*

Passport to MURDER

Passport to MURDER

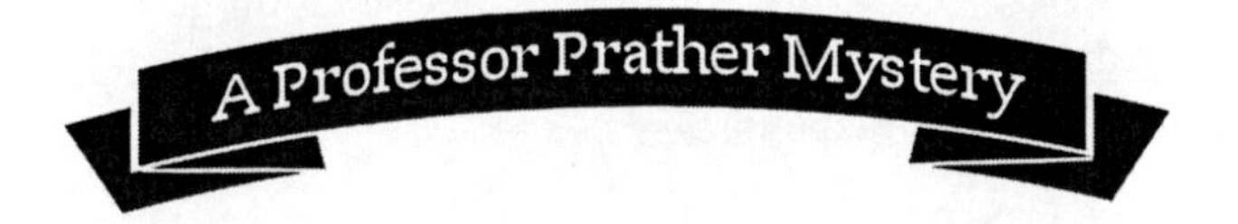

MARY ANGELA

Seattle, WA

CAMEL
PRESS

Camel Press
PO Box 70515
Seattle, WA 98127

For more information go to: www.camelpress.com
www.maryangelabooks.com

Cover design by Tony Astone

Passport to Murder

ISBN: 978-1-60381-653-3 (Trade Paper)
ISBN: 978-1-60381-654-0 (eBook)

Library of Congress Control Number: 2017943406

Printed in the United States of America

Acknowledgments

I AM MUCH indebted to the first important teachers in my life, my mom and dad. Their belief in great things made great things possible. Thank you, Mom, for your willingness to read and discuss everything and anything. I dedicate this book to you.

Although I write new chapters, some things remain the same, such as my husband's unwavering support. Thank you, Quintin. Our family and your love mean everything.

Madeline and Maisie, I am so proud to be your mom. Thank you for being my biggest (and prettiest!) cheerleaders.

The end of the semester coincided with the end of this book, and I had to call in reading reinforcements. Thank you to Amy Cecil Holm, Samantha Engberg, and Elena Hartwell for your willingness to drop everything and proofread my work. Your friendship means a lot.

To my family, friends, and readers, thank you for reading and reviewing. Your encouragement makes all the difference.

Thank you to the Minneapolis Airport Police for allowing me to tour the airport facility and ask suspicious questions while I researched this book. Despite my enthusiasm for murder, you believed I meant no harm.

Finally, a special thank you goes out to Camel Press for publishing this series and to Catherine Treadgold, Jennifer McCord, and Rebecca Eskildsen for supporting my work and ideas. Your considerable help, advice, and revisions are indispensible, and I am incredibly grateful for all that you do.

Chapter One

SPRING WAS CAUSE enough for celebration on the Great Plains, let alone a trip to Paris. When the first green shoots of crocuses pushed their way through the melting mounds of snow, people packed away their fur-lined parkas and donned sweatshirts and hoodies, taking to the fresh air like inmates on furlough. It didn't matter if the day was cold, gray, or windy; the parkas would not return. To bring them back out of storage would only contradict a day on the calendar that would be kept come hell, high water—or the inevitable spring snowstorm.

But snow was nowhere in sight today. It was a bright blue Friday morning I could only describe as cornflower, and I dismissed my stocking cap and gloves with a flick of my wrist. After they tumbled across my porch table and onto the floor with a soft thud, my calico cat, Dickinson, immediately seized them for investigation. Her claws were making short work of the stitching on my hat when I closed the front door, but I didn't bother to stop her. If she turned it into a great ball of yarn, I would be only too happy to roll it in catnip for her and consider it recycled. The winter had been that bad.

It was early morning, and the air was frosty, yet a promise

of warmth lingered in the doorway. I stood for a moment on my steps and inhaled deeply. Then I was off down the street, smiling and thinking of *Mrs. Dalloway.*

"What a lark! What a plunge!" I exclaimed.

"Good morning, Emmeline," said Mrs. Gunderson, my next-door neighbor. Her voice gave me such a start that one of my tan flats skidded out in front of me, setting off a cramp in my calf. When I grew weary of my episodes of insomnia, I reminded myself of Mrs. Gunderson. If she slept, I didn't know when. Although she was in her seventies, it wasn't beyond her to shovel the walkway at five thirty in the morning. If one was up, one might as well get something *done.*

"Mrs. Gunderson, I didn't see you there. Is it planting time already?"

Mrs. Gunderson stepped away from the bushes under her front window. Her white hair was arranged in neat, uniform rolls that covered her entire head, and her pink lipstick shone brightly against her powdered face. This was the other remarkable thing about Mrs. Gunderson: she was more put together than someone half her age—mainly me. "Oh heavens no, dear. It's only mid-March. My bulbs need a little help, that's all. What with this winter, it's a miracle they're alive."

I shook off my leg cramp. "It was one for the books. That's for certain."

For five months, the snow had buried the small town of Copper Bluff, South Dakota, in great piles that sat at the edges of parking lots, growing muddier and murkier with each passing day. During the entire month of January, the temperature never rose above zero, bringing activity in the town to a near stop. The first day of bad weather, the university canceled classes. The second day, too. But on the third day, classes resumed, and students resorted to wearing ski masks and mittens and all the things mothers bundle their elementary children with. In a way, January had humbled us all.

By now the sun had melted away most of the snow, and there

was talk of flowers—and spring break. A smile spread across my face, and I knew I had to keep moving if I were to avoid questions by my nosy neighbor.

"Have a good day," I called to Mrs. Gunderson as I continued walking toward campus, my spring coat swinging back and forth at my hips.

"You too, dear," she replied, watching me leave.

Being an English professor, I usually stayed home during spring break, using the time to catch up on grading papers. But this year, I was scheduled to go to France with a group of students and André Duman. My smile grew wider at the thought of it. It wasn't exactly "April in Paris," like the old tune sung by Billie Holiday, but it was close enough.

André was a French professor who had gone to great lengths to apply for a grant to travel abroad to his native country. While the seven-day trip would cost each participant $2,150, due the first of January, the costs for two professors would be compensated by the grant. The price might seem steep to a college student, until you considered that it included transportation, hotel, two dinners, lecture fees, and event tickets in one of the most expensive cities in the world. André had also managed to obtain discounted Paris museum passes for the students and arranged for a group tour of his beloved Sorbonne University. As the only other professor fluent in French, I was the natural choice to accompany him and the students. He was the faculty coordinator, and I was assistant coordinator. We were to leave tomorrow from Minneapolis, which had the closest international airport, and I was over-the-moon excited.

Ever since I was a young child, I had wanted to travel to France. My great-great-grandmother had been born and raised in St. Emilion, and although I knew little about my ancestor (except that we shared a name, Emmeline) and even less about St. Emilion, I imagined I would feel an immediate connection the moment I stepped on French soil. My father blamed my romanticism on my mother. She, after all, had named me. If I'd had a good, sturdy name like Mary, he said, I would have stayed in Detroit, my hometown, and become a nice high school teacher like my mother. I disagreed with him completely. First of all, high school had comprised the worst years of my life, and second, Detroit was a tough town to get lost in. The city streets always reminded me where I was. From an early age, they instilled in me a reality from which no amount of fiction could ever help me escape for long.

But Copper Bluff was as easy to disappear in as a big fluffy cloud. There wasn't much in town except the university campus and a handful of stores, and I could wander among those without bumping up against any of the predicaments that plagued other cities. Open-minded people with ideas congregated here. It was a safe haven for intellectuals and other dreamers, and the townspeople revered their city not for its smallness but for its autonomy. It was as distinct in its differences as other towns in their sameness.

As I crossed the street to the campus, I focused on my morning class, creative writing. The only reason I was teaching it this semester was because Claudia Swift was on sabbatical. She and her husband, Gene, were on a couples' cruise in Italy. If all went as planned, their yearlong standoff would end and their marriage vows would be renewed. I couldn't wait to hear about the trip. She was a terrific storyteller and one of my closest friends.

"Well you're looking chipper today, Emmeline," said Jane Lemort, our medievalist scholar, as she joined me on the walking path. She was wearing a long black skirt and a dark wool coat and looked like an inky splotch against the cornflower day.

"It must be the weather," I said. "It's nice to see the sun, isn't it?"

She was keeping pace with me now. "I thought it might

be that trip to Paris tomorrow that has you grinning like the Cheshire Cat."

"Am I grinning like the Cheshire Cat? How unflattering," I said with a laugh.

"Em Prather," a deep voice behind us said, "You are the picture of spring in that blue coat."

I turned to face Lenny Jenkins, our American literature scholar, who had come up behind us unannounced. He was six feet tall, and standing next to my petite frame, quite imposing. "Good morning, Lenny. Jane and I were just debating the appeal of the Cheshire Cat."

Still pulling himself together, Lenny was buttoning a dark-gray barn jacket. "Personally, I like the Cheshire Cat. In fact, I am kind of a cat person in general, fictional cats included."

Jane said, "Emmeline is leaving for Paris tomorrow, and she can't stop smiling."

"Who could blame her?" said Lenny. He adjusted his leather messenger bag diagonally across his broad chest. "Have you seen the guy she's going with? Tall, dark, and handsome."

"My excitement is purely due to the academic possibilities of the trip, I assure you," I replied offhandedly.

Lenny came to an abrupt stop. "And Mr. Red, Red Wine?"

Jane stopped, too. They were both looking at me skeptically.

I gave in to my good mood. "Well, his looks are somewhat intoxicating, if you're into that sort of thing."

Lenny shook his head and resumed walking. "What red-blooded American isn't into old-fashioned inebriation?"

Jane sniffed indignantly. "I'm sure I speak for plenty of women on this campus when I say that I, for one, am not inebriated by Mr. Duman's good looks. Appearance is such a superficial criterion to base a relationship on. Wouldn't you agree, Emmeline?"

"I would agree," I said. "However, it might suffice for a one-night stand."

Jane stared at me, open mouthed.

"I'm just kidding," I said.

Lenny gave me a little nudge, and we walked the rest of the way to Harriman Hall in playful silence.

Harriman Hall was an old, plain-brick building that didn't have much to recommend it. It housed the English and Criminal Justice Departments as well as five or six classrooms in the basement. Yet the building was set back from the rest of the campus, further obscured by two terrific maple trees that guarded the entrance like sentinels. I relished the anonymity of it and the quiet beauty too. I didn't mind that it wasn't as regal as Winsor or as stately as Stanton Hall. It was where I belonged—somewhere in the middle, somewhere in between.

My feelings probably had something to do with my academic meanderings. My specialty was French literature, but as we had no French Department or major, there was little need for a French literature professor. So I taught writing and literature classes for the English Department and helped edit the *Copper Bluff Review*, a small onsite literary journal. I hoped that working on the journal would aid me when I applied for associate professor in four years. My pre-tenure review was next fall, and I wanted to show I was on track.

My academic compromise might have been intolerable to some faculty looking for the highest accolades and worthiest publications, but I couldn't say that it bothered me. In fact, I couldn't imagine teaching anywhere except Copper Bluff. With its soft, rolling hills just starting to turn green, smell of dry dirt being prepared for planting, and flat, unending horizon, Copper Bluff had found a convert in me.

The three of us walked up the stairwell of Harriman Hall in single file to the second floor. Jane turned left at the top of the stairs.

"See you later," she called behind her.

Stopping at Lenny's door, Lenny and I looked at each other in surprise.

"Yes, goodbye," I managed to call out after her.

Lenny took out his keys. "She's talkative today."

"I know," I said. "This nice weather has everyone acting out of character."

I followed him into his office. Tossing his coat on the chair, he said, "Let me guess why you're at my office and not yours. One, you gained too much weight over the holidays and can't squeeze into that closet of an office down the hall, or two, you're out of change for the coffee fund." Though most every business in the entire United States provided free coffee for employees, the university did not. Barb, our secretary, forced us to plunk a quarter in the coffee fund for every cup. There was talk this semester of the rate going up to fifty cents.

I sat down in the facing chair, smoothing my blue spring jacket. Really, it was more of a periwinkle. "Just one cup. I have to teach at nine."

He was already fiddling with a coffee filter. "Fine. But you're not going to fill up that damn to-go mug."

"Of course not," I said. "When have you ever known me to overindulge?"

He turned to look at me, despite the fact that he was filling the coffeemaker with a gallon of purified water. Although he had many fine features, such as streaky blond hair and a solid jawline, his dimple was his finest, and now it showed deep in his left cheek. His good looks, similar age, and lively conversation might have made us more than just friends, but our dismal dating records had left us cautious. For now, we both remained stubbornly single.

"Last Friday at O'Malley's ring a bell?"

"That. Well. When do they ever have a special on Jameson?" I said, unbuttoning my coat.

He flipped the switch on the coffeemaker. "Every other week. It's an Irish pub."

"I only had two drinks. We had a good time, though, didn't we?" I recalled the local rock band and their insistence that Lenny join them on stage. "You really are an excellent guitarist."

Lenny was the kind of American literature teacher every undergrad wished for. He was easygoing, passed all his students, and played electric guitar. He performed at many local events, the legion, and even the faculty Christmas party. My first year on campus, I drank too much red wine at the holiday bash and joined in on the vocals to his rendition of the Rolling Stones' "19th Nervous Breakdown." Thankfully, I didn't repeat my performance last Christmas. My second year on campus had taught me a thing or two.

He sat down in his old wooden office chair. "Joke all you want, but you're not the only one with plans this spring break. I'm opening for a band in Minneapolis this weekend at First Avenue."

I sat up straighter. "The Prince bar?"

"That'd be the one. Some amazing tribute bands have played there since his death."

"That is terrific, Lenny. You're like a… a *professional*."

He was pleased by my compliment. "Well I'm from Minneapolis, you know. I still have a few connections up there."

"What night do you play?"

"Saturday."

I frowned. "You'll be missing a fan, I'm afraid. I'll be halfway to Paris by then."

He leaned back so far in his chair I thought it would tip, but instead it just squeaked and moaned. "So I've heard. How did André come up with enough students, anyway? I thought you had to have twelve for the trip."

"We did. We *do*," I said, watching the carafe slowly fill with coffee. "We have thirteen now, including faculty members." With the recent violence and unrest in Europe, terrorism was much more of a concern with parents than we'd anticipated. Not all the students were allowed to travel abroad. In fact, only six students from André's classes signed up. Luckily, several faculty members showed interest from the start, so now we had more than enough.

"Thirteen?" he asked, raising one dark eyebrow, which

contrasted handsomely with his spiky blond hair. "I know how you feel about that number."

According to one of the superstitions surrounding the number, if thirteen sat down to eat, the first one to leave the table would die within the year. Myth or not, the historic Savoy Hotel in London strictly avoided tables of thirteen, providing a fourteenth place setting with a small black porcelain cat named Kaspar as its occupant. It became the hotel's practice after an incident in 1898 where a party of fourteen became a party of thirteen after one of the guests didn't show up. Woolf Joel, a diamond mogul and the host of the party, scoffed the superstition and left the table first. Two weeks later, he was shot. Lenny knew this story, so I didn't bother to remind him.

I folded my hands across my lap. "It's certainly not ideal. But the superstition applies to dinner, not trips abroad." I had been repeating this salve to myself ever since André told me about the new arrangements, but being superstitious by nature, I still had a hard time convincing myself nothing bad would happen. Maybe it was my long-lost French heritage. After all, I had come across several instances of French superstition in my research. Perhaps I had inherited it from my great-great-grandma Emmeline. Wherever it came from, even nine years of book learning couldn't reverse it.

"I know you, Prather. Don't tell me you haven't considered possible bad-luck scenarios? You've read too many mystery novels not to."

I shrugged. "Some of the professors wouldn't be my first choice in traveling companions, but I'd never wish anyone harm." I shuddered, recalling my run-in with murder last fall. "I just hope Arnold Frasier, the chair of the Art Department, stays safe. I want him to be my guide at the Louvre."

"This just gets better all the time, doesn't it?"

"It does."

"I can barely endure art majors while I'm on the clock—let alone off."

"Well," I said, "he's not exactly an art major; he's an art

professor. And hopefully he will be so busy with other artists' work, he won't bother me about his own." Artists could be more pretentious than writers, and that was saying something. I could think of several examples in the English Department.

He pulled out a mug from his desk cabinet and rubbed it on his pant leg.

I reached for my bag. "I do happen to have my to-go mug with me. You needn't fill it all the way."

He was already pouring the coffee. "This is all right, I promise. I got it from my nieces for Hanukkah."

I took the #1 Teacher mug and smiled.

"I'm just happy it isn't another English classic," he said. "For some reason, they think every English professor is into Shakespeare, even though I teach *American* literature."

I nodded. "I have my fair share of his plays."

"They come out in every color over the holidays. Anyway, I'll be staying with my sister and her girls up in Minneapolis."

"Why not with your parents?" I asked, trying not to smile. I already knew the answer. Just as my trips home included a lot of not-so-subtle glances at the Catholic confessional times posted on the fridge, his would include somber walks up to the Jewish synagogue.

Yet we both love our hometowns, despite our lack of desire to live in them, and our religions, despite our temporary lapses. Though I have no siblings and he just one sister, our families are a large part of who we are.

"I'm actually looking to cash in on a little R&R this spring break," Lenny said. "You know, if I stayed there, Mom would have my ass up to the synagogue on day one."

Although Lenny and his sister had not rejected Judaism, their parents were Orthodox Jews. From our conversations, I gathered that he and his sister didn't practice their faith in the same way: they didn't bother with kosher, and they exchanged small gifts during Hanukkah. When I asked him if this was ever a cause of tension between them, he replied, "Only when I'm home."

I took a sip from my cup. "You'll be utterly feminized by the time you return."

He blew on his coffee; the steam came off in tiny gusts. "I'm planning on clocking a lot of time with Dora the Explorer."

"If you come back with a purple backpack, I'll know the transformation was a success," I said, laughing.

"And if you come back with a beret, I'll blame André," he said.

I dismissed the comment. "It's only a week. How much harm can be done in seven days?"

Chapter Two

With Paris on my mind, it was hard to focus on my creative writing students' stories, and during the last draft, I found myself wondering what shoes to pack, what the weather was like, and if I needed an electrical converter for my hairdryer. Although I was capable of vast compromise—as my employment had clearly demonstrated—I refused to go anywhere without my hair dryer and diffuser. Without these tools, my natural curls hung in great ropes that rivaled Medusa's snakes. Of course, I could always resort to a beret, I thought with a smile. Certainly one would do in a pinch.

I noticed Claire Holt, one of my brightest but also my most critical students, cross-examining a classmate whose piece we were considering, and it brought me back to the present. The format of the course was read, review, and respond. Before class, students read each other's drafts, and then in class, we discussed them and the writer responded. Right now, Claire sounded like a lawyer and the writer a defendant. With her square glasses and aggressive stance, Claire looked the part.

"I don't know if we have sufficient evidence to categorize anything with just a few pages of work," I said, cutting off

Claire's extended critique. "Why don't you tell the class your plans for the rest of this story, Kat."

Katelyn—she preferred Kat—was a keen student, except when it came to her own work. Then words escaped her, and she faltered. Her hazel eyes turned gray, her fair skin grew pale, and she disappeared into her omnipresent hoodie. "I saw this mystery on the Hallmark channel…."

A few students snickered.

"What? It helps me relax," she said, clearly embarrassed.

"Just as watching CSI helps many of you unwind," I said, silencing the students. "Go ahead, Kat. Continue."

"Anyway, after seeing the movie, I picked up one of the author's other mysteries, and the plot blew my mind. I never saw the ending coming. And it made me think I could write something like that. Sorry."

"Don't be," I said. "Never apologize for what you're reading—or writing."

"Well, I don't have a plot yet," said Kat.

The bell rang. "Don't worry. Maybe you'll find a plot over spring break," I said with a wink. Kat was one of the students taking the trip abroad to Paris. "Have a good week, class." Students began packing up their bags. "I'll see you when you get back."

As the last students left, I hurriedly packed up my canvas tote. Historically, attendance the Friday before spring break was sparse, but I didn't remember how sparse until only fifteen out of twenty-three students had taken their seats at nine o'clock. The rest were getting a jumpstart on their vacations.

Walking out of my room and into the hall, I saw Jim Giles, the chair of the English Department, dismissing what looked like a full class of students. I shook my head. They had to be upper-level English majors. Why else wouldn't they have cut class?

I caught Giles's eye and waved.

"Are you ready for your trip tomorrow?" he asked, slowly

packing up his worn leather satchel. It took him two minutes to buckle the front pockets. Giles never looked or acted harried, despite the fact that he led a group of habitually harried individuals. Just seeing him reminded me to pause at the end of a sentence.

"I hope so," I said, coming into the doorway. "What do you know about electrical voltages?"

In his late fifties, Giles had a tall forehead with three horizontal wrinkles that couldn't be hidden by his sweep of neat brown hair. I imagined they appeared after many years of questioning students. They rose in question now. "Please tell me this has something to do with a curling iron."

"A curling iron? God, no. A hairdryer."

His lips formed a flat smile. "Hairdryers are standard in most hotel rooms, I believe, even overseas."

"Have you ever used those things? Their airflow, *when* they work, is next to nil. *Pss. Pss. Pss.* And in between sputters, my hair grows curlier and curlier."

Shrugging into his corduroy blazer, he joined me in the hallway. "I'm afraid I'm rather ignorant of the airflow necessary to dry your hair… although I must say I cannot imagine it any curlier than it is. I do know that Pete's Hardware carries voltage converters. My wife acquired one there last year for our trip to Spain."

"Perfect. As soon as I make that purchase, I will be officially ready for Paris," I said.

He zipped his satchel. "I was sorry to hear André didn't recruit as many students as he hoped for this trip abroad. It certainly makes his case for a French major a little more difficult."

Last fall, the dean of Arts and Sciences had promised André that a trip would mean big things for the future of French on campus. But with several students not participating and two failing fall semester, it meant André would have that many more students to recruit next year. His passion and good looks were convincing; that was certain. But the French language itself was difficult and unpopular. The Native Studies Department had a much easier time of recruitment with their authentic pow-wows and fry bread, not to mention the dense population of Native Americans in the state.

"It is disappointing," I agreed, "but it's hard to predict what the future holds with regard to this trip. It could turn into a voyage that our new department takes every year. I can't imagine students not wanting in on that."

Giles looked skeptical. "Some students' idea of a successful spring break is a visible tan line. If I were you, I wouldn't get my hopes up."

I nodded. He had a point. Giles was the voice of reason for the entire department, and most everything he had ever told me had proven to be true.

Turning to me at the end of the hallway, Giles stuck out his hand. "Safe travels, Emmeline. I'll see you when you get back."

I shook his hand and smiled. "Thank you. Have a good week yourself."

"I will." Giles proceeded out the door.

I stood in the entryway of Winsor, one of the oldest buildings on campus, watching the students duck into classrooms and bathrooms and corners and anywhere else where they might have a two-minute conversation. It seemed to me, looking at their youthful faces, that everything they said was vital and had to be said *right now*. I loved that about them—their impetuousness. It made me feel alive or in the midst of something living. Despite the images of dead men and battles fought long ago hanging on the walls, these students lived in the moment, and a part of me lived in it, too.

I continued out the doorway, across the courtyard, and toward Stanton Hall. The hour-long break between my morning classes left me the perfect opportunity to stop by the Foreign Languages Department and see André. When our fall semester plans for the Paris trip had derailed, André was rightly upset.

I had tried to assure him that having faculty join in on the excursion was an even better outcome because of the student-to-teacher ratio, but of course he was disappointed anyway. *I* was disappointed. If enrollment didn't increase soon, I might become a permanent fixture in the English Department.

Stanton Hall was one of the campus's loveliest buildings, constructed of the beautiful rose quartzite for which South Dakota was known. The first structure on campus, it was built in 1883, only to suffer a fire ten years later. It had been fully restored to its original beauty in the 1990s. As I hurried in the door, along with several students running late, I took a quick breath and admired the heavy walnut woodwork and rich cream walls. When the air warmed and the rains came, the cleaning crew would have their work cut out for them to maintain the sheen on the immaculate marble floors.

I peeked through the beveled window of the Foreign Languages Department, noticing two female students and a lean man in his early thirties hovering around André's desk. The scene was stifling. Unfortunately Kristi, the department secretary and my nearby neighbor, was nowhere in sight. She would have kept the visitors organized.

"It's quite a collaboration, isn't it?" the lean man was saying as I walked in. "I'm so glad I get to represent Western State's Paleontology Department. The director of the Institute of Human Paleontology in Paris has given me full access, even to the rock collection said to have influenced Henri Breuil. I'm going to write an article on it that's sure to get published."

His comment confirmed he was as young as I thought he was. All new professors were worried about gathering enough publications in time for tenure.

"Yes, it's extraordinary," André said in his calmest voice, but if there's one thing the French don't do well, it's calm. Little beads of sweat gathered above his dark eyebrows, despite the forced smile. "Tomorrow we will discuss it at length, I'm sure. Ah. Here is Em Prather. Meet Professor Dramsdor."

The man straightened and turned toward me. "Sorry, I didn't hear you come in," he said.

His perfect porcelain skin made him look more model than paleontologist, and I wondered at his brand of sunscreen. It must have been SPF 50 or higher. His well-defined arms and worn cowboy boots were the only testaments to his field experience.

"No problem," I said, smoothing my hair. Several curls had escaped the high ponytail that bushed out on the top of my head.

"I will let you get back to work, André. I can see I'm interrupting. I'm off to see Molly Jaspers in the History Department, if you could just point me in the right direction."

"I'd be happy to show you the way," I said.

André was relieved. "Thank you, Em. That would be most helpful."

"Right this way," I said, opening the office door. The man followed behind. "I'm sorry, I didn't catch your name when we were introduced."

"It's Nick Dramsdor, from Western State," he said. He took my hand and shook it thoroughly. Unlike his smooth face, his hands showed signs of outdoor work and were heavily callused.

"Emmeline Prather," I said, "from the English Department. I'm going to Paris, too."

"Emmeline. What a beautiful name. What is it? French?"

I nodded. We walked in step on the walking path. He wasn't a tall man, and his strides were easy, his boots clicking softly on the pavement. "Yes, I'm named after my great-great-grandmother, who was French."

"I like old names; they seem… sturdier."

I smiled. "My dad rues the day my mother chose that name. He said it put a lot of foolish notions into my head early on."

He turned toward me. "And did it?"

"It might have," I admitted.

He laughed. It was a pleasant sound. If I didn't know he was a paleontologist, I would have guessed he was a cattle rancher. Western South Dakota had a lot of successful young ranchers who exuded confidence. I had met some of them when I presented at a conference in Rapid City. His self-assurance made him no doubt popular with the ladies.

"So, how do you know Molly?" I asked.

"Molly is a good friend of mine; she told me about the trip. As you can imagine, I didn't want to pass up an opportunity to research with her. She's been invited to lecture at the Sorbonne."

Molly Jaspers was fairly well-known on campus for her work in land conservation across the state. She was passionate about leaving the Great Plains exactly the way we found them: grassy, arid, and undeveloped. If it was up to her, buffalo would still roam the greater part of the state, and we would all live in sod houses. She was vocal in her opinions, and not everyone liked the way she inserted them into conversation or meetings. No one could argue with her academic rigor, though. She had been invited to speak all over the country on environmental issues, and I appreciated her enthusiasm for the land; the state needed people like her to champion our natural resources.

"I am excited she'll be joining us," I said. I shielded my eyes from the bright daylight. "It should prove to be a very good time." I pointed toward Winsor. "You'll find her there, in Winsor—that stone building with the turret. Go up the stairs. History is on the second floor."

"Thank you so much, Emmeline. I guess I'll see you tomorrow," said Nick.

"Yes, I'll see you then," I said, turning back toward Stanton Hall.

When I reentered André's office, he was talking with the two girls who had been standing near his desk. Not only was his forehead beaded with sweat, but his cheeks were red with irritation.

"I know you would like to bring Amber," said André. "I would like that, too. But her fee would have had to been paid in full by January. Then there are all the necessary forms to be submitted electronically to Human Resources: the application, the insurance, the health clearance. She has no time to do any of that. This is something to think about for the future. She enrolls in the program, and who knows? The sky is the limit."

Amber frowned. "I told you, Olivia. I knew he wouldn't let me."

Olivia frowned, too. "But Professor Duman, Amber is serious about enrolling. I promise. And I thought those guys in our class failed?"

André shrugged. "They did. Their spots went to faculty members, I'm afraid."

Amber looked at Olivia. "That's what always happens."

I couldn't help but break in. "When does it *always* happen? It seems to me nothing such as this has ever happened before because we've never gone overseas before. Now, excuse us, girls, but the bell is about to ring." I spoke as if a great deal was riding on an event that happened every fifty minutes.

André rubbed his temples.

"It looks like you're having a day," I said, taking the seat across from his desk after the door shut behind the girls.

"Oh, I am having a day all right. People coming in at the last minute. As if I could make a ticket for Amber magically appear when we leave tomorrow. This trip has been months in the making. What are these students thinking?" His usually smooth black hair was rumpled and his voice testy. The shirt under his classic black blazer, however, was still impeccably white.

"They're not thinking," I replied. "Clearly it's too late to get anyone a ticket."

"*Précisément*! I bought the tickets the moment I had the headcount. There was a special on airfares, and I couldn't delay."

"The travel fee is incredibly low. You did an excellent job obtaining discounts."

"I worked very hard with the old connections instead of relying on the travel company many faculty use. It meant more work for me, but it paid off." He took a breath. He was calming down. "You got Nick Dramsdor to History?"

I nodded.

"Thank you, Em. You are a big help. He comes in here talking and talking and talking about all the important things he does with his life. Right now I do not care. I have much to do before tomorrow."

"He's in Paleontology. Is that right?" I asked. Western State University in South Dakota was known for its paleontology degree because of the various fossils found west of the Missouri River, which divided the state in half.

"Yes, right. He is in Paleontology, which might have been obvious by the boots on his feet," he said.

"Boots?" I said.

"Yes, you know. The cowboy boots."

"Ah," I said, "the cowboy boots. A lot of people wear them west of the river."

"Well, he will see no boots like that in Paris, I can assure you." He spoke with clear annoyance.

"No, probably not. I guess I should leave mine at home."

He was speechless.

"I'm joking, of course."

For the first time that morning, André smiled his usual pleasant smile. "I'm sorry. You must think me rude. This trip has been more work than I realized."

"I just wish you'd let me help more. As assistant coordinator—"

André held up his hand in protest. "You are my very dear friend who has never seen Paris; I want this trip to be as enjoyable as possible for you. Besides, it is best to have one person manage these things, and you have done so much already with the itinerary."

Sure, part of André's concern was my enjoyment, but he also had a need to be in control. He wanted to make certain this trip went off without a hitch. The future of the French major depended on its success.

I slung my tote over my shoulder. "All the work will be worth it when we set foot on French soil. I, for one, can't wait."

His was still smiling. "One of your dreams is about to come true, Em."

The thought was almost too much to comprehend.

Chapter Three

THE NEXT MORNING, I arose early to depart for the trip. André had chartered a bus to take our group to Minneapolis, where we would board a plane that flew non-stop to Paris. The bus would leave at seven in the morning, the plane at three in the afternoon.

After deciding the capris I had laid out were ill-advised (after all, it was only thirty-four degrees outside), I donned dark jeans, a white blouse, and a neat navy blazer with white trim. Since Paris was the fashion capital of the world, I had taken extra care with my usually haphazard dress. I had also packed plenty of colorful scarves. One of my many guidebooks recommended that adding a scarf to your outfit was the best thing you could do to fit in on the streets of Paris. That and taking off your bra, which I wasn't prepared to do.

I stood in the middle of my living room, scanning the open space as if the things I had forgotten would line up and jump into my suitcase à la Merlin the Wizard. Everything looked uncharacteristically neat and tidy. There were no papers on my coffee table in the living room, no books on the large bow window in my dining room, and no journals on the wide walnut pillars that separated the two rooms. For once, everything was in its place, except my cat, Dickinson, who lay on top of the television, switching her tail back and forth.

I clapped my hands. “Get down from there. You know that thing is on its last legs.” And it was. Although I wouldn’t have minded buying a sleek new television that would have taken up half the space, it wasn’t a priority. I rarely watched it. Besides, there were so many other things my 1917 bungalow needed, such as central air conditioning and a new roof. Yet I loved working on my house. After living in one dilapidated rental after another during graduate school, home ownership was a very big deal for me. I prided myself on having the wherewithal to purchase a home before the age of thirty.

Dickinson raised one spotted paw and began to lick.

“You know, I have Kristi coming to visit you every day to get you fresh water and food while I’m gone.” Kristi was the neighbor who worked in the Foreign Languages Department and lived four doors down.

Dickinson looked at me as if to say, “Don’t bother.”

“Fine. Be crabby,” I said, taking her from the TV and giving her a quick squeeze before placing her on the couch. “I’m still going to bring you back a treat.”

With that, I rolled my brown hounds-tooth suitcase over the plank floor and onto the front porch, taking care to lock the door behind me and slip the key under the colorful mat that said, “Welcome Spring.”

The travel group was to meet in the parking lot between Harriman Hall and Winsor, so I didn’t have far to walk. As I approached the campus, I noted its perfect silence on this crisp Saturday morning, the first official day of spring break. Like my living room, everything looked clean and in place. No students scurried here or there, no bikes plunged off the walkways, and no laughter floated from the windows. Instead, the buildings stood like guardians waiting for the return of their ever-changing occupants.

The wheels on my luggage labored over the cracks in the walkway as I made my way kitty-corner across campus. As I approached Winsor, I was surprised to see (and hear) the diesel school bus in the adjacent parking lot. I had imagined something more in the line of Greyhound. Knowing the university's shoestring budget, however, I shouldn't have been surprised. The state was more concerned with farm subsidies than education, and just retaining the annual budget without deep cuts was a source of pride.

Several faculty members, looking organized and prepared, were boarding the bus in an orderly fashion. I imagined the students would rush in at the last minute, if their travel habits resembled their classroom habits. André was near the entrance of the bus, cheerfully providing guidance. He was no longer frustrated or angry; yesterday's storm of emotions had passed, leaving the disagreeable André behind. Instead, he brimmed with excitement.

"Good morning, Emmeline," he called out from the bus. He was wearing tight black jeans and a button-down blue and black shirt. Somehow he looked more Parisian than ever, as if anticipating that he would soon be in his element.

"Hello," I said, quickening my step.

"You like our big yellow bus?" André asked as he took my suitcase.

"Very nice," I said, not wanting to dampen his spirits. "Should I sit anywhere in particular?"

"Anywhere you'd like. You have a first-class ticket."

I climbed the three rubber-covered steps and sat in an open green seat near the middle of the bus. Several rows on each side were already filled with faculty members. Nick Dramsdor from Paleontology was seated directly behind Molly Jaspers and her husband, Bennett. Molly was the kind of woman who didn't need makeup; au naturel looked fabulous on her. Masses of natural blonde curls hung just past her shoulders and were tucked neatly behind her ears. When people said they wished for naturally curly hair, this was the kind they meant: wavy locks that piled one atop the other. Her billowy white blouse added the right touch to her straight tan trousers, and the only sparkle came from her eyes, full of energy as she and Nick talked back and forth. Once in a while, Nick, absorbed by her words, would lean in so close it would appear they were all sitting in the same seat. Molly's husband, Bennett, whose hair was black with a two-inch gray streak down the middle, didn't seem to mind. He contributed heartily to the conversation, though he looked more tired and overworked than Molly or Nick. He had broad shoulders and a boisterous laugh, however, and when he let loose with it, his face appeared much younger. Another faculty member occupied a seat across from Molly and her husband, but I couldn't put a name to her face. She was probably nearing sixty, with cropped, dark-brown hair feathered to one side. Thick rectangular glasses disguised her eyes.

"Is this seat taken?" asked Arnold Frasier, the art professor I had mentioned to Lenny.

"Not at all," I said. I was pleased that I would have over four hours to get to know him better. Although I had talked to him a few times during various university events, I didn't know much about him. He was nice looking, in his forties, with a short blond-brown ponytail at the nape of his neck and expressionless eyebrows that framed bland blue eyes. I wouldn't say he was dreamy, but preoccupied. It was as if this world had about half his attention. The other half was lost in a painting somewhere.

"You're in English, right?" he said. He unzipped his khaki jacket.

"Yes. Emmeline Prather."

"Arnold Frasier," he said, sticking out his hand. "Nice to see you again. I'm the chair over in Art."

"I thought so," I said. "I'm hoping to stand next to you in the Louvre."

He smiled. "I hope I don't disappoint you. My specialty is American folk art."

"It'd be impossible to disappoint me. I know very little about art, except the references to Greek mythology. You could probably make up a good deal, and I wouldn't know the difference."

"Well, I guarantee you that your Greek mythology will serve you well at the Louvre. There's nothing those artists enjoyed referencing more."

I shrugged. "Greek myths are popular with writers, too."

The bus was filling up fast as students rushed in, in short bursts. Molly Jaspers stood and hugged a girl who walked in with Kat, my creative writing student, and Nick hugged her too. They all seemed to know each other well. Kat and her friend took a seat in the middle of the bus, Kat high-fiving me as she walked by. Olivia, the girl from André's office, boarded the bus next. She pouted her glossy lips at André as she passed through the doorway with another girl she addressed as Meg. I had a feeling the two groups of girls didn't get along, for Kat and her friend exchanged sour glances as Olivia and Meg hurried to the back of the bus. Two boys, one as short as the other was tall, joined Olivia and Meg in the back of the bus. André was the last to enter, and the door closed with a rubbery slap behind him.

After speaking for a moment with the driver, he stood facing us, waiting for the talking to subside. "Good morning, everyone! We have a nice day for travel, no?" He pointed out the windows. "We make a little stop in Mankato, and then we arrive in Minneapolis by twelve. I will sit directly behind our driver, Ben, here if you wish to pose any questions." With that, he sat down in the seat behind the driver, and the bus began to move in hesitant spurts toward the street.

I never minded a drive through the countryside, especially in the spring. The land wasn't particularly pretty or even green, but the distinct smell of dirt was in the air as if the fields had just been stirred with a giant wire whisk. It was a terrific scent that spoke to the power of renewal after the harsh, harsh winter. With the opening of a bus window, the past four months receded into the folds of a thick blanket. Outside, the seeds of spring were poised to sprout, reenergizing something inside of us Midwesterners that we thought had died with the winterkill.

It was exhilarating, and I found myself inhaling deeply, imagining this trip to Paris as the start of a new chapter in my life. It was the chance I had been waiting for to reconnect with my French background. For almost two years I had taught solely for the English Department. I hadn't minded; in fact, I enjoyed it. I hadn't expected the introductory creative writing class I was teaching while Claudia was gone to be so pleasurable. Now, with the semester half over, I could say it had been one of my best teaching experiences to date. I loved immersing myself in the students' stories and helping them write the next lines. I had always loved fiction, had buried myself in it in my youth, and now I had a chance to participate in its creation. It had been an eventful semester, and with Paris dangling in the distance like a ripe red apple, I couldn't help but anticipate good things for my future.

Mankato, Minnesota, was small but spread out in all directions. Unlike Copper Bluff, it felt like a city, not a town, even though it housed a state university. We stopped at a fast-food chain just past the industrial area for a short break, André emphasizing the word "short" as the bus came to a halt. Although the faculty sat near the front of the bus, the students emptied out first. When they were gone, I waited patiently for Arnold Frasier to stand. My bladder shouted for relief after many cups of coffee, and I made a small commotion as I yanked my purse off the floor, hoping to give him a clue.

"I guess we're here," Arnold said, stating the obvious.

"Time for a stretch." I stood up.

He stepped into the aisle, allowing me to go ahead of him, and I quickly walked to the restaurant, the pungent smell of french fries hitting me as I pulled open the door.

The bathroom stalls were full, and I stood in a line three deep against the wall. Olivia and Meg chatted happily while reapplying lip gloss at the vanity. Kat's friend, who had a curtain of blonde, flat-ironed hair, came out of the stall and washed and wiped her hands without looking up from the sink. She silently zipped up her plaid spring coat and left. As she walked out the door, Olivia and Meg looked at each other and rolled their eyes. Now it was my turn to enter a stall, so I could no longer see their faces, but I could hear them whisper as they rummaged through their purses.

"Whatever. I hope Amanda's not like this the whole trip," said one.

"She's so stuck on herself," said the other.

Over the crinkling of paper towels, I heard, "After last spring, we're through."

"I know, right? It was a test." The other girl zipped her purse shut. "You think she could get over herself long enough for one test."

The door opened, and they were gone. I silently prayed I wouldn't need to moderate between the two groups of girls. With our number totaling thirteen, the trip had enough stacked against it without infighting.

At the counter, I ordered a chocolate malt and french fries, munching out of the bag as I reentered the bus. Some of the faculty stood talking to each other in the aisle. Molly and her husband, Bennett, snacked on vegetables from a Tupperware container, and my seatmate, Arnold Frasier, stood behind them next to Nick Dramsdor. I smiled at him briefly as I plopped down on the seat, the cushion expelling its air as I made myself comfortable. The woman with cropped hair sat reading a book. I still couldn't place a name with her face, but I had a feeling she was associated with administration. She had an air of authority.

Arnold and Nick were discussing the hieroglyphs of the Mayan ruins at some length, and I was surprised to hear an edge in Arnold's voice. The last couple of hours, he had been mild-mannered, even borderline bland, not that I doubted his warmth. He had a quiet passion simmering just below the surface. When I looked into his steady eyes, I could see it there, bubbling.

"Frasier, you're coming at it from an artist's viewpoint. A historian approaches it from a completely different angle. Molly sees it from a social prospective." Nick sounded more like an adoring student than a professor.

"You're exactly right, Nick. That's where Arnold and I have always differed." This was said by Molly. I would have recognized her tyrannical voice anywhere; it nearly beat one over the head with its smug certainty. The woman with the cropped hair looked in Molly's direction. Her eyes narrowed in disapproval.

"Not always, Molly," said Arnold, his voice a little more even. "There was a time when your interest in art went beyond a protest poster."

"Touché!" exclaimed Molly. "And this coming from a man who encourages students to follow their passions."

It was the kind of sparring at which Molly excelled. Although her combativeness infuriated some on campus, I kind of admired her willingness to speak her mind.

"She's got you there," laughed Nick.

Arnold attempted a smile and failed. "I should be getting back." He walked toward our seat, his shoulders slumped. I stuck out my bag of french fries, but he declined with a shake of his head.

"I'm told it's hard to get fast food in Paris. This may be your last chance," I said.

"I'm not really hungry, but thank you," he said.

The bus continued to fill with students, and the noise decibel rose concurrently. "So, you and Molly.... What was that about?" I said.

"She used to be an avid patron of the arts."

I took a sip of my malt. "Not anymore?"

"No, not anymore. Fighting Midwest Connect takes up most of her energy now." Midwest Connect was a proposed pipeline that would transport oil from North Dakota to Illinois. If I remembered correctly, it was supposed to be functional by the end of the year, and I had no trouble seeing why Molly would be against it. I, too, was against it, along with half of the state, including the Native Americans into whose reservation it would cut. The pipeline wasn't worth the environmental risk, especially to sacred lands. One of North Dakota's Native American tribes was already protesting to keep it off their reservation.

His calm eyes turned downward, revealing his disappointment. I knew there was more to the story than his short explanation. "It's too bad. She encouraged a lot of our students when she bought their paintings."

"Yes, the old case of money speaks louder than words," I said.

"Don't you mean *actions*?"

"So many times it means the same thing, doesn't it?" I asked.

"True." He leaned in more confidentially. A few strands fell from his low ponytail, and I tried not to stare at his good looks. Now he looked like the art professor who had caused more than a few girls to change their majors. "It's too bad when professors fixate on a *cause*. It's better for our students when we're integrated as a community. Wouldn't you agree?"

"It depends on the cause; sometimes it's worth it when so much is at stake."

He leaned back; he didn't like my response. But I wasn't about to dismiss the severity of the threat posed by the pipeline entering our state. While I didn't think Molly should put her cause before all else, I could understand why she would. Many professors had a hard time staying neutral on issues that impacted their fields—and even ones that didn't. When a student of mine had died last semester, I'd put finding justice for him before everything. Even Arnold Frasier, if he were honest with himself, would realize that he was doing the same thing—putting his passions above hers. What really angered him was her loss of interest in the art world.

I nodded my head in the direction of the woman with cropped hair. "Hey, do you know who that is?"

"That's Dr. Judith Spade. She's a physician. An absolutely brilliant woman," he added. "She works in the School of Medicine, teaching our student doctors."

I immediately recognized the name, just not the face. Judith Spade had won more awards on campus than I could count; her work had received national and international accolades. When I first came to campus, she won some big award to research at Lancaster University in England. I wondered what brought her to Paris. Perhaps the opportunity to travel internationally again.

The bus door shut, and I settled in with my book, *A Moveable Feast*. It was the only Parisian guidebook I needed as far as Lenny was concerned. Despite the other two guides in my canvas tote, I could see his point. There was one line in the book that I kept coming back to: "Never go on trips with anyone you do not love." No matter how many pages I turned, I couldn't get past Hemingway's warning. It needled me like a guest I had forgotten to invite. I paused, looking around the bus at the perfectly amiable faces that surrounded me. I wouldn't say I loved them (well, I was starting to fall for Arnold Frasier's ponytail), but altogether, it was a pretty good group. I didn't see anything wrong with going on a trip with people I barely knew. Obviously Hemingway had never been on spring break.

Chapter Four

The Minneapolis International airport was equipped with all the things you'd expect to find in a sizable airport: walkways, restaurants, bookstores, a tram, even a shoe shiner. As our group waited near gate 40C, I was surprised, as I always was when I traveled, at how many people inhabited this city within a city. They all looked like professionals with important trips about to begin that would end in new contracts or business or an offshore facility. I, on the other hand, only hoped my wait would end with a Bloody Mary because (as old-fashioned as it sounded) I was afraid to fly. The moment we got through security, I sidled up to the bar nearest our gate with the good-looking Arnold Frasier and downed my first drink faster than you can say thirty thousand feet.

André joined us at the u-shaped bar and ordered. "I see you prefer the cocktail in the afternoon?" The waitress filled his glass with red wine, and he examined it carefully, perhaps wondering about its origin. He tended to believe any wine other than French was a great disappointment.

"I prefer something eighty proof or higher before I board a

plane," I said, taking a large bite of the celery protruding from my glass.

André chuckled. "Em Prather, you surprise me. It is not normal for you to be afraid."

"They say people who cannot relinquish control are afraid to fly," said Arnold.

His ponytail suddenly appeared less attractive. "I have no problem relinquishing control—just not as I am freefalling through the sky."

Arnold laughed. "If that's your notion of flying, maybe you should consider a shot of something stronger."

The idea wasn't completely without appeal. Still, I couldn't imagine taking a shot with students looking on. I could guess how the news would spread through campus when we returned, and while it probably would enhance my enrollment rates, it would make for awkward conversation at faculty meetings. "I think this'll do."

Molly, Bennett, and Nick joined our group, squeezing in beside André. Nick and Molly ordered drinks.

"Congratulations on your invitation to the Sorbonne," said André. "I was glad to recommend you to Dr. Aris, my former mentor. When I told him you knew organic land practices well, he was happy to schedule a lecture."

Molly dismissed his compliment. "I doubt they'll be too pleased with what I have to say."

André looked confused. "What do you mean? You are an expert on land conservation, are you not?"

"My expertise is environmental studies, yes. I received a grant to research the environmental history of the Great Plains two years ago, so I would say my work qualifies me as an expert. But that doesn't mean I'm going to tell them what they want to hear, that organic is the solution to all our problems."

"The Sorbonne is among the world's best universities," André said with pride. "When one speaks there, people listen. You must take care with your words. Dr. Aris is a close friend."

Molly took her glass of white wine from the bartender but remained standing, there being no open seats. The students stood nearby also, leaning against phone chargers and tables. "I'll say what I want to say; you know me. I won't kowtow to an institution no matter what its reputation. People tend to overrate universities based on their names, I've found. I've visited some outstanding institutions, none of which are known by name."

Bennett and Nick nodded in agreement, but André was visibly offended. He had been in Copper Bluff for five years, and was known for his Gallic temper. But he should have also been known for his intellect. He was as smart as he was passionate, and his knowledge of linguistics was impeccable. He taught the upper-level graduate classes in the Linguistics Department that few dared to take on.

"I think any American would be humbled by the prospect of speaking at the Sorbonne." The way he said *American* made us all take note. It was not complimentary.

"Don't be insulted, André. I didn't mean my words to be taken personally." Molly wagged her finger at him. "You need to guard yourself against ethnocentrism. It's a bad habit of yours. I've warned you about it before."

She continued in this vein for several minutes, and I tuned her out. Molly could easily turn any of her statements of opinion into a lecture, and it was often difficult to get her to stop. By the time she finished, André had silently finished his wine, and three seats had opened up on the other side of the bar. They took their half-finished drinks and left, waving to us across the counter.

"That woman," André ground out, "I wish she was not speaking at the Sorbonne. But who was the first one to trot out her CV? She was. She excels at self-promotion."

I nodded sympathetically.

Arnold stifled a laugh. "She wouldn't be where she is without a little PR."

"One day Molly is going to offend the wrong person and find herself in trouble," said André.

I didn't respond. I knew he was upset, and the longer he spoke on a subject, the angrier he would become. I thought it best not to draw any more attention to the argument. Already the students were looking in our direction.

Without my reply, our discussion dissipated into distracted thought, and I focused on the bar's fake waterfall: little silver beads moving down a clear plastic wall. I supposed this was the airport's way of calming passengers who sought out liquid medication before flying. I tried to relax but became aware of a woman staring at me from across the bar. Her blue eyes were piercing and intense. I tried to ignore her by stirring my drink. It didn't work.

I glanced up uneasily. Why was she looking at me that way? She was too old to be a student of mine, so that explanation didn't suffice. Her red hair was like straw, drawn back into a short ponytail with frayed ends. Her face was thin, and her pointy cheekbones stretched the skin. She was a woman on a mission. How it involved me, I couldn't say.

A man approached the microphone at our gate and announced that the boarding would begin with first-class passengers and passengers who needed extra assistance. We slid from our seats, and the students standing next to the bar put away their phones. The red-haired woman stood up. Was she on our flight?

Our group of thirteen congregated near the wall of flight schedules scrolling across the screens, waiting for our section to be called. Because we were positioned in the middle of the plane, it would be several minutes, so I reorganized the books and magazines in my canvas tote from largest to smallest, then A to Z. It helped keep my mind off my fear of flying and the worry that our group was jinxed because it numbered thirteen.

Finally, it was time for our section to board, and Olivia and Meg laughed as they extended the handles of their bulging carry-ons, bumping into one and all as they made their way down the concourse. I slung my bag over my shoulder and stood single file with the others, André behind me, and Molly and Bennett Jaspers ahead of me.

"Is this your first time traveling internationally?" asked Bennett.

Did the death grip on my tote reveal that much? "It is," I answered. "You?"

He smiled. "No. I travel overseas quite frequently for work. These flights are a breeze. You fly so high you rarely experience turbulence."

I wondered if this was supposed to make me feel better.

Molly squeezed his large shoulders. He was a good deal taller than Molly, who like me, was petite. "Bennett's a businessman."

"Actually, I'm an electrical engineer. I graduated from the South Dakota School of Mines. But Molly's right. We own our own business now. Our company makes electrical equipment."

"Bennett's being kind; it's *his* business. I don't know a thing about it. I just use his frequent flyer miles," added Molly with a laugh.

"They come in handy when you have a wife who travels as much as mine does," said Bennett.

She cocked her head to one side, her pretty curls falling over her shoulder. "I was able to use some of his miles on my trip to New Mexico last summer with Nick Dramsdor and an extraordinary group of students, including Amanda," she said, motioning to the back of the line.

Bennett turned to me. "Molly's work in New Mexico earned her national recognition and the Roelker Mentorship Award."

"I seem to remember that," I said, although I had no idea what awards she had won or even how Nick's work connected to Molly's. Still, Bennett's admiration for her was heartwarming, and I felt a pang of jealousy spring up from a place I didn't recognize. It would be wonderful to have someone gush over you like that.

"I am so proud of her," he said.

Molly looped her arm through his. "Come on, Bennett. The last thing Emmeline wants to hear is a colleague's husband bragging up his wife!"

"I don't mind at all," I said, but Molly was already pulling him down the jet bridge. I glanced behind me and noticed Kat's friend, Amanda, standing behind Judith Spade, the medical doctor. Amanda was talking to someone, but I couldn't see whom. She shook her head and turned, pointing in my direction, and I saw she was talking to the woman with red hair.

I reluctantly proceeded down the jet bridge, wishing I could linger behind to see what they were discussing, since it appeared to concern me. I would have liked to know why the red-haired woman was singling me out.

"Welcome aboard!" exclaimed a cheerful flight attendant in a blue suit and matching blue scarf.

I smiled, carefully stepping off the jet bridge and onto the plane. I told myself, *See, the attendant is happy to be flying.* Then I added, *She's also getting paid.* At least she had some compensation for traveling at six hundred miles per hour. I followed Bennett all the way to Row L, where he stopped.

"This is us," he said, shoving his carry-on into an overhead bin.

We were in a good location in the row immediately following the bathrooms, coffee maker, and snack cart. If I had to move from my seat, which I hoped I didn't, I wouldn't have far to go.

The row extended three seats on the right, five seats in the middle, and three seats on the left. André, Amanda, Kat, and I were assigned the middle seats while Molly, Bennett, and Nick were assigned the ones on the right. Judith Spade and Arnold Frasier were behind them. Olivia and Meg, adjusting their matching neck pillows, were seated at the left. Trapped between them sat the tall boy, Jace, who seemed to be enjoying himself. The other boy, Aaron, was stuck in a seat in front of them next to a stranger, an older woman, and had to turn around to talk.

I buckled my belt tightly across my waist. I wished others would do the same because their movement made me anxious, but they continued shoving things in and out of the overhead bins right up until takeoff. The lady to the right of me was working on a PowerPoint despite our impending departure.

Amanda wore fashionable ear buds, ready for takeoff, so I reached across the woman's laptop next to me and tapped her arm to get her attention. I wanted to ask her about the red-haired woman.

"Hey," I said.

Amanda took off one ear bud. Kat leaned in, her hazel eyes flickering with anticipation.

"Amanda, by the way, who was that red-haired lady you were talking to a few minutes ago?"

She shook her head. "I don't know her. She thought you were Dr. Jaspers, but I told her you weren't."

Kat nodded. "I told her you were my creative writing teacher."

"Why was she asking about Molly Jaspers?" I said.

Kat shrugged. "I have no idea. I had to point out who she was." She put her ear bud back in, and I had to assume she and the woman hadn't discussed anything else. PowerPoint looked at me as if to say, *Get a clue.*

"I hope you're aware that your laptop will need to be stowed during takeoff," I said.

She didn't respond.

The plane began taxiing down the runway, bumping along over the cracks and crevices, until it came to a complete halt, third in line for takeoff. As the plane raced down the airstrip and lifted off the ground, I grabbed the first thing within reach, which happened to be André's knee. He patted my hand, and I composed myself, glad for a friend nearby.

A short time later, the captain's voice came on, stating that we had reached our cruising altitude. He sounded too young to be out after midnight, let alone fly us overseas. PowerPoint wasted no time pulling out her computer, and the attendants wasted no time pulling out the drink cart—thank god. We were positioned in the middle of the plane, which meant, despite our unexceptional location, we would be the first ones served from this area. People stood up to use the restroom, grab something from the overhead bin, or simply stretch their limbs.

The plane was abuzz with activity. Molly and Bennett, a stunning couple by any definition, were waiting in line to use the bathroom. Caught up in the excitement and romance of the prospect of Paris, they exchanged a kiss.

I let out a deep breath. I wished I had someone special to share this moment with. I glanced to my left. Of course there was André; I had to admit I was attracted to him. But my feelings were caught up with my interest in French culture, and I had a hard time untangling one from the other. Lenny, on the other hand, was incredibly special to me. I felt closer to him than any man I had dated, yet we were just friends. My dating history was less stellar than my curriculum vitae, and Lenny's could accurately be described as slipshod. In fact, we often commiserated about our bad dating luck. Still, neither one of us was too concerned that one day we might end up like some of the lonely old professors who taught at the university. I was twenty-eight, and he was thirty; middle age and marriage appeared as far away to us as Paris did right now.

By the time the attendant took drink orders and handed out peanuts and pretzels, most of our group were settling in to movies or games or other electronics that would keep us occupied for the next nine hours. But someone in the group was arguing. I looked past André toward the window seats and noticed it was Bennett Jaspers. He sounded disgusted.

"I was assured that this would be a peanut-free flight," he was saying. For the first time, I could detect the shrewd businessman in his voice. When he and Molly worked as a team, they had to be invincible. "I spoke with a manager at your company, who said that no peanuts would be distributed during the flight. My wife is *deathly* allergic to peanuts!"

Cutting off his protest, Molly told him she would be fine. "Don't waste your breath, Bennett. I've learned to deal with people's failings my entire life."

The attendant kept her cool, smiling and speaking in hushed tones. "There's no reason to raise your voice, sir. We could move her to a peanut-free zone if she'd feel safer."

"As if I'd put my trust in strangers," said Molly. "I'm safer around friends than anywhere else."

Bennett began to object, but Molly whispered something in his ear that placated him. He crossed his arms. "I will be contacting the airlines when we land. I promise you that."

The attendant moved on, and I was thankful. Any disturbance increased my unease. I had ordered vodka and a can of Bloody Mary juice, and now I surreptitiously nibbled on my small bag of peanuts, not wanting to draw attention to my selection. I turned to André and whispered, "Did you inform the airline of her allergy?"

He ran his fingers nervously through his hair. "HR did not send me the health forms until after I made the flight arrangements. When I received them, I contacted Molly to ask her what accommodations she would need for restaurants and such. She asked for the flight information at that time and said she would take care of contacting them. I gave it no more thought."

"I wouldn't worry then," I said. "It sounds like Bennett was two steps ahead of you."

"Yes. I'm glad it was him and not me who had to contend with the noncompliance."

André went to take a sip of red wine, and his plastic wine glass dipped as we hit a rough patch of air. Instinctively, I reached for his arm, and he patted my hand.

"Use your imagination to distract yourself from the flight,"

André said. "Think of all the beautiful stops on our itinerary: The Louvre, Notre Dame, the Palais Garnier."

"I will try. It should be good for something," I muttered. God knows my imagination had gotten me into enough tangles over the years, psychological and otherwise.

"The imagination is never a bad thing," André said. He pointed to the book on my lap, a paperback crime novel set in Paris. "Look at your writers. They must have a lot of imagination to think of such things."

I thumbed through the book, finding my dog-eared page. "I can't wait to see how the real Paris measures up to what I've read."

"Ah, but take care, Em. There is a syndrome such as you describe. The Paris Syndrome."

I nodded vigorously.

"You've heard of it, no?"

Yes, I had heard of it; in fact, I had researched it before the trip. Many tourists visiting Paris for the first time succumbed to the syndrome, which took hold of them when reality didn't meet their idealized expectations of the city. They became disoriented, disillusioned, and even disgruntled as they navigated the City of Light. But the truth was, Paris was a big city and could be unkind to those who spoke little or inferior French or expected American-style hospitality.

"I'm fully prepared for a version of the city that doesn't look like the cinematic Paris," I said. "I've scanned articles about crime and corruption, and I've come to the conclusion that Paris can be not only heartless but also cruel."

PowerPoint turned slightly green, but I didn't know if it was from my remarks or the glare of her computer screen. Either way, she turned her shoulder away from me.

André laughed. "Good job. You just keep on reading your… what do you call it, whodunit? Maybe it will distract you from the flight."

I smoothed the page and recalled the day I had purchased

the book at Copper Bluff's bookstore. Ensconced between the bar and jewelers, the tiny shop specialized in collectable books but sold used and new copies as well as all genres. The owner was from California, an exotic location to us, and incredibly wealthy. She was a terrific purveyor of literature, and I spent many afternoons poring over first editions she kept locked in a small bookcase. She was a friend to readers and writers in the area, not to mention jobless eccentrics, and although she didn't host many events (Café Joe had more room), she supported local artists by carrying their work. There was no better friend to the arts.

Despite my book's quick-moving plot, I was unable to concentrate on the words. I read and reread several pages, trying to immerse myself in the narrative. Yet all I could focus on were the bumps and drops of the plane and how the other passengers weathered them with such aplomb. It was as if they were not thirty thousand feet in the air but on a front porch swing.

I looked around. Molly and Nick were having a lively conversation to my left that was growing more heated. That entire side of the plane, in fact, had been a lot more animated and drawn my attention several times.

I soon realized I wasn't the only one eavesdropping on Molly and Nick. The entire middle row was gawking in their direction as Molly's gesticulations grew larger and more erratic. She seemed agitated, and now she tore at her seatbelt.

"What's the matter, Mol? Molly? What is it?"

She was shaking her head back and forth, tearing at her throat.

He grabbed the backpack next to him, tugging at the zipper as it stuck halfway down. He retrieved what I assumed was an EpiPen, a little needle that looked like a child-size marker with a lid he had no trouble removing. The lid dropped to the floor as he stabbed the pen into her thigh with a force that made me jump. She slumped over, and he cried for help. Before the flight attendant could repeat the plea for a doctor, Dr. Judith Spade, our resident physician, was out of her seat examining Molly. The plane grew silent as we all watched in horror, waiting for Molly to regain consciousness.

She never did. Judith shook her head. The pretty Molly Jaspers was dead.

Chapter Five

FOR SOMEONE LIKE myself who suffers from a fear of flying, the disaster was twofold. One, Molly Jaspers was dead, which meant I'd never fly again without recalling this scene. Two, her death popped my false, alcohol-induced bubble of tranquility. I sat paralyzed with dread as the stewardesses huddled in the corner, one talking to the medical hotline and the other to the pilots. After the pilots and airlines reached a decision as to what should be done, the stewardesses moved Molly smoothly, as if relocating her to another seat. But we knew the truth. Molly wasn't relocating to another seat. She had been pronounced dead by Dr. Judith Spade, and her body was being stored out of sight of the other passengers to minimize the chance of pandemonium on the flight. Bennett Jaspers was already out of his mind. His head in his lap, he pulled at his hair, mumbling loud enough for me to hear.

"You, you… damn you. I told them. No peanuts. No peanuts." He shook his head back and forth, moaning. "You heard me, didn't you? They wouldn't listen."

Nick tried to calm him with a hand on his shoulder, but Bennett jerked away. "Don't touch me."

Nick sat back in his seat, his face sullen and white. I wondered if he was in any danger, sitting next to a man half-crazed with grief. The stewardess must have wondered the same thing, for a large man dressed in plainclothes followed her down the aisle at double-quick speed. She politely asked Nick to relocate to another seat a few rows behind ours. The plainclothes air marshal, identifiable by his muscular build and perfect crew cut, took Nick's place as Bennett stared in surprise. I was a little surprised, too. Although I knew air marshals existed, I didn't think our flight had a threat level that warranted their use. Perhaps it was because of our destination and the recent violence there.

"What is this? Could someone please explain? *You* kill my wife, and *I'm* the danger to the airplane? Does that make sense to anyone?" Bennett looked toward us, but nobody said anything. We didn't dare.

"Just here for support, sir. Just want to keep everyone safe," said the marshal.

"It's a little late for that," Bennett said, seething.

The plane began to tilt toward the left, and a moment later the captain's voice came over the loudspeaker. "Hi, folks, you've probably noticed we've begun to turn around. We've decided to return to Minneapolis International Airport for a passenger emergency. If you just hang tight, we'll be on the ground shortly. We can't land on a full tank of fuel, so we'll be circling the area a few times as we drain the tank. Thanks for your patience. We'll have more information for you real soon."

The passengers in the front of the plane groaned in unison; they had no idea what had taken place. Even those of us in the know were disappointed by the captain's words. André appeared crestfallen, as did our entire row. Olivia and Meg looked as if they might cry, and honestly, I could have joined them. Molly Jaspers' death was not just sad, it was tragic, even if we did not know her well. But we had wrongly assumed that our flight would continue. Now we understood that it would soon be grounded.

AFTER WE LANDED, we sat on the runway for what seemed like forever. It was nearing dinnertime, and I was ravenous. Plus I had a mild hangover that required a cup of coffee. Eventually, a stewardess's voice came over the loudspeaker.

"Skyway Airlines wants to thank you again for your patience and let you know that the Minneapolis Police Department will be boarding the plane momentarily. They would appreciate your continued cooperation as they deal with the unexpected emergency on board. When we are cleared to leave the plane, officers will need to ask you some brief questions. If you would please stay in your seats, we will be around with coffee and water while the emergency is dealt with. If you need to use the restrooms, you may do so at this time."

André and I looked at each other.

"Well, at least you'll have your coffee," he said.

"Yes, that will help," I said.

"Why are the police getting on the plane?" This question came from Kat. Her friend Amanda shed silent tears, which dripped into her lap. She and Molly Jaspers had obviously been close.

I shook my head. "I think it is protocol when a person… expires on a plane."

"They're taking away the dead body? Gross," said Olivia, who stood next to our row.

Amanda glared at her, eyes narrowed.

"I'm sure they will wait until everybody has disembarked," I said, trying to defuse the tension.

"What of these questions?" asked André.

I had been wondering the same thing. Growing claustrophobic, I welcomed interrogation over detainment; still, I suspected the police would be disappointed with our answers. I, for one, had been deep in conversation with André when I noticed the disturbance. I had no idea what had transpired in the minutes before Molly's death.

"Yes, coffee here, please," I said to the attendant with the coffee pot and Styrofoam cups. She filled a cup, which she handed to me. I blew on it then drank. I could feel the brew awaking the senses I had deadened with alcohol, the plane becoming not just a mode of transportation but the site of a mysterious death.

I cast new eyes upon the passengers. Everybody was offered a bag of peanuts, everybody had access to the very thing that was lethal to Molly Jaspers, and everybody was mobile once the plane took flight. She could have come in contact with a peanut any number of ways. Despite the various scenarios running amuck in my head, I told myself her death was an accident. She was a respected professor with an adoring husband and a well-formed plan to save the Great Plains one soybean field at a time. She was just the kind of passionate person you expected to see at a university. Why would anyone want her dead?

"I see the potion is working its magic in you," said André. He swirled his hand above his head. "Your brain spins this way and that. Have you devised a way to commandeer another plane to Paris?"

I smiled. Paris was the furthest thing from my mind, but to say so would break his heart. "Surely there must be another flight. We might be able to move forward with our plans."

"Do you think?" asked Kat. Her expression was hopeful. I didn't realize she was still listening to our conversation.

"It's possible," I said, though I highly doubted we would be flying again any time soon.

"Professor Prather investigates every possibility. If there is a way to Paris, she will find one," André said to Kat. "She is a very keen researcher."

I wished André hadn't pinned Kat's hopes on me. "Of course we will look into it. André's put too much work into this trip for it not to happen."

A man in a white shirt and gray blazer appeared from the server's station with a second man close behind. Standing so near, he could have been the older man's shadow. He wore a similar gray blazer and pants. Only his mop of curly hair separated him from the distinguished gentleman in front of him. That, and the large ketchup stain on his shirt. Granted, I was no fashionista, but I owned a stain stick and knew how to use it.

Both men were good-sized, yet while the first man stood tall and straight, the second hunched slightly, making his shoulders appear round and soft. It also made his jacket look a little too big. He fumbled with his inside pocket, pulling out a spiral notepad that had seen better days. It had maybe five sheets of paper left, and I wondered if I couldn't give him one of my notebooks. I had three in my tote bag.

The first man said something to the stewardess, and she nodded, motioning in the direction of Bennett Jaspers. Both men walked quickly toward him, and the air marshal stood and greeted them. Then he walked toward the serving station, where he looked on with a cup of coffee.

"Bennett Jaspers?" said the first officer, sticking out his hand. "I'm Detective Jack Wood, and this is my partner, Detective Ernest Jones, with the Minneapolis Police Department."

Ernest stuck out his hand as well. "You can call me Ernie."

Bennett shook their hands vigorously. "I'm sure glad to see you gentlemen. I want to file charges immediately against the airlines for what's happened here. My wife went into anaphylactic shock after...." He broke off, wiping at his eyes with the back of his hand. "I'm sure you've been briefed on the situation."

"Yes, we have," said Jack, "and let me first say we are very sorry for your loss. We understand you've been married for some time."

"Ten years," answered Bennett.

"When exactly did the attack begin?" asked Jack. Ernest took out a pencil from his jacket pocket.

"It all started when the attendant brought around the snack cart. I saw that she was handing out peanuts and asked her to stop. See, I contacted the airlines some time ago, and they promised me that this would be a peanut-free flight because of Molly's severe allergy. Obviously, my request got lost somewhere in the paperwork because the attendant was not cognizant of my request."

"Did anybody in your row take the peanuts?" asked Ernest.

Bennett shook his head. "Nick and I did not, but who knows what everyone else took."

He pointed in the direction of the middle row, and we stared into our laps. I mentally searched for the peanut wrapper in my seat, hoping I had thrown it away with my cocktail glass.

"As far as you know, did Molly come in contact with a peanut?" asked Jack.

Bennett scowled. "Well, she must have. She's dead, isn't she?"

"What I mean is," restated Jack, "did she eat anything while on board the plane?"

"I don't know. She had her snack here." He reached between his knees and pulled a small Tupperware container out of a carry-on. "But she made this herself. She makes… *made* everything herself. Even the smell of peanuts could make her throw up. That's why I was so upset when I saw the peanuts. The stewardess didn't understand the extent of Molly's allergy."

Ernest pulled out an evidence bag from his jacket pocket. It was in about the same shape as his notebook, and it took him several tries to get it unfolded. "I'll need to take that for further examination, sir."

"Of course," said Bennett, handing him the container.

"Was Molly in possession of this container at all times?" asked Jack.

Bennett nodded. "Yes." Then he frowned. "Well, I believe she was…. It was in her luggage here."

"Did anyone else have access to her luggage?" asked Jack. Ernest stood poised with his notebook, but I didn't know how he could write anything with the Tupperware container under his arm.

Bennett grew flustered. "I suppose… everyone in these two rows." He pointed again in our direction. "We were all traveling to Paris as part of a group from a university."

The two detectives turned their attention toward us. "Are you French?" asked Ernest.

"Yes, certainly," answered André, taken aback by the odd question.

Ernest wrote something in his notebook, using Molly's Tupperware container as a makeshift table.

"Is that a crime?" asked André.

By the color of his face, I knew he was tensing up. I decided to intervene on his behalf.

"Professor Duman and I are taking students and faculty abroad over spring break. We're part of a scholarly expedition, Ernie." The nickname sounded so wrong coming out of my mouth that it startled even Ernest's colleague.

"Would those traveling in the study group please raise their hands?" asked Jack. Everyone complied, and he counted our number in his head. Now he spoke in a louder voice to the middle of the plane.

"Listen up, folks. My partner and I will be leading this section of the plane to police operations. At this time, feel free to find your carry-on luggage and line up single file near the bathroom here. I will lead the line, and my partner, Mr. Jones, will bring up the rear. Please do not leave the line at any time. I can assure you that police operations will have everything you need to be comfortable."

His announcement was followed by bins opening, purses zipping, and feet shuffling. I gathered my tote and placed it on my lap, waiting patiently for the rest of my row to retrieve their belongings. We scooted out of our row when room became available, inching near the front of the plane as the first-class passengers filed out.

When we entered the jet bridge, I realized the enormity of the police officers' task. Besides the airport police, at least two dozen or more MPD officers were helping to disembark the jumbo jet. Jack Wood waited for Ernest's signal before our group began to make its way through the airport toward police operations. The rest of the passengers were being moved in a different direction by officers from various precincts who'd been called in to assist with the emergency.

Considering the size of the airport, I assumed we would have a long walk, but airport police was quite close. The pilot must have been instructed to take the gate nearest security, and good thing, too, because the twelve of us were causing quite a commotion among other fliers. Adults stared, visibly worried, while moms and dads clasped their children's hands tightly as we walked past several small newsstands and a large brew pub. Then we walked down the stairs toward baggage claim and around the corner, where a young, kind-looking female officer sat at a small glass window marked POLICE. The officer immediately stood to open the industrial door, and she and Jack Wood exchanged a few words before the rest of us entered. The hallway was narrow, and our group filled the entire space between it and the small conference room. As we filed into the tiny room, folding chairs were brought in to accommodate the group, who had to sit very close to one another to fit around the oval table.

"If I can have your attention again…" said Jack Wood. He had barely raised his voice, but the room went quiet. "Thank you. We're going to get started right away with our questions. My partner and I will be calling you in one by one to get your statement and pertinent information. If the rest of you need something to drink or eat, or to use the restroom, just let the officer know." He pointed to the woman who had opened the door for us. "Officer Anderson will be happy to assist you. Mr. Jaspers? Come with me, sir."

Bennett Jaspers, Jack Wood, and Ernest Jones walked out of the room.

"Poor Bennett," I said, placing my tote bag on the table in front of me.

"What are we going to do, Em?" asked André. He was seated right next to me. "There is no way we will depart tonight."

"I agree. We'll have to find a place for the group to stay."

André winced at my confirmation.

"But don't worry," I continued, "I've stayed in Minneapolis a few times. I'll try to find a hotel with an airport shuttle." I asked Officer Anderson, who was stationed with us, if it would be okay to use our phones. She said it was no problem, so I began to search the Internet for availability at some of the larger hotel chains.

"A very reasonable hotel, please," said André. "I secured one at deep discount for our stay in Paris."

Arnold Frasier was sitting in a chair nearby. "We're staying in Minneapolis?"

"Who is?" Judith Spade chimed in.

"We will have to," said André, "unless you want to stay at the airport."

"There's a plane that leaves for Amsterdam at ten o'clock," said Olivia. She was scrolling through flight schedules on her phone.

The faculty looked at her, perplexed. She obviously didn't understand the severity of the situation.

"That's less than five hours from now," said André.

"So?" said Olivia.

André started to speak but then, sputtering, stopped.

I broke in, "Molly Jaspers is dead, and we are at police headquarters. There is no telling what the future holds. André and I will find a hotel that can accommodate the group tonight. One thing is certain: we can't split up now."

This last statement put an end to discussion for a moment, and I returned to the Internet. Despite my best efforts, I couldn't find available rooms. Every hotel near the airport was booked.

"How are you faring?" asked André. "Any luck?"

"Not yet," I said. Perhaps our bad luck wasn't surprising, considering the tragedy that had befallen us already. I suspected a gray cloud with our names on it would be trailing us for the remainder of the trip.

"It's Saturday night," Officer Anderson said. "You're going to have a hard time finding a half-dozen rooms anywhere during March Madness."

"We'll just have to broaden our search." I deleted my search restrictions and googled all hotels in the Minneapolis area, finding a hotel downtown that had four suites available. I gave the information to André.

"But they do not offer a shuttle," said André, "and there will be three to a room. The travel fee included double occupancy."

"I know, but nothing else is available. Besides, they're suites. We can make it work. We can take a couple of van cabs from the airport."

André shook his head, clearly displeased with the selection, but quickly reserved the rooms. As he finished, Bennett returned from the interrogation room with Ernest. Bennett appeared to have aged ten years since I'd seen him last. I could swear that the gray part in his hair had grown an inch wider. I told him about the difficulty finding rooms and the makeshift accommodations for the night.

He slumped into a nearby chair. "Thank you, Emmeline, but I won't be staying. I need to call Molly's mom and dad, her brother, the school.... What am I going to say? What can I possibly say?"

"I'm so sorry, Bennett." I had no other words for him.

He turned to Ernest. "How do I get Molly... transported back to Copper Bluff?"

"In cases like these, we have to perform an autopsy, for insurance and legal purposes. To determine negligence. I'm afraid you might as well stay with the group, Mr. Jaspers. Molly's body won't be released any time soon. And it's not good for you to be alone right now."

Bennett began to cry. Nick awkwardly patted his shoulder.

Ernest nodded in my direction. "Miss? Could you come with me?"

I stood and followed him out of the room. "Was your mother a big fan of Ernest Hemingway?"

He turned around. Now I knew what people meant by smiling eyes; they were blue and crinkled happily near the rims of his round, wire-rimmed glasses. "No. She was a big fan of church. My sister's name is Charity."

We entered a small concrete room with a table and three chairs. Jack Wood was already seated. "And your name?" Ernest asked as he retrieved his notebook from his jacket pocket.

"Emmeline Prather."

"Prather," he said as he wrote it down. "Sounds Puritan."

I waved off the comment. "You're thinking of Mather. Cotton Mather. But my great-great-aunt *was* accused of being a witch."

He and Jack Wood looked up from their papers.

I shrugged. "Don't worry. I didn't inherit her abilities, if she had them, as far as I know."

"And your address and phone number," said Jack.

I rattled off both.

"Thank you, Ms. Prather… I mean, Dr. Prather. Or do you prefer Professor?" asked Ernest, fumbling with his pencil.

"You can call me Emmeline," I said with a smile.

"And you can call me Ernie," he said.

If only anyone *could* call him that, I was sure he'd appreciate it. As it was, though, he had the yoke of sainthood hanging about him. He couldn't shake a name that meant "sincere conviction" for all the joys of Christendom.

Jack put down his pen. "Let's return to the airplane. You

were seated near Mrs. Jaspers. How did Mrs. Jaspers seem to you? Did you notice anything unusual about her actions?"

I shook my head. "Not until it was too late. At first, it appeared she was in a lively debate with Nick Dramsdor. I believe they're good friends. But when her movements became erratic, I knew something was wrong. She collapsed in her seat, and Bennett found an EpiPen and rammed it into her thigh. She never regained consciousness."

Ernest wrote hastily in the notebook while Jack considered my answers carefully.

"Were you aware that Molly Jaspers was allergic to peanuts?" Jack asked. From his pallor and bloodshot eyes, I could just imagine the toll his work had taken.

I nodded and recounted Bennett's anger at the flight attendant when she passed out the in-flight snack.

"And did you take the peanuts when offered?" asked Jack. Ernest looked up from his notebook.

I felt my face flush. "Yes, but I wasn't seated next to Molly. I never even left my seat. I hate flying."

Ernest nodded sympathetically. "We're not saying you did anything to Molly Jaspers, Professor. These are just routine questions we need to ask when somebody dies."

I looked to Jack for confirmation, but his serious gaze gave me little comfort.

"Ms. Prather, could you tell me a little bit about your group's trip to Paris? Bennett Jaspers said you were in charge of the expedition," said Jack.

I shook my head. "I'm not officially in charge. André Duman is. But I'm assistant faculty coordinator. His travel expenses and mine are covered by the grant he secured."

"About Mr. Duman, Bennett said that he and Molly had an argument right before the flight. He said you were there and could confirm that."

The mood in the room instantly changed, and I could feel my heart rate increase. I no longer saw Jack Wood's solemn attitude as an occupational habit but something else. Was André a suspect?

"Yes, I was there," I said carefully. "It wasn't really an argument, though. Molly was very… opinionated."

"And what was Mr. Duman's opinion of Molly?" continued Jack.

"He… I don't think he knew her that well," I said.

Jack crossed his arms. "Bennett Jaspers said Molly thought Mr. Duman was a tyrannical Frenchman, so I know that they knew each other in some capacity."

"I guess I can't say how well they knew each other, but I can say their argument wasn't that big a deal. Academics are used to having differing opinions." I needed to take the focus off André's quarrel with Molly. Faculty and students alike would have overheard the squabble and soon would be confirming Bennett's account. Was there some other person who could interest the police? Then it came to me. "Someone at the bar was acting very peculiar."

"Who?" asked Ernest.

I leaned forward. "I don't know her name, but there was a lady with red hair who asked a girl in our group about Molly Jaspers. She mistook me for Molly. It could have been due to my curly hair," I said, pointing to my head. "She stared at me for quite some time, and I was disturbed when I noticed she was boarding our flight to Paris."

"Was she seated near Dr. Jaspers?" asked Ernest.

"A couple rows behind her," I said with enthusiasm.

Ernest nodded and scribbled something in his notebook. He began to comment, but Jack cut him off. "Thank you for the information, Ms. Prather. That will be all for now. We have a lot of people to get through tonight. We may have further questions for you after cause of death is determined."

"Wasn't it… peanuts that caused Molly's death?" I asked.

"We can't assume that," said Jack. "Only a medical examiner can determine cause of death."

I felt like I was missing something.

"You know, Professor...." Ernest recreated the EpiPen scenario using his pencil. Then he shook his head. "Nothing."

"Of course," I said. "If it was anaphylaxis, the EpiPen should have stopped the attack. Why didn't it?"

The question wouldn't be answered any time soon.

Chapter Six

MINNEAPOLIS IS A nice city, and our hotel, built in 1925, was in the heart of it. Although old, the hotel had style and space. The rambling brown and white structure took up an entire city block with its attached bar and restaurant. As I stepped under the scalloped awning that read NORMANDY INN, I was glad we had settled on this hotel, despite having to sleep three to a room. Although we were a ways from the airport, the location was desirable and the price affordable. Plus, from the look of the granite front desk, some of the hotel had been remodeled with modern conveniences and would provide a comfortable night's sleep after our harrowing ordeal.

The lobby held two seating areas, one with a grand fireplace and one with plush leather chairs. The walls were decorated with quaint photos and clocks and memorabilia, and with the hotel's beamed ceilings and heavy woodwork, it was as if we had stepped back in time. The group, looking collectively defeated from the experience at the airport, congregated around the entrance for instructions from André.

"It has not been an easy day, and I know some of you suffer deeply. On the ride here, the good doctor Judith Spade was so kind as to connect me with the Student Counseling Center on campus."

He motioned toward Judith, who nodded.

He continued, "They provide support in situations like ours and will arrange for a special 1-800 number for us to use. When it becomes active, I will text all of you with the number. Your calls will be kept completely confidential, so take advantage of the service as you sort through your feelings about Professor Jaspers' death. Are there any questions about the number or how to use it?"

The group remained silent.

He cleared his throat. "I have paired you up just as we planned to do in France. With a few changes," he added, glancing at Bennett.

Bennett's voice was haggard. "I appreciate your leadership, André, but I could use a little time alone to sort this out. To make some calls. I don't feel right staying here with all that's happened."

"I understand," André said, "but I don't know where else you can stay unless you know someone in town. All the other hotels we contacted were fully booked."

Bennett didn't look convinced.

"The police officers said you shouldn't be alone right now," I said, "and I have to agree with them. We all could use the company."

Glancing around the group, I realized that we looked exhausted from the long day. Perhaps Bennett realized it too.

"I know," he said. "I'm sorry. You lost a good friend and colleague today."

André pulled out a folded piece of paper from his blazer pocket. "We will respect your privacy as much as we can, won't we?" The group nodded, and André unfolded the list. "I have tried to accommodate everyone in the best way possible. All the suites have two beds and a pullout. Nick, Bennett, and Jace will room together. Arnold, Aaron, and I go in another room.

Em, Kat, and Amanda, you are together. That leaves Judith, Meg, and Olivia. Have I excluded anyone?"

We looked at one another expectantly.

"Okay, then. We continue." André led the charge to the front desk, where a young man in a black polo shirt texted on his cellphone. He pushed the phone beneath the counter before looking up.

"Good evening," said André. "I reserved some rooms earlier tonight."

"Your name?" said the front desk clerk.

"My name is André Duman, but there are twelve occupants." Andre took his credit card out of his wallet and passed it across the counter.

"We can't get everyone on the same floor. Is that okay?"

André nodded. "Yes, of course."

"We will get you as close together as possible, though." The clerk looked into his computer screen as if it explained the mystery of the Great Sphinx, typing and clicking at regular intervals. As he searched for rooms, he described the hotel's amenities: bar, grill, pool, and workout facility. He even ticked off all the nearby attractions until he realized by the dazed look in our eyes that we probably weren't here on vacation. Finally he opened his drawer and retrieved the magnetic card keys, tucking them individually into their respective miniature envelopes. He wrote the room numbers on the front. "Floors two and three."

"Thank you, and thank you for the information." André turned to the group, who huddled behind him, and passed out the cards. I took the envelope for Amanda, Kat, and me.

When André finished passing out the last envelope, he composed himself, taking a quick breath. "It's only one night, friends. We must remain together. I know most of you ate at the airport, but if you become hungry, we have the restaurant right here. As the gentleman said, the grill is open until midnight, and you are welcome to order room service if you'd rather stay in. Just be reasonable if you do so. Nothing over twenty dollars. There is also a convenience store not far from here that I saw on the drive in. Any questions?"

Nobody said anything.

"We will meet back here, in the lobby, at nine in the morning to discuss our plans."

The way the boys were eagerly eyeing the door of the hotel told me that the last thing they planned on doing was sticking together. It was spring break, after all, and it appeared even the death of a professor hadn't completely dampened their spirits. Though as for that, people grieve in all sorts of different ways. Meg and Olivia, for instance, were whispering before we reached the elevator. The death made them especially talkative. I was just thankful André had put me with Kat and Amanda, who were respectfully subdued, acting in a manner I thought appropriate to the situation. He probably knew that if anyone could handle hyper Olivia and Meg, it was Judith Spade.

"We are on floors two and three, according to the desk clerk," said André as we squeezed into the elevator. Bennett pushed buttons 2 and 3, and the elevator lurched upward. The movement sent the girls into another burst of chatter.

The door opened on the second floor, and Bennett, Nick, Jace, Judith, Olivia, and Meg got out. Aaron was about to follow until André said, "We're on the third floor, Aaron."

"Call me," said Aaron to Jace before the door closed.

The door opened again to the third floor. We walked down the long hall with our luggage. Our room was right next to André, Arnold, and Aaron's.

"This is us," I said, "305."

"And we are 307," said André. He hesitated at his door.

"You did a very good job back there," I reassured him.

"With Judith's help," he said. "In the taxi, she told me whom to call."

I brushed off his uncertainty. "She's been here a long time; she knows how to handle these situations. Plus, she's a medical doctor. She deals with death all the time." Amanda and Kat waited at the door, and I quickly scanned a room key. "We'd better get settled."

"Yes, we will talk after I call the airlines," said André. "They gave me a special telephone number."

"Let me know what you find out," I said and ducked into the room behind Amanda and Kat.

The large suite had two double beds, with a nightstand in between, and a sitting area with a sleeper sofa, round table, and two chairs. Although we were in the older part of the hotel, the room was nicely renovated with a slim TV and refrigerator. If we purchased beverages at the vending machine, we would have a place to keep them cold. I was more interested in the fully stocked tray of coffees and teas. It was a welcome sight for a coffee addict like me, and I'd put it to good use in the morning.

I switched on the light near the sleeper sofa, and Amanda turned on the ornate table lamp on the nightstand. With a few clicks, our empty suite became cozy and comfortable.

Amanda sat next to Kat on the bed closest to the window, and Kat gave her shoulders a squeeze. Kat was such a caring friend. She was easy to get along with, and even if I weren't her professor, I would have enjoyed her company. I was glad she was there to comfort Amanda because I didn't know her well. She had never been my student.

"Are you feeling better?" Kat said.

Amanda nodded. "A little."

"Did you guys need something to eat?" I heaved my luggage atop the worn luggage rack near the door.

"No," said Kat. "We grabbed yogurt and fruit at the airport."

"So, you're not hungry?"

Kat shrugged off her hoodie and shook out her hair. "Not yet."

"I'm getting a little hungry," I said, sitting down on the other bed.

Kat faced me, cross-legged. She pulled her dark hair forward, revealing emerald streaks I hadn't noticed before. "What's going to happen now, Professor Prather? The cops at the airport were so serious, like maybe we couldn't leave. I felt like I was under arrest."

I sighed. "I wish I knew, but to be honest, I don't have any more idea than you what will happen tomorrow. I think the officers were just being judicious because of the severity of the case. After all, someone died, and they have to figure out how."

Amanda looked pale. I didn't know if it was her pink Oxford shirt or the conversation that caused her complexion to turn. "Do you think she had a heart attack?" asked Amanda.

"Bennett seemed to think she came in contact with a peanut," I said. "And as you know, she was severely allergic. But I don't think anyone is sure yet what happened. We will probably find out more information tomorrow after the medical examiner has inspected Molly's body."

At the word *body*, Amanda shivered, and I changed topics.

"What a day," I said, leaning against the bed pillows and stretching my legs out in front of me. "I wonder how the other girls are faring. Do you know Meg and Olivia?"

Kat and Amanda exchanged a snort.

"Olivia and I were in Professor Jaspers' Western civ class last spring," said Amanda. "She hates me. I got an A, but she flunked. That's why she's not in the sorority anymore."

I frowned. "So what does that have to do with you?"

She looked at Kat, and Kat nodded, silently assuring her that she could trust me. "I don't want her to get in trouble, so please don't say anything, but she wanted to cheat off my exams. Of course I said no. There was no way I was going to chance ruining my good relationship with Dr. Jaspers. She took me on an expedition to New Mexico with *grad students*."

"How cool is that?" said Kat.

"Very cool," I agreed. "You did the right thing. Abetting a cheater could have besmirched your permanent record."

"That's what I said," Kat agreed. "Well, not in those words," she added with a laugh.

Kat's phone buzzed, and the girls began to chat about the text. It must have been something funny because they shared a chuckle. I reached for my canvas tote beside the bed, rummaging for some reading material. Nothing looked appealing. The truth was, I didn't feel like reading. I felt as restless as Aaron and Jace. The anticipation I felt for Paris hadn't gone away just because Molly was dead. I yearned for some sort of release that couldn't be found in a book.

I pulled out my worn leather journal. Writing had always provided relief in the past. As a young girl and only child, I invented things about people or places in my neighborhood in Detroit as a way to make things better, easier. For most of the families, problems were real, insurmountable, inescapable. Reading and writing were the only tangible ways to make them disappear, if only for an hour. As I grew older, an hour became two, and undergrad became grad school, and one day I had my PhD in literature. I realized then, the world I lived in could be largely of my own creation.

Tonight, though, the words wouldn't come. I bent my knees, creating a table of my lap, and removed my pen cap, poised to write. I took a deep breath. I readjusted my pillow. I looked over at Amanda and Kat, who were on their phones. I scratched my head, put down the pen, and thumbed through the last few pages. I stopped and flipped back to yesterday's entry. That's right: Lenny was in Minneapolis tonight, playing at First Avenue! I looked at the alarm clock on the nightstand. It was just nine o'clock. I could still hear him play and talk over what had happened on the plane.

I glanced again at Amanda and Kat. Should I leave them alone? They were both adults; the university wouldn't allow students under eighteen to travel because, while faculty members chaperoned planned stops and events, group members didn't spend all their time together. But after today, I wanted to get their okay.

"If you don't mind, I think I'll go out for a little while," I said, hopping down from the bed and walking toward the vanity mirror. "I could use some air."

"We don't mind at all," Kat said a little too quickly. Perhaps she welcomed the chance to talk to Amanda alone without her professor eavesdropping. "Where are you going?"

"I'm going to see a friend who happens to be in town playing at First Avenue."

Amanda looked surprised. "You have a friend performing in Minneapolis?"

"Friend and colleague. You might know him, too. Professor Jenkins? From English? He plays guitar."

"Cool," said Kat. "I love live music, but I couldn't move ten steps right now. I'm wiped."

I asked them what they planned to do, and they both agreed they wanted to stay in and rest after the long day. I didn't blame them. If I hadn't been so puzzled by the death of Molly Jaspers, I would have stayed in too. But my curious nature always got the better of me, and I looked forward to the prospect of talking over the events with Lenny. The girls, on the other hand, were excited about ordering room service later, which I found endearing. I had forgotten how fun it could be to browse a hotel menu, pondering the array of choices available in a big city restaurant.

I stood up and gathered my makeup bag from my luggage while the girls looked on. At the vanity, I picked through my curls, happy to be released from the up-do. I sprayed a few squirts of hairspray near the top of my head and smoothed the hairs that stood straight up. Then I applied a fresh coat of eyeliner and exchanged my blazer for a leather jacket. A pair of large silver hoops completed my attempt at club attire.

I grabbed a room key and zipped it in my purse. "I won't be late," I said. Then I wrote my cellphone number on the complimentary notepad. "If you need anything, just call. And of course, André is right next door."

"We'll be totally fine," said Kat. "You look great, by the way."

"Really? Thank you," I said.

Amanda agreed, nodding beneath her drape of blonde hair. *A bang trim would really do wonders for the girl*, I thought as I slipped on my shoes. It was hard to read a person who had so much hair in her eyes. I couldn't tell if she was really feeling better.

The door barely sounded as it closed gently behind me, a tiny click in the silent hall. Then I was off to surprise Lenny.

Chapter Seven

First Avenue wasn't far from Eighth Street, less than a mile, but it took the cab driver several spins and turns around the corners of one-way streets to land at our destination. Although I normally would have found a walk invigorating, when I spotted a cab parked outside the hotel, I jumped in to save time. It was after nine o'clock, and I didn't want to miss Lenny's band.

As I stepped out of the cab, I took a welcome breath of fresh air, even though it was frosty cold. The energy surrounding the bar was palpable as music lovers congregated in front of the round building. The whole scene gave off a Saturday night vibe and revitalized my spirit. I had seen the black structure before, just never this close up. My knowledge of the place boiled down to one fact and one fact only: Prince had his start here. Ever since then, many young artists had come here with the same hope—to be discovered. They had even etched their names in the white stars that lighted up the sides of the building with contrasting paint. This was the "it" place to be in the Midwest for musicians, and frankly, as I paid my cover charge and took in the enormity of the stage, I was surprised

Lenny had been invited to play such a prestigious gig, even if only in a warm-up band. The headliners called themselves The Ice-Cold Undertakers, according to the tarp that hung behind the stage.

From the looks of it, I had just missed the opening numbers and, thankfully, what must have been a snaking line outside. There were at least a hundred people pressed against the foot of the stage—perhaps more. I got as close to the stage as I could, which wasn't close.

Lenny was on the left side, near an enormous speaker, the bright stage lights streaming down from the ceiling like rays of smoky sunlight. He wore a black T-shirt and tight blue jeans and looked very much the part of a rock star with his spiky blond hair and nine-o'clock shadow. No one in this crowd would have guessed he was a professor. But I knew how good a musician he was. I had heard him play at bars, bashes, and Christmas parties. His playing went beyond hobby. He radiated pure talent, a quality that, unlike literature, couldn't be taught in a book.

The music pulsated through my body, the drumbeat taking the place of my heartbeat, and it felt good to be somewhere loud. It pushed out every single thought in my head, including the one of Paris. I was happy to be here, watching a very good friend perform. His fingers slid up and down the guitar as if they were part of the instrument, and I wondered how he worked without the benefit of sheet music. Some people were born with that ability, I guessed. They just knew what to do.

Lenny and the band began to build to something, and although I wasn't familiar with the songs, I could tell they were prepping the crowd for the main act, The Ice-Cold Undertakers. The beat grew steadier and more repetitive, and the stage lights turned colors. The volume of the audience rose in anticipation; they were jumping up and down to the refrain. Smoke began to billow from the stage, and four men emerged in death's-heads. The effect was ghostly, but the crowd wasn't shaken. Girls screamed as if at a boy-band concert. When the smoke cleared and the Undertakers began to play, I noted Lenny and the opening group had disappeared from the stage altogether. My heart sank as I scanned the crowd; he had to be backstage.

I managed to get to the bar with a bit of effort, moving in the opposite direction of the crowd. Their bodies formed a dense wall, fortunately one with cracks I could sneak through. The small, open space at the bar was a welcome relief. I smiled at the bartender and ordered a beer.

As he poured from the tap, I said, "I know one of the guys in the opening band. Can you tell me how I can get backstage?"

He placed my beer on the counter, his massive arm a sleeve of tattoos. I especially admired the hourglass covered in thorns. Had we been in a quieter venue, I might have remarked on its metaphorical meaning.

"You know one of the guys, huh?" A large grin spread his thick goatee and revealed a beautiful set of straight, white teeth.

He didn't believe me. I handed him my cash. "Yes, Lenny Jenkins, the guitar player. He's a good friend of mine."

He took the money and punched some keys on the register. "Look, sweetheart, if you want to see your *friend*, I suggest you call him." He slapped my change on the counter.

"That would be a good idea except for the high-decibel noise level." I took a drink of my beer, which was on the warm side of lukewarm. "If you would point me in the direction of the dressing rooms, I could wait outside."

He shook his head and pointed to a plain door at the left. "Dressing rooms?" He laughed. "They come out over there."

I left my change on the counter. "Thank you."

I walked toward the door, but I knew by the size of the two gentlemen standing outside, I would not be allowed to enter. Their shirts didn't say *Security,* but their crossed arms certainly did. Although the general scene was one of complete chaos, the two men stood apart from their surroundings, calm and serene. I had a feeling they sensed my presence the moment I entered their space, though neither looked directly at me.

Before I could devise a nefarious plan to get past the men, Lenny burst through the door covered in sweat and bristling with excitement.

"Lenny!" I called out.

He stopped, looking left and right; then his face lit up at the sight of me.

We came together in a matter of seconds. Caught up in the rock-and-roll atmosphere, I threw my arms around his shoulders, and he returned my affection with a squeeze of my waist.

His hands still resting on my hips, he regarded me from head to toe. "What are you doing here? I thought you'd be halfway to Paris by now."

"It's a long story," I said with a smile. "First, let me say you were great out there. Electrifying."

"You saw me?" he said, leading me to a quieter corner. "When did you get here?"

"About fifteen minutes ago," I said.

He looked off in the direction of the crowd, and I knew he was thinking back to his performance.

"You want to go listen to the band?"

He refocused on me. "Nah. I'd rather hear what the hell happened to Paris. You want to get out of here?"

"I *am* kind of hungry," I said.

"Come on. There's a pizza joint not far from here." He took my hand and pulled me in the direction of the entrance. As we walked past the bar, I flashed a smile at the bartender, nodding toward Lenny. He gave me a wave with his bar rag.

The night air was exhilarating as we walked two blocks to the brick building with the red and white glowing Pizza La Vista sign. Inside, the pizzeria was packed with people grabbing a bite on their way to or from the bar. Two wooden-slat booths opened at the same time, and we made a beeline for the one closest to the window. Street watching would be better than staring at the white walls, which could only be described as drab. There was no décor, unless you counted the neon lights that shouted OPEN, PIZZA, and ATM. Only the half-drunk patrons colored the atmosphere, many of them laughing or talking loudly, but I was happy to be away from the dour travel group and immersed in a carefree crowd.

Lenny squinted at the menu on the long whiteboard above the order counter. "I'm dying to know what you're doing sitting across from me, but we gotta order first. I'm starving. Medium? Large?" he asked.

"Medium should be fine. What about a supreme?"

He smiled. "That's right. You like a lot of stuff on your pizza."

"True," I said, "but I'm up for anything."

He unzipped his jacket, taking his wallet out of the side pocket. "I'm easy."

"Hey, we can split it." I started digging through my purse.

"I got it," he said, standing to go place our order. "A free pizza's not Paris, but it's something."

I watched him order our food, stopping at the cooler to pull out a couple of sodas. I nodded and smiled as he held up the Coke cans. I was so glad I had found him. Although I was staying among faculty members, I didn't know them nearly as well as I knew Lenny. Other than André, I'd had only passing conversations with my colleagues on the trip. None of them were from the English Department, where most of my time was spent, and none of them were involved with the same projects I was. But Lenny and I had grown close in our tight-knit department.

Lenny slid my soda across the table and sat down, our eyes really meeting for the first time that night. "So, what the hell happened on the way to Paris? Someone must have died."

I raised my eyebrows.

His face fell. "Oh god. Someone did die."

"Molly Jaspers, from the History Department," I said.

Lenny paled. "The eco-nut? Jeez. What happened?"

I passed out the paper napkins and plates he had brought back with the sodas. "She died midflight… from a peanut allergy, we think. She was deathly allergic to them."

"Were peanuts on the flight?" he asked. "I know some airlines avoid them altogether now."

I nodded. "Despite protests from Bennett, her husband."

He shook his head. "So I suppose he'll sue the shit out of the airlines."

I took a sip of my pop. "I have no idea. The entire group is staying in a hotel on Eighth Street tonight."

"What a way to spend spring break," said Lenny.

"I think I'd rather be home grading papers." I laughed.

Lenny drank half his soda with one large swig. "Not me. I'd rather face an inquest than read through my survey class's papers. They've been a train wreck this semester."

I gave him a sympathetic look, and we sat in silence for a few minutes. We were both contemplating the situation, or at least I was. He might have been contemplating anything. I took another sip of Coke. "Don't you think it's a little odd that Molly Jaspers died of a peanut allergy when everyone knew she was allergic to them?"

He shrugged. "Not really, considering everyone on the plane had a bag of them. Peanut allergies can be pretty serious. They make the throat totally seize up."

"I wonder…" I said.

He rolled his eyes. "Not this again."

An employee appeared with our pizza, plopping it between us and shoving a spatula beneath one of the pieces before dashing off. Lenny took the spatula and served me a large droopy piece, his eyes still studying me.

I sprinkled my pizza with hot peppers, well aware of Lenny's persistent stare. "You have to admit the whole thing is rather odd. Everyone knew the woman was allergic to peanuts because Bennett protested when the stewardess passed them out. Molly didn't take any peanuts, and neither did Bennett. And then Molly goes into anaphylactic shock? It's all very unusual if you ask me."

Lenny took the pepper shaker and shook it liberally as he spoke. "It's talk like that, Prather, that's going to keep you in Minneapolis all week. You know how cops feed off people's vibes, and your vibe right now reads SUSPECT."

I nodded. "Exactly… that's what I'm saying. I *could* be a suspect. I ordered the peanuts."

"I bet André is bummed," he said.

I loved it when he tried to change the subject. He was so obvious. But I nodded anyway, unable to speak with a mouthful of pizza. The vegetables were fresh and the crust thick and buttery. I swallowed, delicately dabbing my mouth with my napkin. "That's the worst of it. André doesn't know it yet, but the police suspect him. He had an argument with Molly in the airport that everyone overheard."

"André? That's nuts… no pun intended."

I chuckled.

"Well, if they had any proof, they would have arrested him," he said, finishing his soda. "So until they come at him with the handcuffs, I would keep my opinions to myself."

I opened my mouth and then shut it. He had a point. The university would have enough trouble as it was, dealing with an unexpected accident on a sponsored trip. At least no one had thought to take out their phones. Otherwise, Molly's picture might have been all over Facebook.

"Where are you staying again?" he asked.

It took me a moment to remember the name. "The Normandy Inn."

"Oh sure. I know that place." Lenny's brow furrowed. "Are you rooming with—"

"Kat and Amanda," I interrupted. "Students in André's French class. Kat's in my creative writing class, too."

His face relaxed. "Right. Of course. You have students with you."

I was puzzled by Lenny's reaction. "That's sort of the reason for the entire trip, if you remember. Which reminds me, I have to get back soon. The girls might need me."

"Well, I'm parked in a garage not far from here. I'll take you back when we're done."

For the rest of the hour, we munched on pizza and talked about Lenny's performance and First Avenue and what it felt like to play in such a venue. When I joked with him about turning professional, he just laughed, but I wondered if he would have liked to live in the city again, playing shows more frequently. His music was as much a part of him as a hand or foot; anyone watching him perform could see as much. But I had a feeling he was as conflicted as I was about big cities. There was something about them that had driven us away, something we'd never spoken aloud. Maybe it had to do with money. For the wealthy, the city meant specialty stores and Starbucks; for others, it meant high rents, high prices, and little room to move. Or maybe it had to do with injustice. So many had so little yet suffered so much. Whatever it was, the feeling never left me, even after I left.

I waited inside the restaurant while Lenny got the car. When I heard a beep outside, I pulled open the glass door, the cold wind stinging the corners of my eyes. Lenny was throwing food wrappers from the front to the backseat as I opened the passenger door to his Ford Taurus.

"Sorry, this thing is a mess," he said, brushing off the seat with his hand.

"You didn't exactly expect company."

"Did you say the place is on Eighth?" He twisted into traffic, which was heavy because of the downtown events letting out. A cab driver gave him a honk.

I nodded, pulling out my envelope keycard. "Because of the last-minute reservation, we're three to a room."

He grinned. "You can stay with me at my sister's house if you'd like. I'm sure my nieces would be thrilled to wake up to another girl in the house."

The offer was tempting, though we both knew it was impractical given the circumstances. To snuggle into a warm bed in a nice home in the suburbs sounded heavenly. "Don't you think your sister would be offended by your bringing home a strange woman?"

He cocked an eyebrow. "Are you a strange woman?"

I smiled mischievously. "I can be."

He laughed. "My sister's cool. Really, she wouldn't care."

"I wish I could," I said, "but I'd better go back to the hotel. I'm helping to manage this unraveling affair, and I don't know if we're getting on another plane or heading home. We'll find out more tomorrow. One of the police detectives said that he'd want to question us further."

"My advice to you, Em, is to keep it short and simple. Don't go into all the possibilities for Molly's death; keep those safely tucked away in your frontal lobes with all your other conspiracy theories."

"That's not fair. *You're* the conspiracy junkie."

"Elvis?" he said, a large question mark hanging over the word.

I shook my head. "Well, *everybody* knows he's living out his golden years in a Pyrenees tribe…. Hey, this is me."

He pulled up alongside the parking lot adjacent to the hotel, letting the car idle. "Call me tomorrow. I want to know what happens."

"I will," I promised. "André still believes… *who is that*?" I shrank down in my seat.

Lenny looked over at me and then at the parking lot. "What are you doing?"

"Shh. That guy, over there. Isn't that Nick Dramsdor?"

"It depends," whispered Lenny. "Who is Nick Dramsdor?"

"Right. I forgot you don't know him. He's a paleontologist

from Western State. He's in our group." I peeked out the window. "It *is* him."

As he walked around the corner of the hotel, his shadow came into focus. He looked left and right before entering the building.

"Well, that's interesting," I said. "I wonder where he's coming from."

Lenny sat up straighter in his seat. "What's someone from Western State doing in the group anyway? He doesn't look old enough to be a real prof."

"I know. I have to ask about his sunscreen. It's really doing its job." I squinted for a closer look. "I guess he was a good friend of Molly's. *Who's that now*?" As a form entered the light of the streetlamp, I knew in an instant it was Amanda. I would recognize her flat-ironed hair anywhere.

"It looks like a student. Do you know her?" asked Lenny.

I nodded. "It's Amanda, one of the girls staying in my room. She must have left Kat behind. I had no idea Amanda was friendly with Nick Dramsdor."

"What are you saying? The young professor was mingling with a co-ed?" Lenny said.

"Well, it can't be a coincidence, can it? Look at her glancing over her shoulder."

Amanda was doing her best to appear nonchalant as she opened the front door of the hotel, tossing her hair as she entered.

"Looks like she and the paleontologist were out on a moonlit dig to me," said Lenny.

"That is what it looks like," I agreed. "I thought they knew each other through Molly, but I wasn't certain. They both were on a trip with her in New Mexico, though. Maybe they were discussing her death. Maybe they *know* something."

"Maybe, but that sounds like a stretch. Maybe they just hooked up in the heat of the moment."

I frowned. "She doesn't seem like the impetuous type."

Lenny grasped my hands, their warmth radiating up my wrist. “Don’t overthink this, Em. You’ll never sleep tonight. People hook up for all sorts of reasons, or no reason at all. The coldness of a night, even, can bring people together.”

What he said was true. Being in a tight place with a warm body made even the impossible seem possible. “No, I won’t sleep,” I said as his look sent tingles up and down my spine. For the first time, it seemed, I realized how Lenny’s body affected my own.

“Call me tomorrow?” he said but didn’t release my hand.

I nodded, lingering a moment longer. Then I was out of the car, walking into the hotel, unsure of what floor I pushed on the elevator buttons.

Chapter Eight

I DIDN'T SLEEP well, not that I ever did, but my thoughts went beyond Amanda and Nick. Seeing a colleague die right in front of me had shaken me more than I realized. I had never been afraid of death; it wasn't that. From an early age, catechism classes taught me death was natural and even welcome. Later, literature would become my instructor and add its bleaker lessons. But seeing a life expunged before my eyes, not just on a page, made me recognize life's fragility, its brevity, and I valued the moment in the car with Lenny even more.

I had always found him attractive. I doubted there was a woman on campus who didn't. But I ignored my physical attraction to him because, in many ways, we were opposites. Yet our differences, and all the importance I had placed on them, had dissipated in the space between us in the car. What remained was the warmth of his hands in the coldness of the night, and I realized how extraordinary it could be to have someone after everyone has left. I wanted *that* in my life, to care for someone. Perhaps it could be him.

When the sun began to drench the faded drapes Sunday morning, I shot out of the sofa bed like a bullet released from its chamber. I had been awake for over an hour and could lie still no longer. Amanda and Kat didn't stir, and in fact, hadn't stirred all night. They were both sleeping when I entered the room, or pretending to be asleep, and they stayed that way the entire night through.

To be eighteen again, I thought as I flung open the shower curtain. Then I laughed out loud, the sleep deprivation kicking in. I would no more be eighteen again than return to Detroit. At that age, I had kept myself happily intoxicated with historical romances. Who was I kidding? I laughed again as I stepped into the lukewarm water. I was still doing that ten years later.

By the time the group assembled in the lobby a couple of hours later, I had finished one book, thumbed through three magazines, and drunk three cups of coffee, two of them brewed in the room and one of them from a coffee shop a mile and a half away. As I sat in the lobby's leather chair, sipping the last drops from my paper cup, faculty members began to arrive, then students. Aaron and Jace scurried in at exactly nine o'clock, and Olivia and Meg had stumbled in a few minutes earlier. They all looked as exhausted as I felt, and I wondered if they'd gone out together, especially when Olivia greeted Aaron with a wink. Judith Spade appeared to be unaware that anything torrid might have happened under her watchful eye. She looked exactly the same as she had yesterday: clean, smart, and vaguely uninterested. Nick and Amanda said nothing to give away their late-night rendezvous, but they stood next to each other, exchanging secret smiles. Kat leaned against the far wall, silently observing the group. I had a feeling no one but me noticed her there; she really did blend in. The only one missing was André, which surprised me. I thought he would have been the first one down. Just as I was about to call him on my cellphone, he came rushing out of the elevator. I stood and walked over to the group. I knew right away something was wrong. Everyone else knew it, too, because the entire group stopped talking as he approached.

"Good morning," said André, winded.

A few of us returned his greeting.

André coughed. "I just finished talking to Mr. Wood at the police department. He wants us to meet him at his precinct downtown. I have the address." He held up a little slip of hotel notepad paper. "There is new information about Molly Jaspers."

Bennett, who looked tired and pale, came to life all at once. "What? What is this about Molly? Why didn't he have the decency to contact me? I'm her husband."

André shook his head. "I do not know. I am faculty coordinator, and so he contacts me. Maybe he wasn't certain you were with us. He asked and I said, thankfully, yes. You decided to stay among friends."

"What is the new information?" Bennett said.

"He did not say. Maybe they are ready to release her so that you can go home?"

"What about our flight? What about spring break? What about *Paris*?" asked Olivia in a whiny voice.

Her timing couldn't have been worse. Bennett turned to her with hatred in his eyes. "Is that all you can think of? Your little trip to Paris? You selfish child! A woman is dead. My *wife* is dead."

"Mr. Jaspers, you have our sincerest condolences. Please know that," said Judith Spade. "Molly was a dear friend to all of us. But she, more than anyone, believed in the importance of academic exploration. She would sympathize with the students' desire to continue with their trip. They're young. It's only natural."

Judith sounded so intelligent, looked so intelligent, and was so intelligent that nobody responded. We simply nodded our heads. Even Bennett was chastened.

"You're right, of course, Judith. *I* am being selfish. You were all friends with Molly, and you are grieving, too." He looked around at the group. "Forgive me."

André patted his shoulder. "Think nothing of it. Let us go

and find out what this new information is, shall we, friend?"

Bennett agreed.

"It is not far from here, one mile to be exact. The detective gave me good directions for walking," said André.

A few of the students moaned, but André paid no attention. He led the group to the front door and I fell in beside him.

"I was worried about you. I stopped by your room last night, and Amanda said you are gone. Poof!" He made a dramatic gesture with his hands that I assumed was supposed to be a puff of smoke.

"I should have mentioned it, but I came up with a plan at the last minute, and I didn't know if you felt up to going out. Lenny Jenkins, from English, happens to be in town, so I went to see him perform. He plays guitar, you know."

"Yes, yes, I know," André replied. "He played rock and roll one Christmas party. He accompanied you, no? You are quite a singer."

I felt the heat in my face, knowing I was probably the same color as my bright pink scarf, an accessory that would have blended in perfectly with the Paris scenery. It felt like everyone in Copper Bluff had been there for my performance that snowy Christmas evening, an evening that included copious amounts of wine and a discussion between Lenny and me about nonconformity. "Yes, well, thank you. Lenny can be quite persuasive."

"I enjoyed myself very much—except for the wine. I distinctly remember it being tasteless and cheap," he scoffed.

I waved off the comment. "It's always the case at those events." I lowered my voice. "Last night, what time did you come to my room?"

"Right after I unpacked. Maybe nine thirty? Why do you ask?"

"No reason," I shrugged. "I just wondered. Amanda left the room last night, but she was back by the time I returned."

"She was there at nine thirty, so it must have been late, but

I did not hear the door open or close. She probably went to get snacks. I know the boys did. Aaron was digging into his Funyuns bag long after I went to bed. The noise, not to mention the smell, made sleep difficult, to say the least."

I nodded, but I doubted she'd been getting snacks. There was no evidence of food or candy wrappers in the room. If André was right about the time, though, she and Nick couldn't have been out for long. What could they have talked about that needed to be said under the cloak of darkness? I hung back from André, pretending to take in the city streets. Really, I hoped to get in step with Amanda. I hadn't had a chance to question her about last night. I wondered if she would admit to sneaking out with Nick Dramsdor.

It being Sunday morning, the streets were deserted, and the sound of our collective footsteps echoed among silent bars and buildings. Our side of the street was white with bright spring sunlight, and the budding trees in the cross boulevards basked in its warmth. After a few more mornings like these, the leaves would burst open and green up the city and its sister city, Saint Paul. Together they formed one of the largest metropolises in the Midwest but also one of the friendliest. Despite its size and population, I felt at home.

Amanda and Kat caught up with me, and I was enveloped by strong notes of perfume, the same fruity scent all girls their age wore. Had one of them carried a cut watermelon under her arm, I wouldn't have been surprised. It was that pungent.

"I hope I didn't wake you when I came in last night. I was out a little later than I expected," I said.

"No. We had just shut off the light," said Amanda.

"Oh. I didn't realize. I thought you both were sleeping. Did you go out, too?"

Kat gazed off in the other direction. She was good at disappearing into her own world.

"Not really," said Amanda.

Well, *there* was an evasive answer. Either you did go out or you didn't, and I knew Amanda *had* been outside the hotel with Nick. "Were you—" I began, but Kat cut me off.

"I'm hungry. Are we going to eat?"

"I'm hungry, too," said Jace, loping behind us.

I turned around to acknowledge his comment but wasn't sure how to respond. The boy looked as if he had grown another inch since the last time I saw him. I didn't think we had time to stop to eat, yet these students—who suddenly seemed a lot like growing children—were hungry. I felt responsible for feeding them. "I'll talk to André. I'll inform him of the situation."

I had to run to catch up with André, who led the front of the group. He was walking briskly with no one beside him. "A few of the students say they're hungry. Do we have time for breakfast?"

"I don't think so," he said, pulling at his button-up collar. He wore a fitted long-sleeved shirt, black with a subtle, gray-paisley print. It paired perfectly with his jeans, and I had a feeling he knew more about fashion than I did—and probably half of South Dakota. "Jack Wood insisted that we come to the station right now before anyone disembarks."

"I understand," I said, sympathetically. "They will just need to wait until after we find out more information. Did Mr. Wood give you any clue as to what this was about?"

"Not a one. I think he was afraid we were getting on the next plane to Paris, but I spoke to the airline last night and told him this was not the case. Even with our number down to eleven, taking into account Molly and Bennett, the airline couldn't find seats. They have openings tomorrow on a multi-stop flight through Amsterdam, but this makes no sense. We wouldn't get there until Tuesday." He sighed and slumped a little, a picture of defeat.

"Why didn't you tell me you spoke to the airlines?" I was a little miffed he hadn't relayed the information right away.

"Because I had no verification and didn't want to blow your bubble. The airline is supposed to confirm this morning. I was going to tell you then." He gave me a small smile. "Based on my talk with them last night, though, I'm afraid we will be going back to Copper Bluff. I put in a call to the bus company."

He'd only verified what I already knew; still, I felt sad. I had dreamed of this trip so many times that it was not easy to see it fade away into that vague place called *future*. I tried to recall Giles's smart words but couldn't. Sure, I could make the trip to France on my own, and maybe someday I would, but with my hefty student loan payments and low yearly salary, the probability of that happening was on par with getting a full night's sleep. Chances were, it just wasn't going to happen.

André stopped in front of a squat, two-story brick building. "This is it," he said, checking the address against the numbers on the glass front doors, as if he doubted the upper-case letters on the building that read POLICE.

Arnold Frasier, his hair slicked back in a fresh ponytail, held open the door while we filed inside. As the students crossed the threshold, their conversations ceased. The faculty stood quietly aside, allowing André to take the lead.

In the busy lobby was an anteroom with a window like an old-fashioned movie theater's. Above it read the words MINNEAPOLIS POLICE DEPARTMENT. Behind the desk sat a uniformed officer with a tightly knotted bun who motioned us closer. André stepped to the window.

"Good morning, Madam. I am André Duman. My group and I are here to see Jack Wood."

The woman, who was around forty, nodded and smiled without responding. She was obviously stunned by André's good looks and French accent.

"He called us on the phone," I added when the woman continued to stare.

Her trance broken, she glanced at me and picked up the phone. "One moment. You can have a seat while you wait." She motioned toward two rows of plastic chairs, about half already occupied, and pushed a button on her multi-line phone. We were only steps away from the window when Ernest Jones pushed through the metal doors that led to the rest of the station.

Ernest wore the same gray blazer as last evening, but his ketchup-stained shirt had been replaced by a deeply wrinkled white button-up. His smile was the same, lopsided and happy. I couldn't help but return the smile; his personality was infectious. His partner, Jack Wood, was not with him.

Since André stood at the front of the line, he was the first to shake Ernest's hand. Ernest went on to shake everyone's hands, including mine, his curly hair waggling with each pump of a hand. "Good morning. Good morning. Good morning," he greeted each of us.

"We are anxious to be here, Mr. Jones, as you can imagine," André replied. "It has been a difficult night for all of us, especially Bennett."

Ernest was sympathetic. "We will be as quick as possible. Come this way."

We walked through a metal detector and into a boxy room with about a dozen facing desks. Despite it being Sunday, the room was abuzz with activity: officers dressed in uniforms, officers dressed in plainclothes, and civilians, maybe filing a complaint or bailing out a friend from the dry-out tank. In the area were two offices with glass windows and wooden blinds. One was quite large, and a man sat inside behind a big, wooden desk. The other was smaller, and here was Jack Wood from last night. Beside him sat a new man I didn't recognize.

Ernest turned to open the office door. Jack Wood stood, a manila envelope in his hand, but the other man remained seated. He was bald and wore a black suit and black tie. From his dress, he looked like he was with the FBI, but I rejected the idea as cliché. Why would the FBI be interested in the death of Molly Jaspers?

"Good morning, and thank you for coming," Jack said to no one in particular. Although his crisp attire did not betray his fatigue, the bags under his bloodshot eyes seemed even more pronounced. I had a feeling the hardworking Jack Wood hadn't slept any better than I had. "We need some more information about the events that led up to Mrs. Jaspers' death. As you know, last night we were under a time crunch and had to get through hundreds of passengers."

"Anything you need, officers, so that I can take Molly home and bury her," said Bennett. "Her family will be arriving in Copper Bluff in a few days."

"Who's this?" said Olivia, pointing to the man in the black suit.

Although I guessed her mother had never told her it was impolite to point, I was glad she asked. We were all wondering the same thing.

Jack looked at the man in the black suit, then at the group. He laid the manila envelope on the desk. "When we first questioned people last night, we assumed Mrs. Jaspers had come into contact with peanuts, because of her allergy, but we didn't know for sure. This morning, the preliminary examination came back from the coroner stating Mrs. Jaspers died from acute anaphylactic shock."

A murmur rippled around the room.

"Of course I'm not surprised," said Bennett, "but it's still hard to hear. I could have prevented it. All of it." Tears filled his eyes, and he quickly wiped them away. "I'll never forgive myself."

"You can't blame yourself. It's not your fault," said Judith. "Coming from the School of Medicine, I can promise you these fatal reactions are a lot more common than people realize."

Jack continued, "I agree. We weren't surprised by the diagnosis either. But we were surprised that no peanuts were found in her snack, on her clothing, or on her person. So we'll have to investigate further to find out how she was contaminated. We need to determine negligence."

Another murmur passed through the group.

"Getting back to your question," said Jack, nodding toward

Olivia, "the Federal Bureau of Investigation has jurisdiction over any crimes that take place in the air. Since negligence is indicated here, Tom Sanders, from the FBI, will be overseeing the case."

Tom Sanders nodded briefly.

"Unfortunately, we won't be able to release the body today, Mr. Jaspers, but I promise you that we will do everything in our power to release it as quickly as possible. It shouldn't take more than seventy-two hours. In the meantime, you'll want to make arrangements for transport. You should deal with that before you leave."

"Yes, I'll need some help.... Molly wished to be cremated. She believed graveyards were a great waste of environmental resources." He talked like a man in a fog, unable to comprehend the tasks before him.

"Don't worry, Mr. Jaspers," said Ernest. He assured Bennett that he would help him with all the particulars. Then he motioned him toward the chair across the desk from the detectives. He asked the rest of us to wait outside by the TV until he called us in, one by one.

André opened the door, and the group shuffled out. For a moment, we all looked back through the window at Bennett, that is until Tom Sanders, the FBI agent, stood and closed the blinds. I had a feeling the real investigation had just begun.

Chapter Nine

We squeezed in next to each other on three hard wooden benches that lined a quiet nook. Although a TV flickered on the wall with CNN news, it had no sound, just closed captions. Judith grabbed a folding chair from around the corner and positioned it so she was facing the group like a test moderator. I supposed she thought she was keeping an eye on us younger faculty.

To my delight, a coffee pot sat full of dark brew. I took one of the Styrofoam cups from the stack, and as I filled it, I noticed a vending machine across from us and alerted the group. If the students were hungry, a snack would hold them until they got something to eat.

"Poor Bennett," said André, as I sat down next to him. "I have not been as considerate of his feelings as I could have been."

"Me neither. We've been too busy coordinating travel arrangements to think of anything else," I said.

Nick Dramsdor, who sat a bench away, leaned around Arnold Frasier. "Not on your life are you going to leave the country now. Not with an investigation underway."

"If it's an investigation, are *we* suspects?" asked Arnold.

"I would say every person on that plane is a suspect—and should be," Nick answered, stretching his legs out and crossing his cowboy boots. "If someone contaminated Molly, they'd better find out who, or I'll kill the SOB myself. Molly was the best of the best. The best this world had to offer. Her work, her work...." He swallowed hard and his voice broke as he added, "Well, there just wasn't a better person in the world than Molly Jaspers."

"No, of course not," replied Arnold. I'm sure he felt compelled to say something in response to Nick's heartfelt words.

Nick half snorted, and the fluorescent light caught his profile just right, making him appear even younger than he was. "What are you saying, Frasier? You hated her guts. Ever since she picked apart your article on the Mayan ruins, you've been keen on discrediting her."

Arnold's placid face did not change, but he leaned back as if to physically dodge the accusation. "That's not true, Nick. Molly and I had quite an amicable relationship at one time, which you would know if you taught on our campus."

It seemed to me that the pretty Molly Jaspers had several amicable relationships on campus with men inspired by her passionate causes, but I kept quiet.

"Bull." Nick's voice was barely above a whisper. "Everyone heard you fighting with her on the bus yesterday. Obviously your relationship was no longer *amicable*."

Arnold's placid face crumbled. "We were *not* fighting. Tell them, Emmeline. We were having an academic discussion. If anyone was fighting with her, it was André."

Half the group turned to hear my response. I wanted to stand up for Arnold without standing up for Arnold—in case he did have something to do with Molly's death. Besides, there was André's argument with Molly to consider. Out of the two disagreements, his was the more damning. "I can't say

I overheard the entire conversation, but what I did hear was academic in nature."

Arnold smiled. "See?"

Nick was not convinced. "That doesn't prove anything, Frasier. They're going to dig into each and every corner of our pasts, and if you have something to hide, you'd better come clean with it."

Arnold's serene eyes turned frosty. He was displaying surprising vehemence. "Take your own advice, young friend. You and Molly seemed pretty close, despite the fact that she was a married woman. I wonder what they'll make of *that* little secret."

Amanda glanced in their direction, and Nick turned a purplish shade of red. I couldn't tell if he was embarrassed or angry or both. Regardless, I was glad he was a seat away in case fists began to fly.

"What do you know of our relationship with your pictures and buffalos… and, and *ponytail*," Nick ground out. "What kind of guy wears a ponytail?"

I felt bad for Arnold—and his ponytail. Even the students seemed to be silently questioning his manliness.

"Nick," I said, "I'm sure you don't mean that. We're all rather edgy from what we've been through the last twenty-four hours. Let's just take a deep breath before we say any more hurtful things we might regret."

"Many men wear the ponytail in Paris," André whispered to me. "It's the boots—"

I cut him off with a shake of my head, lest the entire argument begin again. The students were as quiet as I'd ever seen them, agog at the professors' boorish behavior. Had they ever wondered if teachers had lives of their own, now they knew and were possibly disappointed. Up until today, they'd probably thought they were the center of their professors' universe.

Judith Spade had thoughts similar to mine. "Please,

gentlemen, keep it professional. We have a responsibility to the students in these unfortunate circumstances; certainly we can demonstrate better leadership in the future. Let's not let our emotions run away with our reason."

Judith's calm demeanor silenced the men. She smiled briefly at the students, who instantly straightened their shoulders, and then she took a book out of her tote bag and began to read, silently demonstrating how to act like a professor. It was a demonstration Nick Dramsdor would do well to emulate.

The students began to talk again, in hushed tones. Their talk was a nice respite from the buzz of the lights overhead, and I cherished the little bits and pieces of conversation that reached me. Life went on for them as usual, despite their unusual setting. Friends, work, a new YouTube video—their worlds kept moving. When they got older, they'd see how a crisis can paralyze you. If one of them were posting a selfie from jail with some kind of clever caption dramatizing the current predicament, I wouldn't be surprised. Though perhaps this was the one situation that warranted dramatics.

I heard the sound of a door opening, and then Ernest appeared with Bennett behind him. We looked at Bennett expectantly; he looked back at us with sad eyes.

"Your friends here will take good care of you, Bennett," said Ernest. "Stick with them until you get back to Copper Bluff."

He nodded. "You're right. It's good to have friends at a time like this. I don't think I could be alone right now." He took a piece of paper out of his pocket. "Thank you for the information. You've been a great help."

Ernest looked down at his yellow notebook. "Ms. Emmeline Prather?"

"Here," I said automatically. Of course I was here. I stood.

"You can come back next," said Ernest.

I walked with him into the room and pulled out the chair across from the detectives. Jack Wood smiled without showing his teeth; Tom Sanders was carefully blank. I readjusted my hard wooden chair, making several tiny noises as I did. It wasn't a comfortable seat, I thought as I adjusted my scarf. In fact, it forced me to sit ramrod straight. That didn't really matter to me, though. I had excellent posture.

"All set?" Jack asked.

"Of course," I answered.

"You are a professor at the university in Copper Bluff. Is that right?" began Jack.

"Right. I teach for the English Department but am fluent in French. That's the main reason I was invited on this trip."

"So you must know the students and faculty pretty well," said Jack. He had deep lines around his mouth that moved with his lips, and I found myself wondering about his story. His solemn eyes, for instance, seemed to conceal a secret. Had he been involved in a tragedy that time couldn't erase?

"I know André quite well, and Kat. She's my student. The others I just recognize from campus," I said. Really, though, I was still speculating about Jack's life.

"Would you say your relationship with André is romantic in nature?" asked Jack. Ernest waited, poised with his pen, for my answer. Tom looked on without blinking.

"No," I said but felt my brow furrow with confusion. "We're just colleagues, though he did say he made a reservation for us at the Jules Verne restaurant atop the Eiffel Tower. One can't help but wonder at his motives there."

"Sounds pretty expensive," Ernest said confidentially, a curly lock of hair falling over one eye. "I would say he's trying to take the relationship to the next level."

"I think you may be right," I said.

Tom's eyes narrowed. Jack tapped his pencil on his legal notepad.

"Ms. Prather, you mentioned a woman at the airport. Someone with red hair," said Jack.

"That's correct," I said. "Now *there's* a woman worth

interviewing. She looked very upset and hostile toward the group… me in particular."

Jack looked at Ernest then back at me. "And when did you first encounter this… hostile woman?"

"Well, I first saw her at the bar in the airport. She was sitting across—" I began.

"How many drinks had you had?" Tom Sanders broke in. The softness of his voice was startling. Because of his bald head and tough build, I expected the sound to be rough.

Wary of the subtle accusation in his tone, I answered, "It makes me very anxious to fly, Mr. Sanders. I had a cocktail to settle my nerves."

"After that flight to Malaysia, who knows, right?" said Ernest. "A plane can disappear out of the sky and nobody may ever know what happened."

I was glad Ernest could relate.

"One cocktail. Continue," said Tom.

I related the woman's unfriendly behavior toward me at the bar and my subsequent surprise when she proceeded to board the plane. "Amanda, a student, told me the woman thought I was Molly. Amanda told her I was not but pointed out the real Molly Jaspers. Maybe this woman had a grudge toward Molly. It appeared that way to me."

"It's possible, I suppose, but if anyone had a score to settle, it was your friend André Duman. Arnold Frasier said his exact words were, 'One day she is going to offend the wrong person.' Isn't it possible that he might have been that person?"

My breath caught in my throat. My instinct had been right: the detectives had focused their investigation on André and would find several students who could corroborate his remarks. I wanted to do everything in my power to advocate for André. I was concerned for him and his academic position. His being under suspicion would certainly put the French program on hold, including any future trips that faculty proposed. If he were charged with a crime, it would be even worse. His career would be over.

"He is just passionate about his native France and took offence when Molly slighted his alma mater, the Sorbonne," I said. "He has worked so hard for this trip; he wouldn't jeopardize it, especially over a silly remark."

Jack put down his pencil on top of his notepad. "As a rule of thumb, Molly and André didn't get along. That's what we've heard."

"Well, Molly could be a hard woman to get along with," I said, leaning forward in my chair. "She was opinionated and self-righteous in her opinions, especially about the environment. She was also very ambitious, and that turned some people off. She probably would have gone on to become a dean or even president of a college had she lived."

"Do you know of anyone who might have had a motive to intentionally harm Ms. Jaspers?" asked Tom. His mouth barely moved, and I wished at that moment that my reactions weren't as animated as everyone told me they were. But I could feel my visage screwing itself into some sort of tell-all novel that was half truth and half supposition.

I checked my enthusiasm, lacing my fingers together in front of me. It was important for me to keep a professional demeanor for the university, André, and myself. Our reputation and possibly our freedom depended on it. "I can imagine several people wanting Molly dead, Mr. Wood. First, there are the professors Nick and Arnold. Both seemed to have relationships with her that were passionate in nature. Then there's her husband, who could have been resentful of the aforesaid relationships. Students, too, can become quite bitter about grades, which can affect one's affiliation with Greek houses and acceptance into student organizations and graduate schools. Not to mention obtaining student loans and angering their parents. A failed class can be a nightmare for any student. And of course there is the lady in red. Very suspicious."

"Are we calling her 'the lady *in* red'? I thought she just had red hair," said Ernest.

Jack watched my exchange with Ernest with a mixture of confusion and dread. Tom crossed his thick arms.

"Well thank you, Ms. Prather, for those enlightening suggestions. You've been very helpful," said Jack.

I opened my mouth then shut it. It was hard to believe he was dismissing me after I had laid so many possibilities at his feet. I thought for sure he would want more details. "If you're certain that's all—"

"Quite," he said.

"So I can leave."

"Of course," said Ernest. "Your presence here is completely voluntary."

I looked to Tom Sanders for confirmation.

"Just remember, Ms. Prather, you are part of an ongoing investigation. This isn't over until we find out exactly how Dr. Jaspers died."

"*Me*?" I said. "I couldn't possibly have any reason for hurting Molly. I'm an English professor."

"And a very convincing storyteller," added Tom.

I decided not to respond. My garrulity had caused me enough trouble.

Chapter Ten

Nick Dramsdor was right about one thing: we wouldn't be leaving the country any time soon. This meant another night at the Normandy Inn. Two nights might prove too many. We would be fielding calls from parents, administrators, or both any minute now. All we could do was ask the group to stay together until André could charter a bus home.

After André and I made hotel and dinner arrangements, I left the precinct to get some air. The rest of the interviews would take at least an hour, maybe more, and André and the students had decided to eat and shop afterwards at the Nicollet Mall downtown. As I had no interest in shopping, and an hour was a long time to wait for breakfast, I dialed Lenny on my cellphone, telling him where I was and asking him if he would like to get something to eat. I wanted to tell him what the detectives had discovered about Molly Jaspers' death.

"So what you're really saying is that you're stuck at the police station without a car?"

Lenny could be so perceptive at times. "Something like that."

"Well, my sister made some sort of egg bake I'm supposed to eat."

"I understand. You eat with your family, and I'll get something downtown. I'm close to everything."

"Just a sec." He covered the phone, ignoring my protests. "Okay, I'm back. She says I have time to pick you up. I'm not far."

"Are you sure, Lenny? I don't want to intrude."

"I'll be right there," he said, ending the call and silencing my objections.

Fifteen minutes later, when he pulled up in his beat-up Ford Taurus, I waved and smiled. He was a bright spot in an otherwise gray day.

"You looking for a free ride into the world of suburban casseroles, lady?" he said, rolling down the passenger window. "We've got 'em fresh, frozen, and ready-to-serve."

I opened the door. "Thank you, Lenny. I really appreciate it. I didn't want to wait for the rest of the group, and André said not to bother. He and the students plan to go shopping when the stores open."

"And how did your interview go? I bet you were an absolute sphinx."

I coughed. "Oh yes. I kept my answers short and on point. But they confirmed Molly died from anaphylactic shock. They're trying to determine negligence."

His brow furrowed. "What's that mean, 'negligence'? They think somebody is responsible for her death?"

"Somebody or the airlines."

"Wait. What about Paris?"

I shook my head. "It's not happening. André is waiting for a call from the airlines, but they pretty much told him last night that they didn't have enough seats on their flights today."

"I'm sorry, Em. I know how much you wanted to go to France."

"It's okay," I said. "I mean it will be okay once we figure this thing out. The FBI agent zeroed in on André, and to be honest, Lenny, I'm afraid for him."

"FBI?" he said. "When did the FBI get involved? After your interview?"

"Ha ha. Very funny. The FBI has jurisdiction over all crimes committed in the air."

At a stoplight, he turned to study my face. I avoided meeting his eyes.

"You say that as if you're an expert on criminal procedure, which you're not. You're an English professor. Okay? An *untenured* English professor."

I settled into my seat as we pulled away from the streetlight. "I'm well aware of my tenure status, Lenny, and believe me, if I could make this trip happen, I would. But it would appear that romance and adventure are two worlds that continue to elude me, so I must make the best of a bad situation. Although we are faced with a dead professor and a disgruntled group of students, on the plus side, I have a dependable friend who is always there when I need him." I smiled as sweetly as I could. "Are you sure your sister doesn't mind my coming?"

"Are you kidding? She's thrilled. She has someone to send leftovers home with."

"Except that I'm staying at a hotel and have nowhere to store leftovers," I said. "I can't remember… did you say she is married?" I knew she was five years his senior.

"Not anymore. She used to be. Her husband left her for some old high school fling on Facebook. A real dirt bag."

Anger tinged Lenny's voice, so I didn't pursue the subject.

"But she seems none the worse for it," he continued, changing his tone. "You'll love the girls. They're funny as hell."

"What are their names again?"

"Adeline and Abigail."

I smiled. "They sound adorable."

"I woke up to a conversation between Ken and Barbie on their boat. Little did I know the couch becomes a Disney cruise ship during the day."

We pulled up to a one-and-a-half-story house that stood

well above the curb. More than ten tiny steps had to be climbed to reach the front door. From the living room window peered two little faces, one just a bit bigger than the other.

"This is it," said Lenny.

As we walked up the steps, I asked if his parents would be joining us, but he said they wouldn't be. They were out of town for the day visiting friends and wouldn't have come anyway; they didn't approve of Julia's non-kosher cooking.

The faces from the window appeared at the front door.

"Hi, Uncle Lenny's girlfriend!" said the younger girl. She had round cheeks and curls to match. She was the epitome of cute. I guessed she was six and her sister eight.

Her comment earned her a jab from her older sister, whose slender face was full of freckles.

"She's not his girlfriend. She's his date."

"Actually..." I began, but then Lenny's sister, who had spiky, short hair and looked nothing like her two girls, appeared from behind the kitchen wall. She was tall, like Lenny, and slim. She could have been a model; her build was just right for the clothes. Her skinny jeans looked like they did on mannequins, fitted but not tight, and her short-sleeved T-shirt revealed toned arms.

"You must be Emmeline. You are even more gorgeous than Leonard described. Let her come in, girls. Come on. Help me dish up." She disappeared again behind the wall.

The younger girl bounded toward the kitchen. The older one moved on more reluctantly.

"*Leonard*?" I whispered. "When were you going to let me in on that little nugget?"

"Never," he said.

The eat-in kitchen was cheery and bright, with freshly painted yellow walls and white café curtains. In the middle was a small round table encircled by four wooden chairs and a fifth folding chair. The girls were carefully placing the napkins on the center of each plate. They had clearly done this before.

"You can sit here, next to Uncle Lenny," giggled the youngest one with curls.

"Thank you," I said. "Are you Adeline or Abigail?"

"I'm Abby," she said. "*She's* Adeline." She pointed at her big sister.

"Well, it's very nice to meet you both. Thank you for inviting me to your house. Is there anything I can do to help?" I asked his sister.

"Not a thing," she said without turning around. She was at the stove, cutting squares of breakfast casserole and placing them on a large white plate. "I'm Julia, by the way. I don't know if Lenny told you."

"Yes, he told me he was staying with you over spring break."

She placed the plate on the center of the table and sat down. Fruit and muffins had already been positioned near a small vase of daisies. She smiled at Lenny, and I noticed she had the same deep dimple. She also had the same punkish hair that was just a few inches longer than Lenny's. I was completely jealous. "We feel honored to have a genuine rock star in our presence, don't we girls?"

"My uncle was on a stage last night," said Abby.

"I know," I said, taking a lemon poppy-seed muffin. "I saw him, and he was very, very good."

"My mom *refused* to let me go," said Adeline, suspiciously poking at the egg bake Julia had placed on her plate. "She said I'm too young."

"Nice verb choice, Addie," said Lenny. Then quietly to me, "Julia's a teacher, too."

"Elementary school. Third grade," said Julia. She placed a napkin on her lap. "When they say kids aren't learning anything in school, it's not my class they're talking about." She looked up and smiled. "So Lenny said you were on your way to France but got stuck here. What happened?"

"Do you speak French?" Adeline asked.

"Say something in French!" said Abigail at the same time.

"*Vous êtes très jolies jeunes filles*," I said. "That means you are very pretty girls."

"No wonder you adore her," Julia said to Lenny.

"I never said that," Lenny muttered.

I laughed. "Anyway, we were on our way to Paris when a professor became ill. The police are trying to figure out what went wrong."

"Did he die?" asked Abigail.

I nodded. "Yes, and *she*."

"That's horrible," Julia said. "But why not continue on to France? There's nothing you can do about it now." She was scooping fruit onto her daughters' plates.

I glanced at the girls, wondering how much I should say in front of them. "There are no seats left on the planes leaving today. Also, the police are investigating the death."

Adeline stuck a piece of cantaloupe with her fork. "That means they think she was killed," she said to the younger Abby.

"So you're involved in a *murder*," said Julia.

"Please don't encourage her with that sort of talk," said Lenny.

"Who's encouraging anyone? I'm simply stating a fact," said Julia.

"Does that mean you're a suspect?" asked Adeline.

Everyone turned to me. "I don't know." Abby inched away from me, and I stifled a laugh. "But if I'm a suspect, everyone on the plane is a suspect."

"Well," Julia said, "I think it's terrifically interesting, although I'm so sorry you missed Paris. What crummy luck. How long will you be in Minneapolis?"

"One more night, if we're lucky," I answered. "We're trying to procure a bus ride home for Monday."

"You can stay here. We'd love to have you, wouldn't we, girls?"

"I could braid your hair," Abigail said.

"No you can't," said Adeline.

"I can, too!"

"It's way too curly, Abby," said Adeline.

Julia shook her head. "Girls!"

"It's okay," I said. "Adeline is right. My hair doesn't take to braids too well, but I do have a lot of scarfs. You could dress up Uncle Lenny."

"Ha ha," said Lenny.

The girls seriously considered the possibility.

"I'm afraid it won't be tonight," I said. "Our group is staying downtown, and the students need me right now. It has been an awful couple of days, and I want to be there for them. Thank you for the offer, though."

"Well, if anything changes, I hope you'll consider our house. All jokes aside, we would love to have you," said Julia.

"Thank you, and thank you for the breakfast. Everything is just delicious," I said.

Afterwards, Lenny and I helped Julia do the dishes. Then we had one more cup of coffee before we left. I explained that I had to drop in at the police station. I also had to get back to the hotel in case André needed assistance with parents or administrators. This prompted several more questions from Adeline and Abigail about André and France and whether or not André wore funny hats. Lenny was only too happy to indulge them, confirming their every stereotype.

I shook hands with each of the girls before saying goodbye, and they returned the handshake with much formality.

"Goodbye, Em Prather," said Adeline. "I hope you don't end up in jail."

"I hope that as well," I replied with a straight face.

"If you do," chimed in Abigail, "we will rescue you, won't we, Mom?"

"Don't be silly, Abby. Only lawyers can rescue people from jail."

Chapter Eleven

Brunch with Lenny's family was a welcome reprieve from the darkness of the day. I felt as if I had known them my entire life instead of just a few hours. When I went back to Detroit, it was just like that: talk, food, and dishes. My mom loved inviting her loud sisters over for big dinners, much to my father's chagrin. She tackled complicated recipes that took two and three people to complete, and there was always much to be done before we could sit down. Books "were for the scholar's idle times," she often said, quoting Ralph Waldo Emerson. But she always made time to pull me aside, afterwards, and ask me about my love life and other figments of her imagination. When I told her it was short on the love, she made excuses for me, saying that she always knew I would find my true soul mate in France. *It's why I named you Emmeline,* she would explain. *So that you would go out and seek your fortune… abroad.* She thought graduate school was a six-year misstep on my part, and my dad agreed with her, though for opposite reasons. *The debt!* he would say. *What young person can ever get out from under that kind of debt.* But all this was said good-naturedly. They knew my career brought me happiness and my goals were different from theirs. I didn't make as much money as I would have, had I taken a job on the East coast as they had hoped; still, they were proud of my accomplishments. We couldn't get as far as the local grocer before my mom would announce to a passerby, "Emmeline's a *professor*, you know." My achievement was a very big deal in the old neighborhood of MorningSide.

As Lenny and I walked down Julia's steep steps, I noticed his smile. But I didn't say anything. I figured he was happy to be back in Minneapolis.

He turned on the ignition of his car. "I would have never guessed you'd be good with children, but you really are."

"I am?" I asked, trying to keep the surprise out of my voice. The thought that I could be *good* at anything but English and French pleased me a great deal.

He was carefully entering an onslaught of traffic, which had picked up considerably since breakfast, and didn't reply.

"Well… yes," I pondered more to myself than to Lenny. "Naturally I'm good with children. I'm a teacher, after all, and… that kid who lives across the street likes me. What is his name? Brendan. Anyway, he always used to come and visit me and pet my cat Dickinson." I thought back fondly to the boy and the rapt attention he had paid to my stories on the front porch. "If I remember right, he was quite a Poe fan. 'The Cask of Amontillado' scared the pants off him, though. I had to walk him home that night. It was October, and you know how the trees whip the shadows into hideous shapes in the fall. I didn't see him much after that night. His mom said he was developing an unnatural fascination with crime and had asked for a police scanner for Christmas. Can you believe it? What's unnatural about that? It's naturally fascinating when someone does something that goes against the laws of human nature."

Lenny's smile had turned into more of a grin. "Mothers. They're such worrywarts."

We pulled up alongside the brick police building.

“Do you want me to come in?” asked Lenny as he parallel parked.

“Would you mind?” I asked. “I don’t know if anyone’s still in there.”

“I’ve always wanted to see the inside of a police station. And somehow, Em, the improbable always becomes probable when you’re around.”

No one from our group was in the lobby, so I gave the officer at the front desk my name and asked if I could go back to the office area.

“Wait here,” she said tersely.

“Pleasant woman,” said Lenny as he sat down.

“Believe me, she was much nicer when André was around.”

“I bet,” he said. “Do you want me to try a French accent on her? Sweet chérie, you are zee most beautiful mademoiselle….”

He sounded a lot like Pepé Le Pew, and I was going to tell him so, when all of a sudden the woman with red hair walked through the metal doors.

“That lady was on the plane the day Molly died. She was asking about her,” I whispered. “The police must have brought her in for questioning.”

“How did she know Molly?” he asked.

“That’s what I want to find out.” I stood abruptly.

He followed me. “What are you going to do? Just go up to her?”

“Yes, that’s exactly what I’m going to do,” I said, nearly in step with the woman now. “Excuse me, ma’am? Miss!” I said loudly as she placed her hand on the outside door.

She turned around, befuddled. Then a look of recognition came into her eyes.

“Yes?” she asked. She still had her hand on the door handle.

“I’m Emmeline Prather. We were traveling on the plane to Paris together before it was grounded,” I said as I caught up with her. “Please, I’d like to talk to you for just a minute if you have time.”

She let her hand drop from the door. "Yes, I remember. You were with the group, with the woman who died."

"That's right," I said. "I teach in Copper Bluff, South Dakota. This is Professor Lenny Jenkins. He teaches there as well."

Lenny gave her a small, silent wave, obviously wanting to stay out of the conversation.

"I remembered you from the airport. Do we happen to know each other?" I asked.

"No," she said, shaking her red head. Today her hair wasn't pulled back into a ponytail. It hung straight to her shoulders, framing her pale face. "I noticed the group when we were waiting for the plane. A girl told me who you were when we were boarding."

"Yes, we were taking a group of students abroad to Paris for spring break," I explained. "I guess we're both here about the death on the plane?"

Lenny took a step closer to the wall. It looked as if he was hoping to become one with it.

"The police had some questions for me since I was sitting behind the teacher who died," she said.

"How did you know she was a teacher?" asked Lenny.

We both glanced at him in surprise.

"Because she wasn't eighteen," she answered.

"So you didn't know Professor Jaspers?" I confirmed.

She shook her head.

"I see," I said. "Will you be traveling on to Paris?"

"No. I was going for a long weekend; it hardly seems worth it now." She moved toward the door again.

"I'm sorry, I didn't catch your name," I said.

"Jean Erickson."

"Jean, thank you for talking with me. I hope you get to Paris another time."

Her face remained emotionless. "Right." She opened the door. "I doubt that's going to happen." Her dull red hair faded in the sunlight as she walked out the door.

"Ma'am. You may go back now," said the officer at the front window. The door buzzed, and Lenny and I walked through in silence. As soon as the door shut and we were past the metal detector, I began to speak.

"I think Jean Erickson knew more than she was telling us. She was acting odd, wasn't she?"

"It's hard to tell how someone would act after being accosted by a curly-headed woman on a mission," said Lenny.

I stuck my hands in my pockets. "I am not on a mission, Lenny. Amanda told me Jean asked after Molly Jaspers, and she just denied knowing her right to my face… and yours."

"Hey, don't pull me into this. I wasn't even on the plane. My plans for spring break were music, beer, and sleep. In that order. But where do I suddenly find myself? At the police station chasing down a woman who may or may not have known some professor I've only met twice. Hmm. What does that sound like? It sounds like Em Prather throwing a monkey wrench into my entire week."

"Oh, oh?" I said, my face turning hot. "Then why did you ask her how she knew Jaspers was a teacher?"

He crossed his arms. "That was for your benefit. In case you didn't catch that she already knew Jaspers was a professor."

"Exactly," I exclaimed with a stamp of my foot.

Before he could respond, Ernest approached us.

"Ernest," I said, "I'd like you to meet my friend Professor Lenny Jenkins."

Ernest shook Lenny's hand. "Good to meet you, Lenny. I'm Ernest Jones, but you can call me Ernie." He smoothed his hair to one side.

Lenny looked from me to Ernest. "*Ernie*? Do you work here?" he said, squinting at his clothes.

"Oh yes, definitely. I'm one of the detectives on the case."

"Don't let him tease you about your name," I said confidentially. "His name is *Leonard*. Which reminds me, you might try another nickname. Maybe E or Jones… or EJ."

He moved closer to me. "Yes, I see what you mean. Jones sort of rolls off the tongue, doesn't it? But EJ… I think my middle name would have to start with a J before I would feel completely honest using it."

"Of course," I said. "We only need go as far as e e cummings to prove that point."

"You've got to be kidding," Lenny said, shaking his head.

"No, I think Ms. Prather is on to something," Ernest said. "Nobody calls me Ernie. I mean *nobody*. It doesn't stick for some reason."

"Are you on your way somewhere?" I asked.

"Right. I was on my way to get your friend Nick Dramsdor a sandwich from the staff vending machine. He's complaining about missing lunch, and I don't blame him, but we need to get through these interrogations as soon as possible. He's the last one."

"Well, we won't stop you," I said. "One quick thing, though. We ran into the lady in red, Jean Erickson? I assume you called her in for questioning."

"Of course I did. Jack Wood, my partner, thought you were trying to deflect suspicion from the group, but I told him it sounded like a solid tip to me."

"See there, Em?" whispered Lenny. "You're not doing yourself any favors by getting caught up in this. You want to get back to Copper Bluff, don't you? I sure as hell want you to."

"Oh she's caught up in this already," said Ernest. "But we didn't get much from Jean. She claimed to have no association with Molly Jaspers whatsoever."

"I need to talk to Amanda again about the conversation. I'm certain she said Jean asked after Molly," I said.

"How do we know Amanda's telling the truth?" said Lenny. "And now this Jack Wood suspects you."

"I like your friend here," said Ernest. "I can see why you brought him."

"Because I saw them talking, that's how," I said, ignoring

Ernest's comment. "And let's not forget I was sitting across the bar from her. The way she looked at me was disconcerting, to say the least. I know it's not much to go on, but it was upsetting to have a stranger stare at me with such hostility."

Lenny spoke to Ernest, putting one large hand on his shoulder. "Ms. Prather here has a very active imagination. She imagines lots of things about lots of people, especially with a few airport cocktails coursing through her veins. She's not used to drinking much and is terrified of flying. But she is also sort of brilliant and incredibly kind. She has nothing to do with this murder. I can promise you that."

A crowd of police officers around a TV screen scowled in our direction. Lenny stepped closer.

"Did she tell you she teaches literature?" Lenny added in hushed tones. Even his quiet voice was loud and deep. "She excels at analyzing stories; that's where her talent lies. You might explain that to your partner next time he gets suspicious. Tell him that's the only reason she's so inquisitive."

I knew Lenny was trying to help, but I didn't need him to defend my actions. I had been nothing but forthright with the police, and if that drew suspicion to me, so be it. I was willing to deal with the consequences as long as I knew I was doing the right thing for André and the university. I opened my mouth to say so and realized Lenny was standing so close I could feel the heat between us. It was almost palpable. I took a step backwards, but my entire retort flew out of my head. I stood silently blinking. Lenny's face broke into a smile, and I narrowed my eyes at him. I hated that he knew exactly what I was thinking.

Unperturbed by our heated discussion, Ernest smoothed a wrinkled one-dollar bill on a nearby office doorframe. "You both bring up excellent points, about the redhead and the literature. But there is that sandwich I need to get, and your friend Nick *is* hungry."

"Of course. We'll tell Nick you're on your way," I said.

Now that we were away from the bustling office traffic, the hallway grew quiet. "I like Ernest," I said. "Jack Wood, his partner, is not as easy to talk to. He's got too much on his plate. He wants to close this case as soon as possible, no matter whom he arrests."

Lenny rolled his eyes.

"Just wait until you meet him. You'll see what I mean."

"He'll probably be investigating me by the time we leave."

The benches were empty now, except the one occupied by Nick Dramsdor. He stood as we approached.

"Emmeline, you're back. André took the students and left a long time ago."

I nodded. "He texted and said they are heading back to the hotel now. By the way, we ran into Ernest in the hall. Your sandwich is coming. This is Lenny Jenkins." Lenny shook Nick's hand. "He happened to be in Minneapolis for spring break."

Nick nodded. "Well, it's not exactly Mexico, is it?"

"You can say that again. Next year I'm stowing away in one of my student's luggage," said Lenny.

"Do you teach in Copper Bluff?"

Lenny nodded. "Yeah, American Lit."

Now we all sat down. "I teach at State."

Lenny leaned back, lacing his hands behind his head. "So, how did you get in on this little shindig?"

"Molly Jaspers and I collaborated on several projects. She invited me because she was going to give a lecture at the Sorbonne on organic farming."

"I bet she was a staunch advocate of that because of her work in land conservation," I said.

"She was surprisingly neutral on the issue," said Nick. "She recently learned of the large carbon imprint organic farming could have on the environment due to the amount of methane that is emitted in composting. I mean, we always knew composting emitted methane, but a recent experiment of hers showed triple the emissions she expected."

"That couldn't have been welcome news for organic farmers," said Lenny.

Nick shook his head. "Nor their supporters. In France, organic is big business, and the government has increased subsidies to encourage even more. France is Europe's largest agricultural producer."

I raised my eyebrows. "And Molly was to speak to this problem—with methane emissions—at the Sorbonne?"

"Yeah. Didn't I just say that?" asked Nick, looking from me to Lenny.

"You look lost, Nick, so I'm going to fill you in on what's happening inside Em's head. What Em is trying to suggest is that Molly was killed before she could share her study at the Sorbonne. Is that a possibility?"

Nick blinked rapidly. Such a sinister thought had never crossed his mind. "It could be. Molly did have a tendency to make enemies when it came to her academic work." Seeing the look on our faces, he continued, "She refused to tell people what they wanted to hear; that's all. She was so intelligent and passionate. She was three steps ahead of everyone else. Even me. People hated that. I didn't, though. I admired her intelligence."

That wasn't all he admired, I guessed. From Lenny's cocked eyebrow, I could tell he agreed. It was impossible to listen to this man and not suppose that he had a crush—academic and/or otherwise—on Molly. His words bordered on hero worship.

"But there weren't any French people on the flight," Nick thought out loud.

"Of course there were. We were flying to *Paris*," I said. "The plane must have been full of French people returning home."

"I mean, we didn't know any of them," clarified Nick.

A smile began at the corners of Lenny's lips, and his eyes

turned from intense to playful. He wasn't looking at Nick; he was looking at me. "*You* know one of them, quite intimately."

Nick scowled. "Who? I don't know a one of them."

But I knew whom he referred to: André Duman.

Chapter Twelve

INTIMACY WAS SUCH a loaded word, especially when used in conjunction with André. You could know someone intimately and not be intimate, or you could be intimate yet not know someone intimately. How well did I really know this man—or how well did he know me? For instance, there were things about myself I didn't share. Period. But could people decipher those things without my telling them? Was that what "knowing" a person really meant? After all, wasn't it easy enough to know a person, in an obvious way, by the things she shared about herself? Perhaps it was the unsaid things, the things people closest to you found out without your saying, that resulted in intimacy.

What did I really *know* about André, then? The adjectives that came to mind were synonymous: good-looking, handsome, and attractive. Yet when I got beyond his appearance—no easy task—I realized that he, like Molly, had one overriding passion, and that passion just happened to be France.

Ever since André came to Copper Bluff five years ago, he had been zealous in his commitment to bring the French language and culture to our campus. He had started as an adjunct, a part-time instructor, and now was a tenure-track professor, leading a team of students and professionals thanks to a grant he'd procured by sheer willpower. His accomplishments spoke to his dedication and fervor. Yet there was more. Despite variable enrollment, he had convinced the dean to consider creating a French major. Failed students wouldn't deter André; he would find a way to enroll more students next fall.

Now I no longer questioned if people *could* suspect André but *would* when it came to his prestigious Sorbonne. He had gone out of his way to procure a spot for Molly's lecture, and what she had to say would have embarrassed him and angered his fellow Frenchmen as well. Maybe people would believe he'd rather poison her than suffer that humiliation. Maybe a part of me wondered that as well. I needed to prove to myself he couldn't have killed Molly if I was going to prove it to anyone else.

In my heart, I knew André didn't kill Molly, but the truth was, I knew very little about his life before Copper Bluff. I shook my head, baffled by the superficiality of our relationship. How could I help defend André when I barely knew him?

Until a laugh interrupted my deliberations, I didn't realize Lenny was studying me on the drive back to the hotel.

"Beret Boy doesn't look too good in this light, does he, Em?" he chuckled. "You might have your work cut out for you."

He was reading my mind again.

"André looks good in any light—candle, fluorescent, or otherwise," I said, nibbling on the Skittles I had bought on the way out of the police station. "The problem is, I don't know much about him. And I'll need to find out everything I can if I'm going to help clear his name. I don't suppose you could fill me in on any particulars you might have gleaned from him over the last couple of years?"

He glanced at me then returned his attention to the traffic. His jaw was set and his expression serious. He was considering my question carefully, but from the look on his face, coming up with no immediate answer.

"I know he likes scarves. I know he speaks French. I know he can't play darts worth a damn." He shrugged. "You're the one who's gone out to eat with him. What did you talk about?"

I picked over several green Skittles, digging for a red one. I couldn't think of a thing André and I had discussed in any depth. "We talked about Paris… he's been there. He grew up in France. Obviously."

"Obviously." Some of the playfulness returned to his face. "Did he say he had family there?"

"Not that I remember. I think I asked," I said, chewing thoughtfully. "Yes, I asked, but he was vague in his answer."

"You're making that up," Lenny snorted. "You can't remember a damn thing except his eye color."

Dark brown came to mind. We sat in silence as I tried to recall the details of our single dinner together, but it had been impromptu. I had been eating alone at Dynasty, the Chinese restaurant in Copper Bluff, when André joined me. We hadn't spoken of our families at all, but he had said he was from an area much like Copper Bluff. Maybe that meant he was from a farming community. What did I know about him that could confirm that? I knew he adored croissants. He drove to the small bakery in a town about twenty miles from campus just to buy them. *Because they reminded him of his mother's.* His mother made her own croissants, her own bread, her own pies. She also canned pickles. "He has a mother who cans!"

Lenny slapped his hands on the steering wheel. "See there? That proves he can't be arrested."

I shook my head. "Actually, it supports the theory that he might come from a rural area."

"Ah. I get it. You think his family might own a farm. But lots of people can pickles and other stuff who don't have farms. They're called *gardeners*," he said.

I threw him a look. "He once said he came from a place

that resembles Copper Bluff, and we have a lot of farms around our area. I need to discover if his family's connected to organic farming in any way, shape, or form. I don't want the police linking André to Molly's lecture, and you know Nick Dramsdor will inform the police of the many merits of Molly Jaspers' talk."

A giant smile spread across his face. "I wish I could be there."

"Where?"

"When you interrogate André," he said. "I wonder if he'll start sweating like he does. Now there's a time when I'd use the word *profuse*."

"*Profusely*." I stuck the Skittles in my bag. "I'm not going to interrogate him. I'm just going to ask him about his family back in France. Really, I should have asked something like this a long time ago. I mean, I know your family so well I could sit down and eat Christmas dinner with them."

"Except that they're Jewish." Lenny laughed.

"I'm sorry. I meant Hanukkah," I said with a wave of my hand. "The point is, I know nothing of André's backstory, and now I wonder if that was intentional."

Lenny pulled up alongside the hotel and put the car in park. He looked at me. "Remember how I warned you about confusing people with characters? You're doing it again."

Lenny had once told me he thought I turned book characters into friends because I was an only child and had no one to play with when I was young. It was a habit, he claimed, that persisted into adulthood. When I heartily disagreed, his reply was, "The lady doth protest too much, methinks."

"Not everyone has a *backstory*," he was saying now, "or even a front story. Sometimes people leave things out because they're embarrassing. Or sad. Or not important."

I shook my head in disagreement. "Everyone has a backstory. What details they choose to leave out are just as important as the ones they choose to tell."

"Just be careful, Em. I'm not particularly keen on the guy, but that doesn't mean I want you to kill your chances of teaching in an actual French Department with a few ill-timed questions. You know how sensitive he can be when he thinks he's being insulted."

I knew what he meant. I loved André's passionate nature—but I didn't relish the thought that he might turn it on me. He could be as stubborn as anyone I'd ever known; once he had his mind made up, it was hard to change it.

"Don't worry. I know what I'm doing. Besides, if this suspicion follows him back to Copper Bluff, there won't be a French Department to worry about."

As I shut the car door, I realized that Lenny was genuinely concerned about my future. He had been teasing me for almost two years about my French literature degree, claiming that I was as ill-suited to it as the Beatles to America. But when I was faced with the possibility of losing André and consequently his much-argued-for French major, he changed his attitude altogether. Lenny was right about one thing: I did need to be careful of insulting André. I didn't want him to think I suspected him, and I didn't—not really. I simply wanted to hear a little bit about his family, and that was how the conversation would need to come off.

The hotel was a menagerie of sights, smells, and people, and I walked through the lobby to the elevator with my head down, ignoring the clumps of guests coming, going, and standing. Instead, I counted the mud spots on the carpet and decided it must have been an unusually wet spring; I lost count before I got to the elevator.

A chubby toddler with muddy shoes was shouting "No!" and arching his back as his bedraggled mother held him tightly. Despite her death clutch, he managed to slide all the way down the length of her body. She tried to wrangle him back into her arms, but the task proved impossible. He fell onto his diapered rear and began to cry just as the elevator door opened.

I waited for people to exit and then stepped through the

steel doors, holding one open for the mother. Her bangs stuck to her perspiring forehead as she pulled her son through the door. She had him in her arms now, but he was still wailing, taking huge gasps of air in between screams.

"How would you like to press the button, little guy?" I asked, feeling confident after Lenny's comments about my being good with children.

He stopped crying and stared at me. I smiled my kindest smile and gestured toward the buttons.

"No!" he shouted.

I blinked. "Look at all the numbers! One, two, three—"

"No!" he shouted again.

The mom reached over and pressed button number 2. I didn't know whom she disliked more at that moment: me or her toddler.

When the elevator opened again, I walked down the hallway with my bulky tote, taking the time alone to think. The investigation wouldn't go away until the police knew for certain what transpired. One side of me wanted to blame the airlines for passing out peanuts in the first place. Perhaps the police would see it that way, too. But the other side of me, the side that grew up in Detroit, knew there was more to the story. The only plausible explanation was that the truth was hidden beneath the surface, and I was going to dig until I found it. If there was one thing my education had taught me, it was how to find the right answer. It was time to put those skills to work.

I swiped my keycard and entered the room. Kat was absent, but Amanda was lying on the unmade bed, her knees bent against her chest. Scrolling through her phone, she looked up as I entered the room. She looked as depressed as I had ever seen her, and that was saying something, considering she had been crying on and off ever since Molly's death. Out of anyone in the group, with the exception of Bennett, the death had affected her the most.

"Hey, Amanda. Where's Kat?"

"Shopping. She found a music store with vinyl records. She's such a hippie that way."

I laughed. "You didn't feel like going?"

She shook her head but said nothing.

"Is something wrong?"

She put down her phone. "Professor Duman talked to the airline. They didn't have enough seats, so we're going back to Copper Bluff in the morning."

I sat down on the edge of the bed, my tote landing on the floor with a thump. "Yeah, he told me that might be the case, but we have confirmation now. Maybe it's for the best, though. It will feel good to get home."

Amanda tucked a long piece of hair behind her ear; her eyes were puffy from crying. "I know. It wouldn't have been that great anyway, not with Dr. Jaspers gone. I was kind of close to her. I mean, for a professor."

"I'm sorry. That makes her death even more difficult for you." I scooted back on the bed, my feet dangling off the edge. "Did you have a lot of classes with her?"

She nodded. "Three. I'm a junior."

"I wish there was something I could say or do to make you feel better. We are all grieving for Dr. Jaspers, each in our own way. It's a cliché, but it will take some time before things get easier. I lost a student last semester, and a day doesn't go by that I don't walk into class and think of him. But it isn't as hard as it once was. I can say his name aloud now."

She was silent for a moment, thinking about what I had just told her. "I know what you say is true. It was like that after my grandpa passed away. I just wish there was something I could do."

This was the perfect time to ask for clarification about Jean Erickson. "There is one thing we can do. We can help the police figure out what happened on the plane. Which reminds me, that red-haired woman.... You said that she asked about me in the airport. Do you remember what she said?"

"The police asked me that too. I don't remember what she said word for word."

"But she thought I was Molly Jaspers, right?"

She nodded. "She asked if you were Professor Jaspers. I thought she was from the university. She sort of nodded in your direction, and I said, 'That's not Professor Jaspers. That's Professor Prather.' I knew who you were from Kat."

I sat for a few minutes while she answered an incoming text message. When she finished, I said, "The lady's name… I found out it's Jean Erickson. Does that sound familiar at all? She isn't associated with the university."

"I don't think so. I don't recognize it." She didn't look up from her phone. "I knew a Skylar Erickson. He was in my Western civ class last spring."

I leaned forward. "Molly Jaspers taught that class?"

She put down her phone. "Yeah. She did."

"Well, that's interesting," I said.

She crinkled her nose. "Why?"

"I don't know." I tapped my fingertips together. "Where is Skylar now? Do you know?"

"He doesn't go to Copper Bluff anymore. I haven't seen him this year. I think he transferred or dropped out."

I let out an audible breath. Here was another dead end.

She returned to her phone, pulling her sleek hair over one shoulder. It acted as a partition between her screen and me, and I worried our conversation would be over with the push of a button. My mind searched for another question. I needed to know if Skylar Erickson was connected to Jean Erickson.

"Was Skylar a decent student? Do you remember?"

"No. Well, yeah." She stretched out her legs. "I mean, he was really smart. You could tell by the stuff he said in class. But he always bombed the tests. I don't think he studied. Plus, he hung out with the guys in the back of the class, and they didn't really seem too interested in the material."

The guys in the back row could do a number on someone's academic standing. "And how did you fare in the class?"

She was surprised by this question. "I got an A."

"You must be a pretty good student," I said. "It sounds like a hard class."

She was confident and keenly aware of the confidence that intelligence brings. "I'm here on an academic scholarship."

I nodded, beginning to better understand Amanda and her academic devotion. She had come to Copper Bluff with the weight of high expectations on her shoulders, but she hadn't faltered. I had a feeling she steeled herself against each challenge, proving over and over again that she could handle anything. Her fortitude was what made her stand out; her professors loved her for it. And their approval reassured her.

"What is your major?" I asked.

"Anthropology."

"Ah. I see. So you're taking French to fulfill your foreign language requirement for the Bachelor of Arts degree," I said.

"Yep. This is my last semester."

A loud knock on the door interrupted our conversation. "Cleaning!"

I stood and began walking toward the door. "Come in."

A maid entered, propping open the door with a garbage can. I looked back at Amanda. She was not quite so sad now. "Are you staying here? I need to find André."

"Yeah, I think so. I'm going to try to take a nap when she's done."

"Okay. I won't wake you." It was probably the grief making her tired—plus the late-night meeting with Nick Dramsdor. I hoped she'd be able to rest.

No one answered when I knocked on André's door, so I took the elevator downstairs to check out the hotel facilities. I didn't have to walk far before I came across a wall of windows and a bustling swimming pool inside. As I peered past the streaky droplets, I saw all the activity associated with a pool: lots of small children, high-pitched screeches, and sudden splashes of water. A blow-up ball hit the window, and a half-drenched girl crawled out of the water to retrieve it. I waved and kept walking.

I passed an ice machine and laundry room before finding the business room. Since André wasn't answering his phone, I thought he could be in here. It had everything he might need, such as a printer/fax/copy machine and desktop computers. But he wasn't here. I thought I heard his voice farther down the hall.

I walked until I came out on the other side of the front desk. André was stapling a packet of papers and thanking the attendant for the office supplies.

"Hi, André," I said.

He jumped. "Em! Were you looking for me?"

I nodded.

"They had no stapler in the copy room. I needed to make copies of our receipts for Dean Richardson, the Global Learning Department, and the grant committee."

I could tell André was frustrated by the way his hair was parted. It looked this way when he had been raking the long top with his fingers. "Let's talk," I said, pointing to the lobby chairs.

"This has been the worst experience, ever," he said as we headed toward the chairs. "Never again will they let me lead a group of students. I could hear it in the dean's voice. He is going to hold me accountable for… all this." He threw up his hands and fell into one of the chairs.

I sat down. "How can that be true? You had nothing to do with Molly Jaspers' death."

"He has been on the phone with Jack Wood. He says for insurance purposes, but I don't believe it. I hear the suspicion in his voice. I'm sure Mr. Wood has told Dean Richardson all about my squabble with Molly. Jack and his partner asked me about our relationship for thirty minutes. I said, 'What relationship?' Someone has them believing I am a great opponent of Molly Jaspers."

Someone, indeed. Someone who was trying to deflect suspicion from him or herself, but who? We were all associated with the university in one respect or another. None of us wanted our names linked to an unfortunate incident. On a small campus such as ours, it didn't always matter if a rumor was true or not. What mattered was how many times it was repeated.

"Don't worry, André. When we get back, I will go straight to Dean Richardson and tell him exactly what happened. Let's hope he will understand you had nothing to do with Molly's death."

He patted my hand. "That's very kind of you, Em, but you have not been on campus as long as I have. He won't put much faith in your testimony."

I started to object, but I knew what he said was true. It was only my second year on campus. I would need to be pretty convincing if I were to prove André's innocence.

"But it doesn't matter. I have other fish to boil. Dean Richardson is upset. Parents are calling him with reports of our *dire* situation." He flung up his hands in the air. "It could be worse. We could be stranded at the airport."

"That's very true. We're lucky we were able to reserve this hotel for one night, let alone two."

"They want to get home for their little spring breaks." He pinched his fingers together as he spoke. "They have missed the greatest experience of their lives, and they don't even know it. The Avenue des Champs-Élysées, Montmartre, macarons at Pierre Hermé."

"I'm sorry, André. I can't tell you how sorry I am."

He shook his head but didn't reply.

I cleared my throat. Maybe this would be a good time to ask about his family. "I suppose you were planning on seeing your parents when we got to Paris."

"No," he said. "They live too far outside the city."

I was encouraged. "Do they live on a farm?"

He smiled. "Not the sort you imagine, Em. You've been in the Midwest too long. My parents grow grapes—for wine!" He laughed.

It couldn't get any better, could it? No wonder he knew so much about wine. "Your family owns a winery?"

"I'm surprised you didn't know," he said. "I thought I mentioned it."

Although I admitted to being somewhat distracted by André's good looks—every woman was—I was certain he hadn't mentioned a winery. I would have remembered. "No. Never."

"My brothers operate it now, for the most part. My parents are old. My dad, though, he still has a mind for business." He tapped his forehead.

"Didn't you want to stay in France? To help them with the winery? It seems like a pleasant way to live, immersed in grapes and the French countryside."

"No. No. Not for me. My brothers, they are lazy."

A mom and dad with a passel of kids in tow entered the lobby. Between the ages of five and ten, the children made as much noise as a small parade. Two of them began chasing each other around our seats as the parents approached the front desk.

"Come on," said André. "Let's get some air."

I buttoned my blazer and followed André, pausing a few times as the children ran in front of me.

It was late afternoon, and the sun was warm but the wind was not. We went around the corner of the building for shelter, and the air felt ten degrees warmer.

"My brothers," he explained, "they have no ambition. They just live off my dad's hard work. I couldn't live like that and not become bitter."

I was perplexed. "Surely they must help in some way."

He unzipped his sweater. “Oh, they do. But my dad has had to bring in more help than he should need to. It’s a five thousand-case winery. There is no reason my brothers cannot be out in the fields during harvest. But they like to stay in the tasting room, where they can be playboys.”

I was interested in wine enough to know that organic wineries were becoming fairly popular in the United States and Europe. After Italy, France was the top wine producer. All I had to do was look for the label in the corner of the bottle to know if a European wine was organic. I wanted to find out if his family’s winery was but needed to be subtle. He was aware that I knew Molly was speaking to the Sorbonne on land conservation. I didn’t want him to think I suspected him. How could I get an answer to my question without arousing suspicion? I tried the roundabout approach.

“You mean to tell me that your father has to supervise all the work in the fields? Your brothers don’t help with, say, pesticides?”

André’s dark eyebrows came together. “What? What are you saying?”

I sniffed. Unfortunately Lenny was right; I wasn’t as smooth as I thought I was. “I just meant your brothers must help with… with irrigation and fertilization and pesticides, like farmers do in the Midwest.”

“No. My dad still does things the old-fashioned way.” He leaned against the building, putting one black boot on the white stucco. “Now my brothers, they would do anything if it meant less work.”

I tried another approach. I would easily be able to find out more about the winery if I knew the name of the wine. “What is the name of the wine, may I ask? I would like to order a bottle.”

He smiled. “I will get you one myself. It will be my pleasure. It is called *Trois Frères*.”

Three brothers. Of course.

Chapter Thirteen

There is one constant among families: they are all different. I used to think that every family was like mine until I went to college and had roommates with brothers and sisters and stepfamilies. It was a second education. But every time I went home, I remembered exactly why I had immersed myself in the blithe world of Copper Bluff. Detroit presented real problems; the university presented theoretical ones. It made a huge difference in the way I lived my life. Most of the troubles I tangled with were found between pages, not people. And I had grown accustomed to that. Perhaps André could relate to my experience. Although owning a winery in France sounded like a fairytale to me, it meant real problems for André. There was the business side of it, which was as foreign to me as the German language, and there was also the family side of it. How could a family run a business without tearing one another apart with their differences? I chuckled to myself. My mother's sisters couldn't even agree on what food to serve for Christmas dinner or who would host. I couldn't imagine them coming together to bottle five thousand cases of wine.

From our conversation, I gathered his family's winery could

be organic. That meant it was possible that André might not have wanted Molly Jaspers' study to be shared because of the damning information it contained. Though that offered a possible motive for his murdering Molly Jaspers, it also proved that he probably didn't do it. The fact that the winery was named "Three Brothers" and one of the brothers was noticeably absent gave me enough reason to assume the rift in the family was real. His father had expected his three sons to take over the winery and run it as one unit, together, but André had split up the family when he decided to come to the United States after graduating from the Sorbonne. He obviously didn't have a vested interest in the winery or his brothers, whom he described as lazy; in fact, the only interest he showed was in his father. But I knew how strong ties could be between parents and children. My parents grew more special to me every year. Perhaps André's concern for his father's traditional methods was motive enough.

After André left, I remained camped out in one of the plush hotel lobby chairs so as not to disturb Amanda. She was probably fast asleep by now. After the fiasco with breakfast, André and I had reserved a table at a nice French bistro that served authentic food at a reasonable price. It was about two miles from our hotel, but I assured him college students were used to walking. Besides, I could ask Lenny if he wanted to drive the faculty members since he was in town. André thought that was an excellent idea, but I wasn't so sure Lenny would agree.

I mentally prepared myself for Lenny's objections before calling him: one, he was on spring break, as in a break from the faculty; two, he was honing his guitar skills, which didn't jive with taking time out to go to a French restaurant; three, he was spending quality time with his family—the girls were growing up so fast.

I heard a scuffle as he answered the phone. "Hello?"

"Ask her if she's in jail!" one of his nieces whispered.

"Are you in jail, Em?" Lenny asked.

I looked out the window at the buildings across the street. "No, I'm still at the hotel."

The girls sighed in unison.

"But it's kind of like I'm in jail. I can't leave until tomorrow," I added.

"They're already bored. A hotel to them means vacation. So what's up?"

I uncrossed my legs and leaned forward. This was going to take finesse. "Oh, nothing. I was just relaxing a bit before we go out to dinner."

"Who's *we*? The dirty dozen?"

"You can joke all you want, Lenny, but I'm stuck here without so much as correct change for the vending machine."

"I'm sorry," he said. "I know how much you like vending machines."

"Anyway, the point is that we are going out for a nice dinner tonight, and I'm really looking forward to it."

"I'm happy for you?" he said, not sure where the conversation was headed. "Where are you going?"

"A French restaurant. I went there once when I presented a paper at the University of Minnesota. André thought it was a great idea. At least the students can practice ordering in French. We're leaving tomorrow. André booked the bus ride home."

He moved to a quieter location. I could tell because the girls' chatter turned into a dull buzz. "So they're letting you leave? I guess that means nobody's been arrested."

"No, not yet, but poor André.... It sounds like Dean Richardson is coming down on him pretty hard. He wants André to get the students back as soon as possible. So, why don't you come along tonight? It'll be your last chance to see me before I leave."

"With the whole gang? I dunno. It might turn into a night of badly pronounced entrees. 'Gimme an order of escargot,' " he said, voicing the silent "t."

"It won't. I promise. The group is too disjointed to speak much French."

"Well, I told my nieces I'd take them to school tomorrow…."

"It won't go on too long, I swear."

"Come on, Uncle Lenny… go! What are you, *chicken*?" said one of the girls. The other girl started making clucking noises.

I laughed. "Your nieces are right, you know. These people are completely harmless."

"Except for the murderer, right?" he said under his breath.

I twirled a curl around my finger. "Well, there is that one exception."

"You know what this means, Em? If I come, there will be thirteen for dinner."

I was silent; it hadn't occurred to me.

His laugh busted up the silence. "Are you sure you want to court death again on this already ill-fated trip?"

I let out a huff of air. "I know you're mocking me, Lenny, but this is no laughing matter. One faculty member *is* dead."

"I know, I'm sorry. It wasn't about her. So what time is this French meeting of the minds?"

I hesitated. Superstitions aside, I had reservations about his coming. I had been brought up in too Catholic of a house not to be. Blessed salts, holy water, rosary beads—they were my ammunition against all things unholy. But against a curse? What power did I have? Yet he had told me before: he could take care of himself. And I would be there, watching carefully. "Seven o'clock. Oh, and Lenny? You might want to make room in your backseat. A few of the others will be riding with us."

With this, I pushed the End button as fast as I could. I waited a couple seconds. When there was no return call, I happily tucked my phone into my purse and pulled out *A Movable Feast*. My feast had certainly moved. Perhaps it had disappeared altogether. But the truth was I wasn't as upset as

I thought I would be. For years, Paris had been a dream of mine, yet here I was, stuck in the Midwest over spring break, looking forward to an evening with Lenny. Minneapolis might not offer a genuine Parisian café or an ancient cobblestone boulevard, but its spring streets were pleasant enough.

The sleepless night began to catch up with me, and I felt myself nodding off over my unturned pages. Once in a while, a cry from a baby or a honk from a car horn would propel me to the next page, but mostly I dozed for the next two hours. When I awoke, my eyelids were stuck together, and I had to blink several times to get my contacts in working order. Putting my book back into my tote, I stretched my arms above my head, stood, and walked to the elevator. I'd make use of the coffeemaker in the room before getting ready for dinner.

When I came into the room, Kat was nowhere in sight. She must have still been shopping. Amanda, though, was sleeping, curled up in a tight ball atop the covers. She looked very much like a child, and I felt profound sympathy for her. Although she had concerns, her studious façade concealed her anxieties so well they were almost imperceptible. Only now, when she was asleep, did her face relax.

I was filling the coffeepot when I heard a phone vibrate. I turned back and peeked around the corner. Amanda didn't move. The phone buzzed a second time. I walked toward the bed. She was still taking the regular breaths of a sleeper. Quietly, I leaned over the bed, trying to read the message on her iPhone. The sender was NAD. Nick, middle initial A, Dramsdor? And there was only one line of text: *meet tonight after dinner?* I stepped back—right onto a pile of magazines next to my bed. They were slippery, and I lost my footing. Amanda stirred, and I quickly jumped onto the other bed. I put my arm above my head, trying to appear nonchalant.

"Hey," I said.

She looked around for her phone. It was more addiction than device for a lot of students. "I must have fallen asleep."

"Right," I said, stretching. "I'm going to make some coffee. Do you want some?"

"No." She was texting back. "Thanks, though."

I walked toward the sink and filled the four-cup coffeepot. I placed two pre-made coffee bags in the top of the machine. Hotel coffee was nearly like drinking hot water; I had to make my cup as strong as possible. "Where's Kat?" I called out.

She chuckled. "Still shopping. She should be here any minute."

"Does she know we're going out for dinner tonight?"

"Yeah, I told her." she said. "She just stayed away so I could get some sleep."

When I came back to the bedroom, she was brushing her blonde hair vigorously.

"She's worried about me," she continued.

"Kat is a good friend. Are you feeling any better after your nap?"

Amanda stopped brushing her hair. "I am. But I'm still bummed about the trip."

"There's always next year," I said, trying to sound upbeat. "I believe Professor Duman will do some great things for the Languages Department in the future."

"Next year won't be the same," she said. Her voice had a note of finality in it.

"Because of Professor Jaspers?"

She nodded. "It won't be the same group."

Fresh tears in her eyes, she stood and walked into the bathroom, leaving me feeling as if I should do something, but I didn't know what. Maybe she just needed a few minutes to herself. We could all use that right now. I poured myself a cup of coffee and sat down on the sleeper sofa, giving her as much privacy as the room afforded. She had been on expeditions with Molly and Nick before, and she was one of Molly's pet students, if the other girls' jealousy was any indication. It would take more than a day to grieve.

Amanda was in the bathroom for a while before I heard her flush the toilet and wash her hands. I busied myself with my suitcase, searching for an outfit for dinner. I had bought a red dress for such an occasion, and after attending fifty spin classes, I was going to wear it. Gathering my clothes in my arms, I smiled at Amanda as I walked past the vanity, where she was putting toothpaste on her toothbrush. Just then, Kat burst into the room with two large bags, one nearly nicking me.

"Oh, I'm so sorry, Professor Prather! I didn't know you were there," said Kat.

"Don't worry. You missed me. It looks like your shopping trip was successful?"

"Totally. Most of the records are used but in good condition. Hey," she said to Amanda, "did you take a nap?"

Amanda nodded, her mouth still full of toothpaste.

"I'm starving," Kat said, plopping the square bags on the bed. "I can't wait to eat. Amanda says we're going to some French place. I hope we don't have to pay. I think I spent all my money."

I laughed. "No, two of your dinners were included in the price of the trip, most of which will now be refunded."

She was wrapping her hair into a bun. "You know that story I started?" she said, taking a hair tie from her mouth. "I think I have a plot."

I moved closer. "Oh? What is it?"

Her hazel eyes glinted green. "Nope, can't tell." She reached over to her bag and pulled out a notebook. "It's bad luck to talk about a work before it's finished."

I think I was starting to rub off on the girl.

Chapter Fourteen

A HALF HOUR later, we met up with the rest of the group downstairs in the lobby. André looked good in his leather jacket and tight black jeans, and he wasn't the only one. The entire group was dressed up; we finally had somewhere to go that didn't include a police station. We smiled at one another as if the last twenty-four hours were just a bad dream. Except for Bennett. While he was clad in khakis and a polo, his face was unshaven and fatigued. He was talking quietly on his cellphone, presumably about Molly. The next few days would be trying for him, making arrangements from afar. He hung up as Amanda, Kat, and I approached the group.

"I'm glad you decided to come," I said to him.

He motioned toward Nick. "Nick talked me into it. I'm not even hungry."

"You'll need to keep up your strength the next couple of days. For Molly," said Nick.

Bennett nodded. "For Molly."

"Good evening, Em," said André, approaching us. "You look *magnifique*!"

"And you, too," I said, smiling around at the group. "Everyone looks great."

"It is good to have a distraction," André said.

"Agreed," said Arnold. But I had a feeling he was distracted enough without dinner.

"Em's good friend Lenny Jenkins has offered us a ride, but I do not see him yet?" André looked at me for confirmation.

"He'll be here. It's early."

"Now, students," André said, "I have printed out directions on the MapQuest. All you do is walk one mile and take a right. Then keep walking." He handed the printout to Amanda.

"Oh, I've got it on my GPS, Professor," Amanda said, flashing André her phone.

"Take it just in case. One never knows when the technology will fail." André looked at the rest of the students. "All stay together please, and follow Amanda."

Olivia rolled her eyes. "*Follow Amanda*," she mimicked him under her breath. Her friend Meg smiled.

"Ah! There is the man of the minute," exclaimed André.

I turned toward the door and saw Lenny visibly pause. I think he was deciding whether to continue walking.

"Lenny!" I hollered. His jaw relaxed, and he walked toward the group.

He gave me a wink. "Wow. You look good."

"This is Lenny Jenkins," I said. "Most of you know him from English. He happens to be in Minneapolis visiting his family. He agreed to give us a lift tonight."

"The guitarist," said Arnold, sticking out his hand. "I've heard you play at O'Malley's. I'm Arnold Frasier."

"Yeah," said Lenny, shaking his hand, "the buffalo guy. If we could combine your art with my guitar, I'm pretty sure we could become South Dakota's most famous duo."

Arnold laughed. "Nah. You and Emmeline are the only famous duo around there. I wouldn't want to step on her toes."

I rolled my eyes. The Christmas party duet was more unforgettable than I remembered.

"Hello, Lenny," said Judith.

"Nice to see you again," said Lenny.

"This is Nick Dramsdor, from State, and Bennett Jaspers, Molly's husband."

After shaking hands with Nick, Lenny reached out to Bennett. "I'm sorry for your loss. Molly was someone special on campus; she will be missed."

Lenny impressed me with his sincerity and must have impressed Bennett as well, for Bennett returned his handshake heartily.

"I will see to it that her good work continues. I promise you that," Bennett replied.

Lenny counted the faculty members. "I don't know if Em told you, but I drive a Taurus. There's no way all six of you are going to fit in my car. Five, tops."

"Em is small," said André. "She can sit on my lap."

Lenny frowned.

"Hey, I can walk with the students," offered Nick. "André said someone should, and he and Emmeline have done so much already. Besides, it's a nice night. I could use a little fresh air." He smiled at Amanda, and her face flushed.

"Good idea," I said, pretending I hadn't seen Amanda's reaction. "Let's get started."

Fitting four of us in the backseat of Lenny's car took some finagling. I ended up sitting half on the seat and half on André's lap. Bennett, the largest in the group, sat in the front seat with Lenny, who glanced at me from the rearview mirror.

Arnold and Judith were discussing student retention rates, but Bennett had lapsed into silence. He looked miserable as he stared out his window into the dark, empty streets. Maybe insisting that he come along wasn't such a good idea after all.

Lenny noticed his preoccupation, too. "So, Bennett, I'm guessing you're not a teacher. What do you do for work?"

"Work. Oh. Well, I got my degree in electrical engineering. That's how Molly and I met. But that's about the extent of my college experience. Now I own a company that contracts out for various engineering projects. We have some very smart people working for us. A lot of new things happening in the world of electronics."

"Technology is always changing, and we depend on it more than ever. I guess that's job security for you," said Lenny.

"You couldn't be in a better field. If you can make it, someone is willing to buy it. Drones, cameras. They're huge right now. We want to monitor things from far and wide."

Lenny turned on his blinker. "I suppose yours is a pretty lucrative business." Then he muttered, more to himself than Bennett, "I could use something lucrative in my life. Teaching in the Midwest hardly pays the bills."

Bennett agreed. "Don't I know it. Molly cursed technology, but we never could have lived off her salary. She was applying for the associate dean position in Arts and Sciences, though. She said that paid more."

I glanced at Arnold and Judith. Arnold was as surprised as I was that Molly would have considered a largely administrative position such as dean.

"Molly, the associate dean?" questioned Arnold. "I can't imagine her settling down to the life of a paper pusher."

"You can hardly equate the job of a dean with that of a paper pusher," said Judith. "It's a prestigious position that requires relentless devotion to academic rigor. I'm considering the position myself."

"Oh, I'm sorry, Judith. I didn't mean to insinuate—"

"You're right, though, Arnold," Bennett broke in. "Molly wouldn't stand for the status quo. She talked about 'revolutionizing' the office."

Judith huffed a breath. "There is something to be said for history and tradition. Molly, as a trained classicist, would have realized this. Changing the environment is one thing;

changing the office of the dean is quite another. Everything has its boundaries."

"She no longer saw boundaries, only obstacles." Bennett chuckled.

Arnold grinned in agreement. "She had many admirable qualities; her stubbornness wasn't necessarily one of them."

I smiled politely, but my mind was replaying Judith Spade's offhand comment. She was interested in the open associate dean position, as was Molly. I couldn't conceive of two more different candidates. One would have changed everything; one would have changed nothing. The School of Arts and Sciences would have taken on an entirely new direction with Molly in the office. I couldn't imagine Judith agreeing with that direction, even though I tended to believe that the School of Medicine was more inclined to look toward the future than, say, the Humanities Department. But from Judith's reaction, I had to wonder if my assumption was wrong.

We arrived at the restaurant, and Lenny got out and opened the rear door.

"Thank you, Lenny," I said, taking his hand. We were in front of the cream-colored brick building with the name written in large red script above the door.

André stepped out and patted Lenny on the back. "Yes, thank you, old friend. The ride was much appreciated."

"I bet," Lenny said.

André looked up and down the street. "Let's have a cocktail before the students arrive, eh?"

"Cheers to that," Arnold said. He held the door for the rest of us. "Do they have a bar?"

"If I remember correctly, one side is reserved dining; the other side is informal dining with a small lounge," I said.

Because it was early Sunday evening, there were lots of open booths and tables at the restaurant. In each one of them, a dim candle glowed at the center. Although there were several round tables available at the bar, we all remained standing around the counter after we ordered our drinks. We assumed we didn't have much time before the students arrived, and we were right. I had taken only a few sips of my French 75 when Amanda and Nick entered the restaurant, looking like a couple. There was something about them that said *together*. Maybe it was the way their hands always brushed or the way he held open the door for her. Under different circumstances, I would have said they were cute, the all-American girl and her cowboy.

Kat, who was a step behind them, waved to me, and I waved back. Olivia, Meg, Jace, and Aaron followed behind.

"Can we take these with us?" Lenny asked, holding up his beer.

"Yes," I said. "Come on."

"Prather, party of… thirteen," I said.

"Right this way, mademoiselle," said the host. "We have a table prepared for you and your guests."

"Very nice choice, Em. I like it very much," said André.

"Are you sure I won't have to take out a loan to buy supper?" whispered Lenny.

"Completely," I answered. "The velvet curtains are truly deceiving."

The host took us to a large table in the corner. A tiny triangle of street showed beyond the curtained window, and I wondered what a passerby would think as he walked by our happy little window. Would he think we were part of a family reunion or a church mission trip? He would never assume that our group was a gathering of possible murder suspects.

I sat between Lenny and Bennett. Amanda sat on Bennett's other side, along with Kat. André busied himself with the rest of the seating, making sure students and faculty were intermixed at the table. I realized too late that I should also have been making sure everyone was at ease since I was assistant faculty coordinator. But I had become ensnared in a conversation with Lenny and had temporarily forgotten about everyone else. This was a bad habit of ours. Christmas parties, potlucks, faculty meetings—we had a way of tuning out crowds when we landed on a topic we both enjoyed.

The waiter began passing out the single-sheet menus, while informing us of the day's special: *sole meunière*.

"*Très bien*," exclaimed André. "One finds *sole meunière* in Paris every day, students. Here is your chance to taste authentic French cuisine."

The students didn't look convinced and neither did Lenny.

"*Escargot*? You've got to be kidding me," he whispered, reading the menu. "I was joking."

I brushed aside his comment. "You can order the special. *Sole meunière* is nothing more than fish fried in butter, served with lemon and parsley. What's so shocking about that? You eat fish, don't you?"

"Fish," he said, "as in trout. Halibut. Shrimp."

I pointed to the *steak au poivre*. "You like meat. This is a steak with a cognac and heavy cream sauce. You'd love it."

"I like cognac…" he considered.

"And steak," I said.

"I don't know."

"Remember, I've been here before. The food is good."

I turned toward the group. Everyone was intrigued with the menu. The students were studying it and asking questions, and André was thrilled to answer. I'd never seen him more animated. I could tell he wanted everyone to enjoy the meal as much as he would. His enthusiasm was contagious, and even Lenny was excited when it came time to place his order. For the first time, we were acting like a group with similar interests. The trip, I realized, would have been a success, had we made it to Paris.

Bennett must have been thinking the same thing. Surveying the table with a wistful smile, he told me, "She would have loved this, you know. She wouldn't have wanted to be waylaid, mind you, but she would have loved the academic company. She thrived on it."

I nodded. "Nick said she was going to present a paper at the Sorbonne. Was she excited about it?"

"Very much," he said. "She had discovered some new emission findings linked with organic farming and couldn't wait to expose the *dangerous* amounts."

"Were they really dangerous?" I asked, taking a piece of bread from the basket.

"She thought they were, but she thought everything was dangerous. In terms of the environment," he added.

Not for the first time that spring, the character of Mrs. Dalloway came to mind: *She always had the feeling that it was very, very dangerous to live even one day.* "Wasn't she afraid that someone would be angry with her for disagreeing with a land practice that seems to support the environment on so many levels?"

Bennett raised his eyebrows. "Molly wasn't afraid of anything, certainly not of the environmentalists. They worshipped her fanaticism. I tried to tell Molly that every action causes a reaction." He unfolded his napkin on his lap. "She said the thing to do then was not to act." He shook his head. "I don't know how you apply that to the real world."

" 'Be the change you seek in the world,' " said Amanda in an innocent voice. "That's what Professor Jaspers always taught us."

"Who still quotes Gandhi after ten years of teaching? I dropped it year two," whispered Lenny, biting into a bun.

"That sounds like Molly," said Bennett, smiling at Amanda.

Judith agreed. "You had to admire her ability to inspire students."

Amanda nodded. "She knew big changes were ahead for the Midwest, and she said we had to resist them. Changes like the Midwest Connect Pipeline."

"*Midwest Connect*," Olivia groaned. "That's all she talked about in class last spring."

"She probably had a good reason. What was the class?" Nick asked defensively.

"I don't believe we offer a class on pipelines." Sarcasm tinged Judith's words. "At least I hope we don't."

"Western Civ," Olivia said. "No connection whatsoever."

"Professor Jaspers saw a similarity between the Roman Empire and the pipelines," Amanda explained to Bennett. "It was a terrific metaphor."

Kat nodded in support of her friend. "She was always pulling in contemporary references. It's what made the class interesting."

"Exactly. But you had to *get* the references," said Amanda. Her voice was haughty. She turned to Olivia. "You're just mad because you didn't pass."

Olivia crossed her arms, tossing her hair over one shoulder. "True, but neither did half the class. It was more work than anyone could handle. That guy you were crushing on? He shot himself a month later."

Amanda looked at Nick. "I was not *crushing on* anyone. And what do you mean he shot himself?"

"I mean he shot himself in the head. He committed suicide."

"I have no idea who you're talking about," she said. Her voice began to tremble.

"Yes you do. Skylar. Skylar Erickson."

I looked at Lenny. He recognized the name.

Kat touched Amanda's shoulder, but she didn't notice.

"He killed himself?" Amanda said, her voice barely a whisper. She put down her butter knife. "I thought he dropped out."

Olivia's eyes narrowed. She was happy to be causing Amanda distress. "Well, now you know. He didn't."

Kat glared at Olivia, her eyes steely gray. "I don't think this is the kind of thing we should be talking about right now."

André responded at once. "I think Kat is right. We have had enough sadness in our lives. You see the wine I've ordered," he said, holding up his glass in the light. "This is a Bordeaux, which comes from Southwestern France. The river Garonne cuts the region into the right bank and left bank. Together the blending of Merlot and Cabernet wines creates the Bordeaux." He took a drink. "Now, if the winery is on the left bank, the Bordeaux will have more Cabernet; it will be stronger and bolder. If it is on the right bank, it will have more Merlot and be milder. This wine definitely comes from the right bank."

"You know quite a bit about wine, André. You must drink a lot," said Nick, lightening the mood.

Arnold chuckled.

André shook his head. "Yes, I do admit to drinking a fair amount of wine, but my family owns a winery, not in Bordeaux but in Bourgogne. Bourgogne is a small region known for its fine Burgundy wines, Pinot Noir and Chardonnay. I'm sure you know it?"

"Of course," Bennett said. "It produces the best wine in the world. When I'm overseas, that's all they drink."

André beamed with pleasure. "Yes, you know it. Would you like a taste?"

"No. No thank you," said Bennett.

He knew a lot about wine, but I never saw him drink. I suppose it was the grief of losing Molly that made him refrain.

"What makes the wine good?" asked Jace. "The grapes?"

"Well," said André, leaning in as if he were going to tell us a secret. "It's not just the grapes but the land. We call it *terroir*. See, we have the combination of the grape, soil, climate, and *esprit*. You taste a burgundy, you taste Burgundy itself." Looking at the group's confused faces, he added, "It is difficult to explain. When you visit, you feel as if you have stepped back in time."

"Textbook organic," Lenny whispered.

I nodded. It sounded as if the Burgundy region was known as much for the land as the grapes themselves. In that respect, André wouldn't want chemicals involved in his wine process anymore than Molly would have wanted the pipeline to cut through her Midwest.

"What's the name of the wine?" Lenny asked. "I might check it out."

André smiled. "I did not know you were a connoisseur of wines. I thought you drank the bourbon."

He raised his wine glass. "Well, I'm trying to class it up for Em here."

André laughed. "It is called *Trois Frères*—Three Brothers."

"You've got three brothers?" Lenny asked.

André took a piece of bread from the basket. "No. I have two brothers. I am the third. Ironically, my father also had two brothers. The winery has been in our family for a long time."

Lenny took a glug of his wine and grimaced. "I hope it's better than this stuff."

André nodded enthusiastically. "It is very good. My dad and his brothers never compromise on anything."

"Are your uncles still in the wine business?" I asked.

"No, my father bought them out years ago." He shrugged. "They had girls."

"How sexist," Amanda said.

"I have to agree," said Judith.

André looked at me for help, but I had none to offer. The thinking was antiquated.

"I suppose it does sound that way, but I assure you it is not. It's just the way things have always been."

"The definition of sexism," said Lenny with a laugh.

"I am not helping my case," André said. "What I mean is that my family has changed nothing for years. If my cousins had wanted the winery, I am certain my father would have considered it. They probably would have been better stewards than my brothers," he added with a sniff of disgust. "They are idiots when it comes to growing wine."

"Does that mean you have no plans to go back to France? Seems to be quite a profitable business to be in," said Bennett.

His hand shook as he took the bread basket from Amanda, and I felt a new wave of sympathy for him. I applauded his commitment to participate in spite of his grief. "The land alone is worth a fortune."

"Profits are all my brothers think of," said André. "No, I could never get along with them. I still can't. We have different brains for business."

Bennett took a sip of water then replied, "Well, unfortunately, profits must come first. They have to if you want to get ahead."

"What does that mean, 'get ahead'?" asked André. "Get richer? There must be a better goal in life than that."

"I can't think of one," said Jace to Aaron. Aaron laughed.

Bennett shook his head. "It's about being successful. You can't be successful without the profits to back it up. That's just common sense."

André nodded. "I'm sure you have a point, but if you met my brothers, you would see what I mean. They value profits above *all* else—even the land that has given them everything."

Our food arrived, and we ate heartily, despite some of the unfamiliar menu items. It was as if we were starving, not just for food but for companionship. We ate and drank and ordered dessert when it was offered. As my crème brûlée was served, I worried about the bill, but then I remembered we would be going back to the campus tomorrow. This would be the only outing worth mentioning from the entire spring break. So I dove into the pudding, which was still warm, one delicious spoonful at a time, regretting nothing.

When it was time to leave, André insisted on paying for Lenny's food since he'd provided us with transportation. Lenny resisted, but André was adamant.

"It was a few blocks," Lenny said.

"Well, it was worth it to ride those few minutes in comfort," André said. "We need to guard ourselves as much as we can against this Midwest weather."

"Are you sure?" Lenny said. "You don't want to have to

justify your receipt to Arts and Sciences. You know how they get. I don't want to muck up a chance for you and Em here to plan another trip."

André waved away Lenny's concerns. "*Allez.* We have an extraordinary circumstance, no?"

"It certainly falls under that category in my mind," I said.

Lenny let the subject drop and started to shrug on his coat. Suddenly I remembered the curse of the thirteenth dinner guest: the first one to leave the party would die within the year. I jerked at his arm.

"Your concern is flattering," he murmured, "but you know I don't go in for voodoo."

Nick stood and pushed in his chair. "I will walk with the students."

He was obviously unaware of the myth or our discussion of it.

"That's okay. I'll take my turn," said Arnold.

"No, really. I want to," said Nick. He pulled on his coat.

Arnold looked at him quizzically, and Nick added, "I ate way more than I should have. I need to walk it off." As he zipped up his jacket and left, Amanda was the first student to fall in line behind him.

"I am only too happy to ride in the car again, my friend," André said to Lenny, patting his shoulder.

"I agree," said Bennett. "Thank you for driving. I don't think I could make it back to the hotel without a ride. I'm exhausted."

He looked exhausted. Engulfed by grief, he walked with a newly hunched posture as if his shoulders were pressed forward by some physical weight. His eyes, hooded by dark, saggy skin, didn't lift from the ground. I wondered if he was getting any sleep at all.

"You must be tired," I said as we walked to the car. The students were hurrying down the street.

"I am. I'll be glad when this is over and I can give Molly a proper funeral."

"Did the police say when?" I asked.

"They said I might as well bus home with you tomorrow. That way I will be there when Molly's parents arrive. Molly's remains won't be shipped for a couple more days. I hate to leave her here, but I don't know what else to do."

He coughed to hide a sniffle, and I looked away, giving him some privacy. He had put up a solitary battle for this woman. He had fought for her causes, he had defended her positions, and he had funded her passions. And now that she was gone, so was the better part of him. I continued walking, saying nothing. I could think of nothing to say except that I was sorry for him. But this time, I meant it.

Chapter Fifteen

LENNY PULLED UP next to the hotel and left the engine running. Bennett was the first to shake his hand as he shut the passenger door then quickly ducked under the awning and disappeared inside the building. Lenny opened the back door for Judith, and the rest of the group began to dislodge themselves from the backseat. I dallied as long as I could to grab a few minutes alone with Lenny.

"Em, are you coming?" André asked.

"In a minute," I said. "You go on up without me."

I waited for André to continue walking, and then I turned back to Lenny. "Did you hear what Olivia said about that student? Skylar *Erickson*?"

Lenny nodded. "It's the same last name as the red-haired woman. Do you think there's a connection?"

"Of course there's a connection. There must be."

"I never heard about it on campus. Did you?"

I shook my head. "No, but who knows what happened over the summer? Amanda said she knew a kid by that name from spring semester. She said he was smart enough but that he started hanging out with some of the guys in the back row and quit coming to class."

A shot of wind blew open Lenny's jacket, and he quickly pulled it shut. "Maybe that's why we didn't hear. Maybe he left campus."

"He must have. But who is Skylar to Jean Erickson? That's what we need to find out." I began to rummage through my purse for my phone.

"Come on. You think you're really going to find your cell in that suitcase? And if you do, will it even be charged?" He took his phone from his pocket. "Here."

He had a point. I had a bad habit of not keeping track of my phone. Although the twenty-first century had adhered most people to their technology, it had done nearly the opposite to me. I was so tired of students bringing their phones into the classroom that I resisted dependence on them entirely. But now I was glad Lenny's cell lighted up the dark night with its fluorescent glow. It became a beacon of hope for shedding light on Skylar's fate.

I typed his name into the Safari app, and after a few seconds, I got several hits. But only one was an obituary from a funeral home's website in Minnesota.

"That one," said Lenny.

I touched the link, and slowly Skylar's picture began to populate the screen. The first thing we noticed was his bright red hair.

"They have to be related!" I said as I began to scroll through the obituary. "It says he was a history major at Copper Bluff. Survived by his brothers… sister… parents. Tom and *Jean* Erickson."

We stared at each other for several seconds.

"What do you know," said Lenny.

"The red-haired woman is his mother."

"Do you think she blamed Molly for her son's death?"

I nodded. "That's exactly what I think. He was a history

major, and she failed him in what must have been a critical course."

"Yeah, but lots of people failed. They didn't kill themselves. You heard that student."

"Amanda. I know. There must be more to the story."

I was already writing it. Jean Erickson was crazed with grief; it showed in her sallow skin, her dry hair, her thin body. She sent her son to a good university, and instead of an education, he was given a failing grade. He gave up. Someone would pay for failing him, and that someone was Molly Jaspers.

I looked up and noticed Lenny studying me. The light from the streetlamp illuminated his lips and chin; the rest of his face was in the dark. The result was dangerously handsome. His lips curled into a smile.

"What are you thinking?" he asked.

I looked at the hotel and then back at him. His teeth were perfectly straight. "I am thinking about, um, you know, everything."

"*Everything*? You know you're an open book?"

"I assure you, you have no idea what I'm thinking." And I doubted he did. I couldn't imagine that he could guess that I found myself wondering what it would feel like to kiss him.

"Oh yeah?" he said, moving one foot forward. "Should we put that theory to the test?"

"I don't think so," I whispered but didn't move. My heart grew louder and louder until its beating filled my ears. My lips scarcely parted, but the movement was enough for Lenny to tilt his head toward mine.

Suddenly I heard footsteps and laughter. Aaron pulled Jace from the front door of the hotel.

"You cheated," Aaron said.

"No, I didn't. I'm faster than you. Just admit it," said the long-legged Jace.

The boys shoved each other back and forth in a playful way. I took a step back, and they realized we were at the curb.

Aaron dropped his hands to his sides, and Jace pulled open the door. Olivia, Meg, and Kat weren't far behind, with Nick and Amanda trailing by several steps.

"So I guess I'll go," said Lenny.

"Yes, me too," I said louder than I intended.

"Will you still be in Minneapolis tomorrow?"

"Until eleven. That's when the bus takes off. But I want to tell Ernest what we found on Jean Erickson before we go. Do you want to come with me?"

"You mean, will I take you to the police station? Sure. Why not. I'll call you in the morning," he said as he got back into his car. "Turn on your phone."

I waved. "Of course."

As I walked toward the hotel, I noticed Kat lingering by the door, waiting for Amanda. But Amanda and Nick didn't seem to notice her. They didn't notice me either. They were absorbed in conversation, and I doubted they knew anyone else existed right now.

"Hey, Professor Prather," said Kat. "I really liked dinner. It was cool."

"It was good, wasn't it?" I said. "Even if we didn't get to France, we did get to try some authentic French food." I nodded toward Nick and Amanda. "What's that about?"

Her face turned nonchalant. "What's what? They're both fossil geeks."

Amanda noted Kat's voice and quickened her pace. "Sorry. Are you waiting for me?" She was distressed, if not by the news of Skylar's suicide, then by her amorous conversation with Nick. She knew I had noticed.

I held open the door. "No, not at all. I just got here." We paused for a moment in the lobby. "Last night of vacation."

"What about the police?" said Nick.

I shrugged. I wasn't about to admit that I planned on talking to them tomorrow. "I don't know. André told them about our plans to leave."

"It's ridiculous, if you ask me," said Nick. "They shouldn't even be involved. It was a very unfortunate accident. The rest is all conjecture."

"Well, not quite all," I said.

"So you agree someone is responsible for her death?" said Nick, starting toward the elevator.

Kat and Amanda looked at me for the answer.

"I'm not saying that. The police are."

We walked the rest of the way to the elevator in silence.

Chapter Sixteen

MONDAY MORNING WAS cloudy, and the threat of snow lorded over my thoughts. What if we couldn't get out? Spring in the Midwest could be elusive; snow could still bring plans to a standstill. After a few weeks of warm sunshine, it could turn gray and dark, extending winter into the late month of May. Maybe the weather mimicked life, or maybe it was the other way around. Either way, Midwesterners had little choice but to persevere, not just for days but generations.

I checked the window again, straining to see as far as I could into the steely clouds. No flakes—yet. It was nine o'clock, and Amanda and Kat were still sleeping. I was amazed that anyone could sleep through the noise of my hairdryer, but they pulled off that feat without a single stir. They had come back to the room late last night after having met the other students down by the pool. At least that was what they had said. If anything, the impromptu pool party gave Amanda an excuse to meet with Nick in private. But I didn't care about that relationship, at least not today. I was more concerned about her relationship with Skylar and how it related to Jean Erickson.

I opened the drapes, but with the thick clouds, the room

barely brightened. I continued to pull until the large window was fully exposed. Still, Amanda and Kat didn't move. I coughed and cleared my throat. Nothing. I started digging through my purse, which *was* more like a suitcase, for my lip balm. I had the perfect shade of pink that would match my linen sweater, and finding it would make enough noise to wake the dead. Sure enough, halfway through my quest, Amanda turned over and moaned. It was enough for me to start a conversation. I wanted to inform them I was leaving and remind them what time we were departing for Copper Bluff, provided we could beat the snow out of town.

"Oh, good morning, Amanda."

She mumbled, "Is it late?"

Kat rolled over and put her pillow over her head.

"Just nine o'clock," I said. "I have a meeting to go to today, so I got up early and showered."

She rubbed her eyes and looked at her phone, which was charging next to her bedside. She propped herself up on one elbow. "When are you going?"

"Soon. Lenny is picking me up."

"Professor Jenkins?"

"Yes, Professor Jenkins. The musician from Minneapolis."

She smiled. "I didn't know you guys were a thing."

I sat down on the edge of the bed. "Oh, we're not. We're not a thing."

"Okay," she said, but she didn't believe me.

Her comment on my relationship with Lenny gave me the opportunity to follow up on Skylar. "What about the boy Olivia mentioned at dinner? Skylar? Were you a 'thing'?"

"No. Not even close. Olivia just said that because Nick…" she stopped short. "Olivia and I used to be friends. When we took that class together, everything changed. Then she flunked—and blamed me. She ended up getting kicked out of her sorority because of her low GPA."

She shook her head and continued, "Skylar quit coming to class. But I had no idea…." Her eyes shone with tears.

"I'm sorry, Amanda. Were you close to him?"

"I was, but more intellectually than anything. He was smart. He was well-read. I liked talking to him about things. I can't believe he killed himself. He seemed so interested in everything, in life."

"Did Professor Jaspers like him?"

She nodded. "She did. Especially at first. But then when he kept slacking off, she told him he didn't have the 'academic rigor' to pursue the degree. He just quit coming to class afterwards."

I raised my eyebrows. "That's a little harsh."

Her voice turned defensive. "Professor Jaspers was like that. She expected a lot from her students, and we expected a lot from her."

"Would a comment about his academic performance affect him in that way? Was he sensitive to criticism?" I asked.

"No. No way. He was a smart guy. He respected her. And besides, it sounds like he moved off campus."

I thought some of her opinion had to do with her friendship with Skylar and some of it with her admiration for Molly Jaspers. I couldn't imagine her believing anything sinister about one of her professors.

My phone began to ring, and I rifled through my bag. "I just put that thing in here. How could it have sunk to the bottom… ah ha! Hello?"

It was Lenny.

"Hey, I was about to give up."

"No, my phone is fully charged and in my front purse pocket… or it will be when we hang up."

He laughed. "I'm on my way. I will be there in fifteen minutes or so."

"Perfect," I said. "That gives me enough time to talk to André about the bus."

"I'll text when I get there."

"Okay," I said and ended the call. "That was Lenny," I said

to Amanda. "I'd better talk to André before I leave. I want to make sure we're still scheduled to leave at eleven."

"Hey, let me know, will you? Text me?" she asked. "I'm going to start getting ready."

"Of course." I grabbed my coat off the back of the hotel chair. Then I walked next door, to André and Arnold's room, hoping both men were up and decently dressed. I knocked.

"One moment," André called from behind the wooden door. After a minute, he pulled it open. "Emmeline! It's you. Come in, come in."

His hair was slick from the shower, and his red shirt clung to his damp shoulders. The room smelled of expensive cologne, and the sound of the shower whirred in the background.

"Arnold is in there," said André, indicating the bathroom door, "and Aaron is in there," pointing toward the bedroom. "The boy snores like the bear, and we don't sleep." He rubbed his eyes.

"I bet you can't wait to get home. Neither can I. Please tell me we haven't been canceled because of the forecast."

"No. I have just confirmed with the bus company. *Voilà!* We still leave at eleven o'clock, check-out time at the Normandy Inn."

I clapped my hands. "Thank god. Have you told Dean Richardson?"

He nodded. "Yes, I have. He was glad to hear it. He said he has had many phone calls from parents the last two days."

"I bet," I said. André had answered more than a few of them himself.

"I will have everybody ready by check-out time." He glanced at my coat. "What are your plans? You are on your way out?"

I didn't want to confide in André; he had enough troubles without worrying about why I was going back to the police station. What was important was getting to the bottom of Molly's death and clearing his name. Only that would solve his problems. "Lenny is picking me up, but I will be back at eleven… sharp."

He ran his fingers through his wet hair, and a few dark locks scattered about his forehead. "You and Lenny. You are *good* friends."

It wasn't a question, but it felt like one. "Yes, we are, I suppose."

"You two are so different from each other," he said.

"That's for certain."

I thought he was going to say something else, but he said, "It is good to have good friends, especially at a time like this. I look back on the last two days and cannot believe what's happened." He glanced toward the window and shook off his melancholy. "I hope the day is propitious for travel."

I gestured toward the open curtain. "I don't know. It looks like snow, doesn't it?"

He opened the door for me. "Do not say that word, Em. To me, it is a four-letter word."

I chuckled. "I'll catch up with you later." After texting Amanda to confirm our departure time, I walked down the hall and into the elevator. Downstairs, I was happy to see a coffee carafe placed in the lobby—until I realized it was empty. After listening to it sputter for a few seconds, I gave up and tossed the cup in the garbage.

Lenny was waiting in his car outside the building. I tied my coat, opened the door, and leaned into the wind.

"I was just texting you. Where are your fuzzy mittens?" asked Lenny.

"I didn't think I'd need them. I thought I'd be halfway around the world by now," I said. In the winter, I didn't travel anywhere without earmuffs and mittens. I'd heard on the news once that frostbite could occur within five minutes in extreme wind chills.

I buckled my seatbelt, pulled down the visor, and flipped open the mirror. The wind had instantly volumized my hair, making it appear as if it had grown five inches—straight out. "This is exactly why I don't wear it down," I mumbled, smoothing it.

"Prather, are you worried about your hair?" asked Lenny.

"No, I just want to look… professional."

"Ah. *Professional.* I've seen that look on you… once, before your review," he chided. "I think it's charming that you think a ponytail can make or break you."

"If you were a woman, you'd understand. You wouldn't believe how often we're judged on our appearances. If that FBI agent is there, I want to be ready. I got the feeling he suspects me of something. Besides, I need coffee. The carafe in the lobby was empty. Can we stop?"

Lenny calmly pulled into traffic. "I think you're nervous. I think you want to make a good impression on Mr. FBI."

I glared at him. "Can we get coffee or not?"

He laughed. "All right. And don't worry. You look great. I love it when you wear your hair down."

"Really?" I asked.

He looked over at me. "Really."

After securing two large cups of coffee through the Dunn Brothers drive-thru, we headed toward the police station. While driving, we talked about last night's dinner and whether or not Jean Erickson had anything to do with Molly's murder. Lenny doubted that she had gotten close enough to Molly to contaminate her, and I argued that she had. Furthermore, she had confused Molly and me because of our curly hair and had been looking for Molly when we boarded the plane. She could have contaminated her before we were seated.

"I don't know, Em. You said nobody knew she had an allergy until the snacks were passed out," said Lenny.

"Yes, well, she might have googled it before the flight."

Lenny raised one eyebrow, a skill I often tried to imitate. "Could she really google Molly's allergies?"

"My students google everything. Besides, maybe Skylar told his mom about Molly's allergy," I said, making a mental note to ask Amanda if Molly had mentioned her allergy in class.

"Maybe," he said, looking skeptical. "But what about André?

Did you see how red-faced he got over his brothers? He's just crazy enough to go off. And I'm not the only one who thinks so."

I took a long drink of my coffee. "He's not crazy; he's passionate. But you're right. The land seems to have quite a bit to do with the grapes. Still, André had a lot riding on this trip. If he wanted to kill her, I can't imagine why he wouldn't have done it months ago. Why wait until now?"

He laughed. "So you don't doubt that he's capable of killing. You doubt the timing? That's so like you."

"Well, I'm just saying that the timing is highly unlikely."

Lenny parked in front of the police station. "I hope we're not here all day. Believe it or not, I had plans for my spring break, none that included spending time at a cop shop."

"Don't worry. We'll be in and out. We leave at eleven o'clock for Copper Bluff, and that's one meeting I'm not going to miss. André confirmed with the bus company this morning."

I opened the car door slowly so that it wouldn't be taken by the wind. Then I jumped out and gave it a slam. Lenny was already holding open the door to the police station.

Inside, people packed the lobby. Young, middle-aged, old—the assemblage was loud and diverse. If we looked out of place, there was no indication. Nobody bothered to glance at us when we walked in, and I felt confident as I walked up to the window, no longer new to the inside of a police station.

"Good morning," I said. "I am here to see Ernest Jones."

"Do you have an appointment?" the young officer asked.

"Kind of," I said. "My name is Emmeline Prather. I texted him last night."

The front-desk officer pushed a few numbers on his phone, then said, "Emmeline Prather is here to see you. She said you're expecting her. Okay." He hung up the phone. "He'll be right out."

A moment later, Ernest came through the double doors, looking harried. "It's a Monday, isn't it?" He held open one of the doors, tucking in his shirt. "I've had three calls already. Haven't even had breakfast."

"Or finished dressing," Lenny added.

We walked through the metal detectors to the same interrogation room from Sunday. This time, it was dark; Jack Wood and the FBI agent were nowhere in sight.

Ernest flipped on the light. "We'll have a little more privacy in here. My desk is no place to have a conversation right now." He pulled a Snickers candy bar out of his front shirt pocket and began opening the wrapper. Motioning for Lenny and me to sit across from him, he said, "So you said in your text you had some news about Jean Erickson." He took a big bite of his candy bar.

I nodded and proceeded to tell him about Amanda and Olivia's conversation at dinner. "When I realized Skylar's last name was the same as the red-haired woman's, I googled the student. He was her son."

Ernest leaned across the table. His round shoulders curled into an upside-down U. "So you're saying Jean Erickson might have killed Molly Jaspers to avenge her son's suicide?"

Our curly heads met in the middle of the table. "That's exactly what I'm saying."

"I like that theory. I like it a lot." After a long moment, he leaned back in his chair. "The only trouble is, her story checks out. She does have a sister who lives outside of Paris, and she was meeting her for a little R&R time. She disclosed her son's suicide to us upfront; she said it had been a hard time for her and her husband and that she needed to get away. They're considering a divorce."

Although a surprise, the news didn't completely dissuade me. "But don't you think it's quite a coincidence that she was on the exact same plane as we were *and* asked about Molly Jaspers?"

He nodded. "It's more than coincidental. It's suspicious."

Lenny let out a breath. "It sounds like the woman's been through enough. Maybe you guys should hold off on charging her until you rule out other possibilities."

"Oh I don't have enough evidence to charge her—or anyone else for that matter." He tossed his candy wrapper in the garbage. "The truth is I have a little evidence on a lot of people who could be responsible for Mrs. Jaspers' death. Honestly, the entire world of academia is a little baffling to me. Assistant… associate… emeritus? What do all those titles mean?"

"That's why you need me," I said. "I know the ins and outs of university life. I could be your eyes and ears when I get back to campus."

Lenny shook his head, but I persisted.

"Besides, academic research is just another form of investigation. You and I are really not that different. We both read between the lines to get to the truth."

He nodded. "Believe me, Ms. Prather, anything you could do to help our case load would be appreciated. My partner's wife is about to leave him over all the hours we've been putting in. And I'm afraid his schedule's not going to get lighter any time soon. Especially with the FBI involved, we have to stay on our toes. Keep me informed, will you, if you hear anything else?"

"I will." I was glad Ernest considered me an ally. "We're returning to Copper Bluff at eleven o'clock. Did André tell you?"

Ernest patted his pockets for his cellphone. "He probably did, or maybe he told Jack. My morning has been one crisis after another."

"Don't worry. It doesn't show," Lenny said, smirking.

I pointed to my lip. "You have a little chocolate right there, Ernest." He grabbed a tissue and wiped it off.

We stood up and shook hands with Ernest. I told him I would be in touch if I found out any new information and asked him to do the same. He assured me he would. Just as I had promised Lenny, we were in and out of the police station with time to spare.

Chapter Seventeen

As Lenny drove back to the hotel, the sky turned metallic and it began to snow. The flakes were large and white and hit the windshield with wet splats. It was the kind of snow that made terrific snowballs and snowmen, that piled up heavily and quickly, that could delay airplanes and buses. It was different than the snowflakes that fell in December, which were tiny and fluffy and magical. This snow held a different kind of power, the kind that changed plans.

Lenny and I exchanged a look.

“Don’t even say it, Lenny. I am not staying in Minneapolis one more night. It’s only a little after ten now. If we leave right away, we’ll be fine.”

“If you get out ahead of it, you’ll make it,” he said.

I was grateful for his assurance, however halfhearted. He was a pretty good judge of most situations, even the weather.

We drove for a few minutes in silence, listening to the sound of the windshield wipers moving rhythmically back and forth. “What are your plans for the rest of the week?” I asked.

“I gotta see my parents. My mom will probably drag me up to the synagogue before I leave. I have a couple friends in St. Paul

I'm meeting up with." He shrugged his shoulders. "Nothing's going to be as exciting as your murder mystery, Prather. I'm going to miss you."

I glanced at him to see if he was serious; I couldn't tell. "If you really feel that way, I'm sure we could stow you away on our school bus. Tons of room in there."

Now he quirked an eyebrow. "Even your charms have their limits."

I gave him a little shove. We were in front of the hotel, and I gathered my purse and unbuckled my seatbelt. "I will see you when you get back, then."

He nodded. "Be careful, Em. These people have been cooped up for a couple days; there's no telling what they'll do when they get on that bus in the middle of a snowstorm."

"It's not a storm. It's a few flakes." But as the wind took the car door, my voice lost all conviction. "I'll be careful. Call me when you get back."

I dashed into the hotel, glancing at the parking lot. No yellow bus yet.

André was in the lobby, talking to the front-desk person and presumably paying the bill.

"André," I called out, "everything on schedule?"

"Em, you're back. Good. Yes, everything is on time." He looked at my hair as if counting the snowflakes. "We are going to drive out of this. I checked the weather app on my phone."

I nodded and kept walking toward the elevator, but in my mind, I was recalling our bad luck so far. It had started with the number thirteen and had ended with the number twelve. If snow had to fall, it was going to be on us.

I swiped the room key. Amanda's suitcase was already sitting by the door, but Kat was still shoving clothes into her luggage on the bed.

"Is it time?" asked Kat. Frantic, she pulled on the zipper, which promptly stuck.

"Don't worry. The bus isn't here yet," I said, giving Kat a

hand. I gently pushed down on her luggage, overstuffed with records and clothes, as she zipped it shut. Amanda, who had been flat-ironing her hair, stuck her iron in the front pocket of her luggage. I gathered my books and magazines and placed them in my tote bag. All my other belongings were packed.

Amanda walked to the window. "What about the weather?"

I rolled my suitcase to the door.

"We're going to get ahead of it," said Kat, pulling her hoodie over her head. Even the students knew how to talk weather.

I nearly bumped into Arnold and Aaron as I opened our door.

"Finally," Arnold said. "I can't wait to get out of here."

"No kidding," said Aaron.

In the lobby, everyone was assembled a full thirty minutes ahead of schedule. No one wanted to miss the departure, especially with the snow, which was certain to worsen as the day progressed. André, talking to the bus driver outside, motioned to us with a frenzied gesture of his hand. It was as if he was worried our transportation might disappear in a piling mound of snow before we reached it. Just that quickly, we were on the interstate back to Copper Bluff, wondering if the last two days had been a bad dream.

For the first hour, the bus chugged along heavily and without incident. Despite a stop at a fast-food joint, we were making good time. We ate our food quietly as if doing so would prevent any delays in our progress. Our heads bobbed along with the ruts in the road. Then we began to converse in louder tones, maybe because of the road noise, or the speed of the bus, or because with some distance behind us and Minneapolis, we actually believed we were going home. I was sitting next to Arnold Frasier. In fact, everyone had taken their original seats, except for Nick and Bennett. Since Molly was no longer with us, they sat together. Only André sat alone. I stood up and excused myself as I made my way up to his seat.

He was surprised when I sat down beside him.

"Em!"

"You looked as if you were in another world just now," I said.

"I would give anything if I could redo this trip." He glanced around at the faces on the bus. "Had I been more vigilant about Molly's allergy, maybe her death could have been prevented. I could have reminded the airline. I could have—"

"Bennett contacted the airlines. It was their mistake. You did nothing wrong," I assured him. "You were the person who spearheaded this trip to Paris. And despite the tragedy, you've kept everyone together and the mood positive. No one could have handled it better. I mean that."

He shook his head. "I don't think Dean Richardson will see it that way. He talked to officer Jack Wood, who blames me because of the fight I had with Molly." He leaned in so close that I could smell his expensive cologne. "I think they suspect me of poisoning Molly."

He said it so quietly I barely heard him, yet I looked behind us to make sure no one was listening. "I got that feeling, too," I whispered. He started to respond, but in a louder tone, and I shushed him with my hands. "Of course I don't believe them, but until we find out what really happened, I would stay as mum as possible on the topic. You know me, André. I won't be satisfied until I discover the truth. I know you didn't commit a crime, and I'm not going to let you take the blame for anything that happened on this trip."

His bushy brows came to a perfect point. "And the dean?"

"I'd be happy to talk to him on your behalf." We both knew my efforts might come to naught, but it was worth trying anyway. I had been at the university almost two years and was four years away from tenure—or exerting any influence.

"Thanks, Em. It is very kind of you to offer," he said.

He returned to the window, where the flakes outside were falling less and less. Watching him gaze though the glass, I knew he was not responsible for Molly's death. André wore his emotions on his sleeve, and he was devastated by the situation.

He had put up a strong front in Minneapolis, but now that the trip was almost over, his sadness was evident. He'd admitted he felt responsible because he had set up the travel arrangements. Although I didn't have proof, I knew he had done nothing to prevent Molly from speaking at the Sorbonne, family winery or not. When I got back to Copper Bluff, I would work doubly hard finding out what really happened aboard that airplane.

I was about to return to my seat when I heard a bit of conversation behind me. Nick and Bennett had been revering Molly and her work since I'd sat down. I had caught several snippets of their discussion as André and I talked, but now their voices grew hushed, and I strained to listen. It wasn't easy with the windshield wipers slapping back and forth on the front window of the bus, but from what I could hear, Nick was telling Bennett that Molly would have wanted something. It had to do with money. I listened as closely I could, hoping to learn more.

"What do you know?" Bennett said. "You're just a kid. Did you live with Molly? Did you support Molly? Did you *love* Molly?"

I wanted to know the answer to his last question, too, for I had wondered it many times myself.

But Nick's answer was noncommittal. "Of course I loved Molly. Everyone did."

"Oh, I know about you, Dramsdor. I know about your little infatuation with Molly. So did she. She found it amusing. She had a lot of hangers-on. Did you think you were the only one?"

Nick didn't speak for a long moment, and I felt embarrassed for his sake. I hated the way Bennett spoke down to Nick. Just because Bennett was a few years older and few dollars richer didn't give him the right to humiliate.

"I was not infatuated with Molly," Nick said finally.

Bennett snorted. "That's not what she said. She said you followed her around like a lost puppy on your trip to New Mexico."

"She knew very well I was involved with…" he stopped. "Ask anybody who was there. Ask Amanda Walters. She'll tell you. I didn't have a crush on Molly."

"It doesn't really matter now, does it?" said Bennett. All feeling had left his voice.

"I suppose not," Nick said.

A conversation I thought would end in blows was over just that quietly. I looked over at André. If he had overheard the testier parts, he didn't let on. I knew Amanda had been on expeditions with Molly and Nick, so Molly might have known about Amanda and Nick's relationship. That was probably what Nick meant when he told Bennett to ask Amanda. Still, I was surprised that Molly had told her husband that Nick was infatuated with her. Maybe she truly did find it amusing. Or maybe she was jealous of Nick and Amanda's tender relationship and wanted to thwart it by flaunting Nick's high regard for her.

I stood to return to my seat. Only then did André glance over.

"I'm sorry I have not been better company," he said.

"Not at all," I said. "I have to get back to my seat. I can't have Arnold thinking I'm avoiding him."

He nodded, and I walked down the rubber-lined floor of the aisle, still pondering Nick and Bennett's conversation.

Chapter Eighteen

IF SPRING BREAK came in like a lion, it went out like a lamb. Before the week was over, I'd finished my grading, updated my students' scores online, and even washed my hardwood floors. It was good to be home and busy. When I had something on my mind, it was easy to immerse myself in the daily tasks I usually avoided. Now I welcomed the prospect of dusting the bookshelves and shaking out the rugs. It gave me time to think about Molly Jaspers.

I had heard nothing from Ernest Jones or Jack Wood, and if not for the evidence of my unstamped passport, I could have believed the entire trip was a bad dream. But it wasn't a dream. Not even close. A person had died, and even though I didn't know Molly well, I was sure her absence would be felt all over the state. The Great Plains had lost a fierce champion and Copper Bluff a spirited professor.

Despite the loss, life marched on to its steady drumbeat. Classes resumed Monday morning and so did my schedule. But before meeting with my first class, I met Jim Giles, our department chair, who'd appeared with a sober face at our office doors. He was concerned for my wellbeing and the students' and asked if I was okay. I said I was, and he gestured toward his office so we could continue our talk in private.

Giles's office was right next to mine, and Lenny often teased me that my room was actually Giles's storage closet. Our spaces were connected by an interior door that we rarely used, but our proximity had made us good friends. Although he never said it, I had a feeling he liked my impetuousness, or at least was entertained by it. A quiet thinker, he did not act rashly.

"I heard the news about Molly from Dean Richardson. You were there. Tell me what happened. I want to hear it firsthand," he said, unlocking his door. I noticed how much lighter his office was than mine. It had two windows, and his bookshelves were bright white. They were also meticulously organized.

He sat in his desk chair, and I took the folding chair next to his desk.

"It was the oddest thing," I began. "One moment we were on the flight to Paris, the next, Molly's husband was jabbing an EpiPen into her leg. She died right there on the plane."

"I heard she had a peanut allergy," Giles said, crossing his legs. "Didn't she have another… what… EpiPen?"

I shook my head. "Obviously not. With the prescription prices of those things going through the roof, nobody can afford more than one."

"How did she get ahold of a peanut anyway? You would think she'd have taken extra precautions." He began tying his worn leather shoe.

"She did. Bennett informed the airlines of her allergy months ago and threw a hissy fit when the stewardess passed them out. But the police confirmed she died of anaphylactic shock."

"Well, I suppose she did, if she was allergic."

I leaned in closer. Giles didn't seem to understand what I was telling him. "The police don't know how she came into contact with the peanuts. When they figure it out, someone will be charged. The FBI is involved."

Giles finished with his shoe and leaned back in his chair. "The FBI? Whatever for?"

"When a crime is committed in the sky, it falls under the FBI's jurisdiction."

"I don't even want to know how you know that, Emmeline. What I do want to know is how André took it. I can't imagine he'll ever receive a grant again after this fiasco. And the students? How are they faring? Student Counseling just made an announcement."

I nodded. "The students are doing well, considering, but André is devastated. What's more, he feels responsible for the whole mess. He had a fight with Molly at the airport, and now everybody's pointing invisible fingers at him."

Giles was about to retie his other shoe but stopped.

"What is it?" I asked.

"Nothing. It's nothing." He pulled his foot to his leg. "It's just something Richardson said."

"What'd he say?"

"He implied André might be in some sort of trouble."

I clapped my hands. "I knew it!"

Giles's foot fell to the floor. "Emmeline, leave this to the police. A jail cell is no place for an English professor."

"Or French," I added.

"I'm serious. You have your whole life and career ahead of you." The deep grooves in his forehead relaxed, and he looked more like a father than a colleague. Conversations such as this one reminded me that a twenty-eight-year-old was a youngster in his eyes.

"That's what people keep telling me."

"Because it's true," he said. "You don't want to get snookered into this. People will start to think you have a strange affinity for crime. And lord knows we have enough strange affinities around here."

I couldn't help but laugh.

"Anyway, Dean Richardson also told me that Molly's

visitation is tonight at Sanderson's Funeral Home at six o'clock. I didn't know if you had heard."

"It's been *nine* days since she died," I said.

"I know. I guess Bennett had a heck of a time getting her remains transported from Minneapolis."

"Poor Bennett," I said. "I bet he'll be glad when tonight is behind him. This ordeal has gone on longer than it needed to."

"So I will see you tonight," said Giles, "without a spyglass?"

"I will be there, but I can't promise I won't be wearing a trench coat." I stood up.

He looked doubtful.

"It's cold outside."

He smiled. "Do you have creative writing this morning?"

I nodded.

"I've heard good things about that class. Good things. You know, Emmeline, I think you might have a bit of a knack for storytelling."

I started for the door. "Story listening, perhaps. These students come up with the most fascinating plots. A few weeks ago, a boy wrote a story about a bathtub swallowing him whole. And it was from the bathtub's point of view."

"Fascinating, indeed," muttered Giles as I left his office and unlocked my own.

The air was stale; I hadn't been here since before spring break. I switched on the light and opened the window to catch the fresh spring breeze. The sights and smells of new life were everywhere. The sun was warmer, the sky was bluer, the days were longer. In the fields surrounding Copper Bluff, farmers were beginning to plan and dig and till. Nowhere was it more evident that the seasons had changed.

It was lucky that Minneapolis's snowstorm had skipped Copper Bluff, I thought as I turned on my computer. According to Lenny, it had snowed eight inches, and he'd been trapped inside for a full day with his nieces and their Easy-Bake Oven. I wished I could have been there.

I waited patiently for my computer to boot up. It was a relic that I planned to replace with the money I didn't spend in Paris. I sighed. Despite the sensible investment a laptop would make, I would have preferred to fritter away my money in French cafés, perfumeries, and museums.

My creative writing students submitted their work to an online drop box where the class could read and comment on the stories before class. Although students were supposed to drop in their work at least one full day before we met to give others time to read, they didn't always meet the deadline. Today, I had a late submission from Kat, and I wondered why. After all, her spring break plans, like mine, had been drastically cut short. She could have had her story in well ahead of deadline.

I began scanning it and felt my lips curl into a smile. Here was the reason. Often, writers wrote exaggerated versions of their own lives. If we had a thunderstorm on Saturday, a monsoon would appear Monday in their poems or short stories. If we had a snowstorm, a blizzard. It came as no surprise, then, that Kat had written a mystery-most-noir.

By the time I reached the end, I was thoroughly intrigued, not only as a professor but as a reader. Growing up as an only child, I read a lot of books. They were my companions. Within them were so many more chances for happiness and adventure and love than on my street. In my circle, a dream meant a nine-to-five job and a weekly paycheck. It had little to do with passion or talent or interest. But in books, the most extraordinary things could happen to the most ordinary people. Even me.

I packed my folders and grade book into my satchel and logged off my computer. My class was in Winsor, which had been a women's dormitory in the late 1800s. Composed of purple-red bricks and a three-story turret, the building was connected to my building, Harriman Hall, by a rickety passageway. The passageway was known to those of us who taught in the buildings but very few others—thankfully. I was certain that if it saw any more foot traffic, it would surely crumble.

My classroom was on the first floor, so after crossing the passageway, I descended one flight of stairs and walked into the far room at the bottom of the turret. The windows were bowed in a half-circle shape, and the students' seats were raised, theater-style. I had twenty-three sophomores in the introductory class. Since it was a few minutes to the hour, most of them were present and ready to begin.

"Good morning," I said as I shoved my satchel under the desk facing the students. I sat there instead of standing at a podium because creative writing courses worked like discussions rather than lectures. "First of all, I hope all of you had an enjoyable spring break and have refueled your tanks of creative inspiration." This garnered a small laugh. "Second of all, if you haven't checked your emails since returning, you might want to do so after class. The Student Counseling Center sent out a message about the death of Professor Jaspers. They are extending their hours today."

As I waited for questions, I downloaded the first short story from the drop box, which also happened to be the last one submitted, and brought it up on the overhead screen. This method saved students the hassle of printing out the stories themselves. It also meant they didn't need their laptops, which always proved to be distractions.

I scanned the room. "If there are no questions, we have four stories to discuss this morning, so let's get started. Kat, your story is up."

A few murmurs passed through the room, and I inquired about the problem. Claire Holt said, "Some of us didn't read this. It must have been submitted late."

"It was," I said. "But that's okay, given the circumstances of spring break. We'll let Kat summarize it for us, though we don't usually have the writer talk about the story first. This will help those of you who didn't get a chance to read it."

Against her jade-color sweater, Kat's hazel eyes appeared green; the gray in them was all but gone. I could tell she was excited and ready to talk. "Okay. So, it's a story about a group that takes a trip overseas. They're *going* to take a trip, I should say, but then someone is murdered, and they can't go. So now they have to figure out who the murderer is. That's all I got so far."

"Didn't you go to France?" asked Jason, a boy who sat next to her.

She looked at me. "I was supposed to go but didn't."

"Was Professor Jaspers on that trip?" asked Sabrina, the girl two seats away from her.

I answered for Kat. "Yes, we were all going to France on a university-sponsored trip, but when Professor Jaspers died unexpectedly, the trip was canceled."

I cleared my throat. "So let's continue with the story. This is what's called a 'whodunit' mystery. The writer should know who did the murder. Do you know, Kat?"

She bit her lip. "No, I don't."

I said, "That's an important part of the plot."

"But how do I decide who did it?" Kat asked. "It could have been any number of people."

Sabrina said, "They couldn't have *all* wanted her dead."

Kat braided a piece of hair that had come loose from her sloppy bun. "They kind of could have. Like in *Murder on the Orient Express* by Agatha Christie."

The room was silent. I had the feeling nobody read Agatha Christie.

"I got it," said Jason, slapping his hand on her desk. "The murderer kills somebody else."

I became enthusiastic. "You're right, Jason. Good idea. In some mystery novels, the murderer miscalculates. He makes mistakes. He goes back to the scene of the crime, he retrieves a piece of evidence, and he may even kill again."

Kat wrote something in her notebook. "Yeah! That's a good idea."

A few other students chimed in with suggestions that sounded like they came from the latest season of CSI. The story was going from mystery to thriller, and the room was buzzing with all kinds of possibilities.

"Even so," said Claire, "what's the purpose? Where's the moral?"

Jason and Kat exchanged glances. So did a few of the other students. Then they looked to me.

I smiled. "The purpose is to find the truth, catch the killer, and ensure that justice is served. What else?"

After class, Kat stopped by the computer, where I was shutting down the overhead equipment.

"Professor Prather? Can I submit another draft to the drop box on Wednesday even if I'm not scheduled? I got some really good ideas today."

"Definitely," I said, logging off my account. "We'll try to squeeze it in at the end of class." Now I gave her my full attention. "How was the rest of your spring break?"

"After what happened, there was no place for it go but up, right?"

I nodded.

"Amanda and I hung out. We finished our presentations for Student Fest." Student Fest was a conference that gave students in various fields the opportunity to present papers on topics of interest. It would start in a couple of days.

"How is Amanda doing?" I asked. "She was pretty upset by everything."

Kat nodded. "She was close to Professor Jaspers."

"What about Nick Dramsdor? They seem pretty close, too."

She shifted her weight from one Vans shoe to the other. She didn't know how to answer.

"Kat?"

She was deciding whether to confide in me, her hazel eyes growing wide and intense, and I knew it must have been serious for her to hold back. She and I had become close friends the last several weeks of class, and this ordeal had brought us a bit closer.

"I'm worried about Amanda. She was so disappointed by the trip. She's not acting like herself."

I leaned against the podium. "What do you mean 'not acting like herself'? Are you worried she will harm herself?" If that were the case, I had a duty to report it to Student Counseling and notify the university.

"No," she said quickly. "Not that. I mean she's acting kind of weird. Kind of crazy."

"Do you think her behavior has to do with Molly Jaspers' death? Or does it have to do with her relationship with Nick?"

Her eyebrows rose in surprise.

"I know they were seeing each other in some capacity, Kat. Since he wasn't her professor, I'm not concerned about the indiscretion. I *am* concerned, though, about her."

She looked relieved that someone else knew the secret. She let out a long breath. "Me too. That's the only reason I'm telling you this. See, she had the impression that Nick might propose to her in Paris."

"Propose?" I said, trying not to show how stunned I was. "Were they *that* close?"

"I think so. They are both kind of idealistic that way. Amanda said he had hinted at proposing before the trip."

I wondered if the myth of Paris didn't have more to do with the idea than Nick himself. It was, after all, the city of light—and love. I said as much to Kat.

"Maybe," she said, "but Amanda's normally pretty level-headed. She's been on lots of trips—even with him. Whatever he said, it must have been convincing for Amanda to believe it. She's not what I would call gullible."

I agreed. From what I knew of Amanda, she was serious to

a fault. Had it been Kat, the notion of being head over heels in love might have been more believable.

A few students began to trickle in for the next class, and I gathered my satchel. "Don't worry, Kat. I will keep an eye on Amanda, and if anything else comes up, be sure to let me know. You have my cellphone number."

"Thanks, Professor Prather. I will. I promise. See you Wednesday."

I finished straightening up the podium and walked out the door, my mind still on my conversation with Kat. Something bothered me about Nick and Amanda's relationship, and I decided it was their equal fondness for Molly Jaspers. Bennett even suggested Nick's admiration went as far as being a crush. Perhaps Bennett was jealous and overreacting, but from what I had seen on the trip, I would also call it a crush. Academic or otherwise, Nick's interest in Molly may have complicated his relationship with Amanda—and prevented him from proposing. But was the complication reason enough to do away with Molly? This was what I needed to find out.

Chapter Nineteen

Although Lenny didn't like being on campus Mondays, he couldn't avoid it this semester, for he had a Monday, Wednesday, Friday class schedule just as I did. As I walked back to the English Department, I thought I would stop by his office to see if he had returned from class yet. I hadn't seen him since Minneapolis, but we had caught up on the phone. I found myself wondering about his sister and nieces, and well, Lenny himself. I had learned a lot about him in Minneapolis, about his music and his family. Even his real name: Leonard! Somehow it suited him. Underneath his carefree demeanor was a serious side that he hid very well, a little like his name.

I knew right away that Lenny was in his office because I could hear the Beatles' "Lovely Rita" playing as I walked down the hall. Before I could enter, Barb, the English secretary whose office was across from Lenny's, stopped me. She was a large, nondescript woman with a face that looked good devoid of makeup. It was plain and remarkably unwrinkled, even though she was in her late fifties. Perhaps because she spent so much time indoors, her face was as pale as the moon.

"There you are, Emmeline," she said.

"Yes?" I said.

"I have something for you."

I followed her into her office. If my office was unorganized, hers was atomic. Although her desk looked relatively neat, cardboard boxes were stacked haphazardly in every corner of the room. Some were open and had university forms and letterhead paper in them. Others were closed and probably filled with copy paper. Copy paper was one item she parceled out like military rations; another was Dixie cups for the water cooler.

She pulled out a large Get-n-Go travel mug from her desk drawer.

"I've been looking for that everywhere!" I exclaimed. "Where did you find it?"

"In the break room. On the bookshelf," she said.

The English Department had a double bookshelf with glass lift-up doors in the break room. It held some lovely old books. I liked looking at them while I waited for the coffee to brew.

I went to take the cup from her. "Thank you, Barb."

She turned the to-go mug over in her hands as if she were looking for the fluid ounces it held. "This has got to hold a half a pot of coffee."

"Oh, I don't think so."

"Nevertheless, I don't think donating two quarters to the coffee fund would be out of line when you use this mug. Wouldn't you agree?"

Since the university didn't find it economically feasible to provide employees with free coffee, the coffee fund was one of Barb's pet projects. She made sure that faculty members donated a quarter whenever they indulged in a cup. The coffee was purchased out of the English slush fund, but one would think the money came from her own pocket the way she monitored our intake.

"Completely. I agree completely."

She smiled, returning the mug.

As I turned to leave, I said, "I still haven't received my student evaluations from fall semester. Do you know when I will have them?"

She folded her hands. "Soon. They haven't come down yet from the dean's office."

I nodded but was unconvinced. Had I asked Giles, Barb's favorite teacher and boss, about his class evals, I knew he would have students' comments typed, the scores stapled, and the results sealed in his desk drawer. The rest of us would have to rely on Barb's goodwill.

Lenny was laughing as I entered his office. "How did the inquest go?"

I plopped down in the chair across from him, dropping my satchel on the floor. "Did you tell her that was my mug?"

He raised one eyebrow. "I might have suggested you were the only one in the department who could drink that much coffee in one sitting."

I crossed my arms. "Thanks."

"Come on, Prather. You couldn't expect me to take the fall for you; she knows you and I are the only coffee addicts on this floor."

"Did you get your evals?"

He opened his top desk drawer, rummaged through some papers, and took out an unopened envelope. Examining it, he said, "Nah. This is from last spring."

I was astonished. I opened my evaluations the second I received them. "Haven't you opened it?"

He shrugged his shoulders. "It was a crappy class. I don't need these to tell me that."

I smiled. I wished I had some of his carefree attitude. It would have done me a world of good in so many areas of my life.

"So how was the bus ride home? Did everyone arrive alive?" he asked.

I nodded. "There *was* a tense moment between Nick and

Bennett, and Kat just told me that Amanda thought Nick was going to propose to her in Paris."

"Marriage?"

"Yes, marriage. What else?"

He tapped his pencil. "I can't see any professor asking a student to marry them, even from a different campus. And Nick.... He was pretty hip on Molly Jaspers as far as I could see."

"That's what makes it so odd. They both adored Molly. I bet they will be at the visitation tonight. Are you going?"

"Do you want me to go?"

"Yes, of course," I answered. "I mean, if you want to. I could pick you up."

He laced his fingers behind his head. "You know, Em, this sounds like you're asking me out on a date. On a date to a funeral home. You know how weird this would come off to any other guy? No wonder you got no game."

I could feel my cheeks grow warm. Despite several attempts, most of my dates in Copper Bluff had ended in dismal failure. Some men didn't like my cat, some didn't like my aversion to their cellphone use during dinner, and some were just plain rude. But if my track record was sketchy, Lenny's was scribbles. He had more flavors of the month than a Baskin Robbins.

"Oh, I have game," I said. "I have a big game going on right now with lots of players on the bench just waiting for me to give them a call. Any one of them would die for a chance to take me to the funeral home."

Lenny raised an eyebrow.

"No pun intended," I added.

His hearty laugh filled the room. "I bet. If they were smart, they would be. But if you will allow me the honor, I would love to escort you to the funeral parlor tonight. What time will you pick me up?"

I stood up. "It starts at six and goes until eight."

"I will see you at six, then."

I tossed him a smile over my shoulder and walked out the door.

AFTER TEACHING MY afternoon class, I returned home. The spring air had turned colder as the afternoon wore on. The campus was quiet, and I had a feeling that many students had extended their spring break. It was the time of the year when people had a hard time returning to classes, finishing papers, taking tests. On the trees, leaves were beginning to bud, and after a long winter, any sign of life made one's own seem that much more precious, too precious to spend in a hundred-year-old classroom. I couldn't say that I wasn't affected. With the warm weather so near, I found myself in the seed aisle of the local hardware store a good deal now. In fact, I had purchased five packets of wildflowers to date. I was no gardener but thought there couldn't be much to growing wildflowers. They were, after all, wild.

My cat, Dickinson, greeted me with a swerve when I entered the house, and I knew she had been waiting for her canned cat food. I tossed my satchel on the couch on the way to the kitchen.

"Yes, yes, I see you, Dickinson. Just a minute," I said aloud as I found her cat food under the sink. After feeding her and giving her several scratches behind the ears, I walked into my office, determined to work on my research.

Although I had published a few essays, mainly taken from my dissertation, my book-length project was ongoing. The subject was early creative outlets for women. And now, when I did have a few hours to spare, I found myself wondering about the wall color and if that new paint at the hardware store really did cover in one coat. This, too, was a danger of spring. It conjured up ideas of *house projects.*

I turned on my desk light and pulled a large book on the twelfth century from the top of the stack. Without any new research from the canceled trip, it was back to the books for me.

I had clipped the first three chapters for reading. Three chapters could easily be accomplished before I picked up Lenny. But as I began to scan the pages, my mind wandered to the death of Molly Jaspers. Dean Richardson had said something to Giles about André. Were the police closer to charging someone than I realized? It was possible. It had been a week since our stay in Minneapolis. Maybe they had found more evidence linking André to Molly.

I put down my book and picked up my phone. An Internet search yielded nothing for *Trois Frères*, not even on Amazon.fr. I tried again, in English, but still no results. The winery must have been as traditional as André professed, not to have a webpage.

Finished with her dinner, Dickinson jumped on the chair and began licking her paws. My lap made a good bathing area, it seemed, and I continued to pet her long after she finished. Laying aside my phone, I tried to resume reading but couldn't. If I didn't help André, who would? He had no family in the United States, and despite his popularity with females, he had no serious relationship with one. His only hope was for me to find out who murdered Molly and why. Unfortunately, I was no closer to finding that someone than finishing my book.

A couple of hours later, I had made a start at the unread pages. However, it was time to dress for the visitation. I pushed in my desk chair, shut off the lamp, and walked to my bedroom, happy to call it a day. This being an old house, the bedroom closet was miniature. I always kept its size in mind when I went to the mall. Although I didn't shop often—department stores were an hour away—when I did, I tended to buy clothes that were colorful, bold even. But I did have a black dress suit tucked away in the back of the closet for occasions that required it. I laid it across my bed, examining it for wear. After finding no problems, I dressed quickly. My black kitten heels gave me just enough height and a spray of light perfume gave me just enough scent for the informal service for Molly Jaspers. I'd had enough of Lenny's teasing for one day, and I didn't want him to accuse me of turning this outing into a date.

I tied the belt around my short trench coat and walked out to the garage in the alley, where my '69 red Mustang awaited. My uncle in Detroit had sold me the car at a bargain price. Although it wasn't refurbished, the vehicle was my pride and joy. I loved hearing it rumble to a start, and I supposed my admiration had something to do with growing up in Motor City. There, a car meant something; it was part of your American heritage. It was the lifeblood of the city, and whether you considered yourself an enthusiast or not, you cared deeply about the future of the industry. In my neighborhood, to drive a foreign car was almost sacrilege. You would certainly never admit to buying one on a lease deal.

Lenny didn't live far from me. Maybe ten blocks. But in those ten blocks, the houses changed drastically. I lived in a 1917 bungalow; he lived in a 1970s ranch. Every house on my street was different; every house on his street was similar. But despite the difference, I liked his lane a lot. The residents took good care of their homes, and the road always looked neat and tidy. My street was more haphazard and was inhabited by an eclectic mix of students, professors, and widows. There was no telling what they would do to their houses or at what hours.

I pulled up to Lenny's olive-green house and honked my horn. Lenny appeared a moment later, dressed in slacks and a wool toggle-button coat. With his broad shoulders and square jaw, he could have passed for a seafaring captain. It was a bad habit of mine—imagining entirely different lives for people, even me. Sometimes it was hard to shut off the ongoing storyline in my head.

"Hey," he said as he buckled his seatbelt. Then he gave me a glance. "You look nice. And smell even better."

"Thanks," I said as I backed out of his driveway. "I love that coat."

"Where is this place anyway?"

"Sanderson's Funeral Home. It's on Main Street, before downtown." Sanderson's was a square mansion, white with navy trim, that took up half the city block. It was integrated into the residential section, so we would have to park on one of the side streets. A couple roads were already dotted with cars. I found a spot a block away and swiftly parallel parked, a skill I was proud to exhibit with Lenny in the passenger seat.

"Show-off," he said as he opened the car door.

The house had two entrances, one that looked like a front door and one off center that was marked "visitors." But since some people were entering through the front door, we followed them in. The entry was massive, the size of my living room, and an L-shaped staircase led to unseen rooms upstairs. To the right was an old-fashioned parlor with heavy brocade drapes and wingback chairs. Each of the tables held a vase of flowers from well-wishers. A coat rack stood near the entrance. I untied my coat and hung it up, and Lenny did the same. To the left was a basket for sympathy cards. There was also a guest book, which I signed before placing my card in the basket.

"Did you put my name on that?" Lenny whispered as he signed his name in the book.

"You didn't ask me to."

"A fine date you are," he said.

The large room had pews for sitting, but the program I picked up at the guestbook table said there would be no formal service. Around the perimeter of the room were poster boards of Molly as well as her awards and some of her published works. In the front were several arrangements of flowers, a large photograph of Molly, and an urn with her cremated remains. I didn't see Bennett, so we started in the far corner, making our way around the room, looking at the displays as we went.

On the poster boards, Molly's world came to life. She appeared as a young girl and then woman in the pictures with her family. She had a younger sister and an older brother, and with a glance around the room, I could see they were in attendance, shaking hands all around. Molly's sister was pretty, like Molly, with wavy blonde hair; her brother was tall and thin. Molly's mother and father had to be the older couple crying in the front row directly behind them. Grief-stricken, they left the condolences to their children.

One poster board drew my attention because it looked as if a student or a group of students had made it. It had colorful bubble letters and pictures of Molly, students, and grad students. I noticed a couple of pictures with Amanda and Nick and pointed them out to Lenny.

Lenny raised an eyebrow. "One big, happy family? Where do you think the pictures were taken?" he asked.

"I think somewhere in New Mexico. I remember Molly mentioning it on our trip."

"Look at this," he said, pointing to a stack of pre-addressed envelopes.

Above the envelopes was a printout that detailed Molly's opposition to the Midwest Connect Pipeline, asking sympathizers to donate to the fund to stop the pipeline in honor of Molly. I took one of the envelopes and put it in my purse.

"Really, Prather? I thought you were going to take your extra Paris money and finally get rid of that eyesore on your desk."

"I am. This is for informational purposes only," I said.

He shook his head. "Information on how to get yourself and me off the road to tenure and on the express route to adjunct city."

"Professor Prather, do you like it?" came Amanda's voice from behind me.

I turned around. Amanda wore a long black blouse with black leggings, and her bangs were pinned demurely to one side. I agreed with Kat. She *did* look different; she moved with a new purpose that had supplanted her grief. "Hi, Amanda. Did you make this? It's lovely."

She nodded. "Some of the students from class helped me. Nick and I are going to make sure Molly's work continues. He's already talked to Bennett about setting up a fund."

Kat was right. Amanda had an aggressive tone in her voice that I wasn't used to hearing.

"Is Nick in town?" Lenny asked.

"Yes. He came back for the visitation. He's over there." She pointed in the direction of Molly's parents, whom he was consoling with a half embrace. He looked regal in his dark suit jacket and tie, and had it not been for his black cowboy boots, I would have never guessed he was the same rugged explorer from the pictures.

"And how are you holding up?" I asked.

"Better," she said. "I feel like her death wasn't in vain now. I feel like she will live on in her work."

"She will," I said. "She definitely will."

A group of students waved to her from the door. Meg and Olivia stood behind them. "There's some of our class. I'll see you later."

"Sure," I said.

Lenny and I moved toward the next display and the front of the room. This display was mostly of Molly and Bennett. Many of the pictures showed her winning various awards or giving speeches, and he, the devoted husband, was at her side in every one. I looked around. I still didn't see him.

Lenny motioned toward a picture on an easel near a grouping of flowers. "One guess as to who painted *A Buffalo at 5 o'clock*," he joked.

We moved closer to it. It was a painting of prairie grass, the waning sun, and in the far corner, a buffalo. "Arnold Frasier," I said, pointing to the small initials in the corner.

"What was the deal there anyway?" asked Lenny.

"He said Molly used to buy quite a few paintings and donate

to art exhibits before she was consumed by her zeal for the environment. Maybe this was a parting gift."

We continued toward Molly's sister and brother, and Lenny shook their hands first, explaining who we were. After I offered them my condolences, I asked if they had seen Bennett. Molly's sister motioned toward the short hallway.

"He's in there. Help yourself to cookies and coffee," she said.

We walked through the dark hall to what must have once been a dining room. Tonight, the sideboard was filled with cookies and bars, napkins and cups, juice, and coffeepots. Additional tables were set up for seating. Bennett had just pulled out a chair for Judith Spade, and Nick was already seated. As we approached the table, he encouraged us to sit. I told him we would, as soon as we helped ourselves to coffee.

"I'll get it. I was just getting Nick some anyway. Take a seat," said Bennett.

"Lenny, Emmeline," said Judith, "it's good to see you again."

"Hi, Judith. Hey, Nick. You make the long trek from Rapid City?"

Nick nodded. "I got a sub for today and tomorrow. I know we just had a week off for spring break, but there was no way I was going to miss this. Molly's work was too important."

"Amanda said you talked to Bennett about setting up a fund?" I asked.

"Yes, as soon as possible. That's another reason I'm here."

Bennett returned with the coffee, handing a cup to Nick.

"Let me help you," I said, standing.

"No, no, I got it. It helps to keep busy." A moment later, he brought back two more cups for Lenny and me.

"Don't you want one?" I said, taking the cup.

"No. I've had too much already." He sat down next to me. "I'll never sleep tonight."

I believed him. His hands were shaking. "Thank you. It's good," I said after taking a sip.

"Mine is a little… cold," said Nick, making a face.

Bennett started to stand again. "They just put out a fresh carafe. I'll get you a different cup."

"No, no. Sit down," said Nick. "This is just what I need after my drive, a little wake-up juice." He took a long sip to prove it.

"Have you heard any more from the detectives?" I asked Bennett. I was wondering if there was news about André. I hadn't seen him yet, but I was sure he wanted to be here. With all the administrative gossip, though, I wouldn't blame him for not attending.

"Not a word," said Bennett, "and I don't think I will, either. They were just as disgusted as I was with the airline and insurance companies. Those folks made it very difficult for me and the police to bring Molly home. I had to get my lawyer involved."

We all shook our heads to show our mutual disgust.

Sorry to have brought up the subject, I switched topics. "Judith, have you heard about the associate dean position?"

Her lips turned up ever so slightly. "Just today, in fact, so nothing has been officially sent out. I accepted the position this morning."

"Congratulations!" I said. I wondered if her help on the trip propelled them into making a prompt decision.

"Yes, congratulations, Dr. Spade," added Bennett. "That's good news."

Nick put down his empty Styrofoam cup. "Now you'll have the chance to implement some of Molly's plans."

Judith looked puzzled. "I'm not sure what Molly's plans were, but of course I will do everything in my power to preserve her memory and her work." She glanced at Bennett, who nodded gratefully.

"I'd be happy to sit down with you before I leave and tell you what she told me," said Nick, rubbing his hands together. "See, she thought the College of Arts and Sciences placed too much emphasis on publication. She wanted to emphasize action—the impact her colleagues' work had on the real world. Like a carbon footprint, only good. It would be central to promotion."

The idea of having my tenure tied to my societal impact caused me considerable dread. If I had left an impression, it was slight and only visible on my students' faces. Maybe scientists and historians such as Molly and Nick fared better with tangible effects; still, I had the feeling a great many academics would bristle at the suggestion. Judith, in fact, sat perfectly rigid.

"That's a worthy notion," said Judith, "but one that can hardly be put into play in our college. We have teachers like Emmeline and Lenny here who cannot be expected to measure their contributions to the literary world in a quantitative way."

"Agreed," said Lenny. "Unless you include rejection slips as part of my legacy, my chances of getting tenure would be next to nil."

Nick shook his head vigorously. "This is exactly the kind of opposition Molly's ideas met with. She was the only free thinker among you, do you know that? She was a visionary. A visionary!"

Nick looked a little wild-eyed, and honestly, I couldn't think of a response. Even Bennett appeared baffled. But Judith readily assumed the role of administrator as she had on the trip.

"She was extraordinary," Judith said. "I understand you worked with her quite a bit in the field."

"Yes, I did. We were… friends. We went on a few expeditions together." His eyes welled up with tears. He blinked rapidly and wiped them away with the back of his hand. "The students loved her. Amanda loved her. She's here tonight."

"Amanda. What a good student," said Judith. "I had her last year. She is a talented individual."

"Isn't she?" I said. "I got a chance to know her a little bit in Minneapolis. She's a bright young lady."

Tears began to gush down Nick's cheeks. "You'll never know, you'll never know," he repeated into his hands.

"Hey, man," said Lenny, "are you okay?"

"I'm fine," said Nick, looking almost normal. Then he became inconsolable again. He stood. "I just need some air."

Those of us who were left at the table turned to each other for answers, but none of us had any to give. The answer, however, became shockingly clear the next morning.

Chapter Twenty

NICK DRAMSDOR HAD been found dead in his hotel room. Overcome with grief over the death of his colleague and probable lover, he had committed suicide. One single shot to the head by his own gun left little doubt in our minds that he had indeed been in love with the distinguished Molly Jaspers.

Although Nick's death came early enough to report on the Tuesday morning news, that wasn't how I heard it. Around eight o'clock in the morning, I received a text from Kat that relayed the dreadful information. Though Lenny thought I was insane to give out my personal cellphone number to students, it hadn't been a problem. He said that was because I didn't carry my phone with me enough for it to become one. Luckily I had my phone charging next to the coffeepot when the text came in, and I answered it immediately.

When I saw the message, I was surprised but not shocked. I'd had my eye on Nick ever since he was the first one to leave our table of thirteen in Minneapolis. I wondered since then if something bad would happen. Now Kat confirmed that it had and was desperate over her friend Amanda. She begged me to *do* something. I told her to bring Amanda and meet me at the grocery store café because, really, it was never a good idea to skip breakfast.

Copper Bluff Food and Stuff was a little grocery store situated on Birch Street, which was the second main road into and out of town. The next city, if you could call it that, was ten miles away and had a population of fifty. Copper Bluff Food and Stuff not only sold groceries, it also sold toiletries. Chances were if you didn't find what you were looking for downtown, you would find it here.

Sometime during the eighties, the store had added on a small café. Light wood paneling marked off the addition from the rest of the store as did the lacy-curtained windows. The counter, which seated four diners max, always had a few people standing around it, talking with the cook, the waitress, or a friend. Some ogled the three-tier glass case, choosing a morning donut or an afternoon piece of pie. It didn't take long for the goodies to disappear, especially with the wonderful smell of cake wafting through the entire store, and I was relieved to see a variety of donuts remained this morning. Although it was just nine o'clock, many customers grabbed a sweet confection on their way to work.

I spotted Kat and Amanda right away; they were seated at one of the five tables in the tiny addition. I sat down next to Amanda, and giving her shoulders a half-embrace, asked how she was doing. Not that I needed to ask. Her hair was pulled back in a messy ponytail, and the dark circles under her eyes told me she hadn't slept well.

"I can't believe this is happening again," she said, wiping her nose on a napkin. "First Professor Jaspers, now Nick."

I reached for the tissue pack inside my purse and handed it to her. "I'm surprised too. He was distraught last night, but I never imagined he would take his own life."

A waitress approached the table, and I ordered coffee. I asked the girls if they wanted anything, but they said they weren't hungry. I ordered three homemade donuts anyway.

Copper Bluff Food and Stuff's cake-like confections were too tempting to pass up.

"He did not commit suicide," Amanda said when the waitress left.

I looked at Amanda and then Kat.

"See, Amanda has an idea about Nick's sui—death…" Kat began.

Amanda interrupted, pulling her sweatshirt sleeves down over her fingers. "Nick and I were going to the bank today to set up a fund for Dr. Jaspers. Why would he kill himself? We had other plans… plans for the future. It doesn't make sense."

I couldn't say that I disagreed, yet in her current state of mind, I didn't want to encourage her. "But last night at the visitation…. Maybe he was more broken up about Molly's death than you realized. Maybe they were… closer than you knew."

Amanda shook her head. "No, I know what you're saying, and it's not true. Nick admired her, but so did I. They were not seeing each other romantically."

The waitress returned, placing the plate of donuts in the middle of the table and the mug of coffee in front of me. I thanked her and then continued, "Do you know for certain they weren't seeing each other?"

"Yeah, I'm one hundred percent certain." She looked at Kat, who nodded. "Nick and I were dating. It was getting serious."

I reached for the large donut with chocolate icing and nuts.

"Oh, I know the stereotype—young student falls in love with hip professor—but that wasn't the case. He had never experienced anything like this, and neither had I. It was true love."

I wanted to dismiss the idea as a first love but couldn't. I had read enough romance novels in grad school to know that what she was saying was possible. Despite what others might think, I believed love could happen in the most unexpected places. "I don't buy into stereotypes. I believe you," I said.

Amanda let out a breath of relief, and Kat broke into a smile.

"I told you she would understand," Kat said, reaching for a maple-glazed donut.

Amanda took a drink of water. "I haven't told anyone, except Kat. I've kept it a secret because I feel… embarrassed."

I tried to put her at ease. "You've never attended one of my classes, have you, Amanda? I've had some of my most embarrassing moments in front of a class of twenty-three."

Kat laughed. "A couple weeks ago, a cat toy fell out of her bag and she screamed like a little girl."

"It was a very lifelike mouse," I explained. "And I hardly think you can describe my small exclamation as a scream."

Amanda's lips turned up ever so slightly. Our joking lightened the mood. She relaxed.

"The point is, you don't have to worry about being embarrassed. Not in front of me. Now tell me, why don't you think it was suicide?" I asked.

"Last night I talked to him on the phone after he left the visitation. He said someone was watching him from the window."

I put down my donut. "A man or a woman?"

"I don't know. I told him he was being paranoid and to shut the curtain," said Amanda.

I silently cursed Amanda's pragmatism. We could have used a little more description. "What else did he say?"

She leaned closer. "Professor Prather, he sounded *crazy*. Like I'd never heard him. Like he was on drugs or drunk. I told him I was coming to the hotel, but he said not to come near him."

"Did you go?"

She shook her head. "Honestly, I was so mad about the way he was acting that I hung up on him. I was grieving, too, and I thought he was being selfish. I had no idea…." Fresh tears formed in her eyes.

I patted her hand. "It wasn't your fault. You need to know that. Promise me you'll talk to someone at the Student Counseling Center?"

She nodded.

"What else can we do?" Kat asked me.

"Have you talked to the police? Have you told them about the person outside the window?"

"No," said Amanda. "After what happened with Dr. Jaspers, I don't want to say anything about… a murder. First my professor, next my boyfriend. I know how that would look for me."

I agreed. If Nick were murdered, she would certainly become a person of interest, not only for the reasons she stated but also for the reasons she didn't. Just yesterday morning in my creative writing class, Kat had admitted to Amanda's acting erratically. It was possible that others had noticed her odd behavior and would be willing to testify to it. And Amanda was smart, smart enough to get away with murder. I had a hard time believing she would kill her true love, especially with Molly Jaspers dead. Still, the police needed to know what she had just told me. The question was how to tell them.

Kat grabbed my arm across the table. "It's just like what we were talking about in class. The murderer always messes up… or leaves something behind or… or…."

In her excitement, she became tongue-tied, but I had no trouble finishing her sentence. "Or murders again."

AFTER PAYING FOR breakfast, I left the café with the idea of talking to Sophie Barnes, a previous student of mine who had been hired to the Criminal Investigations Division on the Copper Bluff Police Force. Sophie loved stories, especially dramas, and had been an excellent student in literature class; she would do an all-star job analyzing cases. She hadn't been a detective long, just since last fall, so I needed to make certain my stopping by would cause her no difficulties. I would make my visit brief and to the point, relaying the information from Amanda about the person outside Nick's window.

The Public Safety Building was attached to the old county

courthouse and housed not only the police department but also the jail. It was a brick building with ivory trim, and upon entering, I noticed how different it was from the Minneapolis Police Department. In Minneapolis, the building was buzzing with noise and activity. Here it was quiet, even friendly. The officer at the front desk was pleasant and inquired about my purple sweater. She said just looking at it reminded her it was spring and if I could stay a moment, she would grab Sophie Barnes.

I waited in the lobby, and Sophie came out minutes later. She was a pretty girl with a headful of chestnut hair, which few people would realize because she kept it tied back for work. I put down the newspaper I had picked up and stood to give her a hug. She was taller than I was, but not tall, with wide shoulders and hips, the latter accentuated by a gun belt.

"Professor Prather! It's good to see you again," Sophie said.

"You don't have to call me 'professor' anymore, you know," I said with a laugh.

"I know. It's a hard habit to break." She motioned past the front desk. "Do you want to come back? I have an office now."

"This shouldn't take long, and I know you're busy, but it *is* confidential. Is sitting here okay? Or would you rather go to your office?"

She took a seat next to mine. "There's no one here. What's up?"

I sat back down. "It's about the man who killed himself last night, Nick Dramsdor. I knew him. We had just been on spring break together with several other faculty and students; our trip was cut short by Molly Jaspers' sudden death. He was in town for the visitation."

"I heard about that," she said, nodding. "Jack Wood from the Minneapolis Police Department talked to Lieutenant Beamer last week. We are collaborating with them on the investigation. I guess I didn't remember right off that Nick was part of that group."

"As you know, Minneapolis was pursuing charges, and I worry foul play might be a factor here, too. Are you sure Nick's death was a suicide?"

Sophie's head bobbed up and down as she spoke. "Nick Dramsdor killed himself. There's no doubt about it. There was gun residue on his fingers, and the gun found at the hotel was registered to him."

I thought over this new information.

"Do you have reason to believe it *wasn't* suicide?" Sophie asked.

I leaned in closer. "Last night I was at Molly's visitation with Nick and several other faculty members and students. He seemed okay at first. Then, all of a sudden he became… unhinged. I don't know how else to put it. He was not acting like himself. He left abruptly."

"It sounds like he was grief-stricken." Hand over her heart, she added, "The poor soul!"

"But afterwards," I said, "his girlfriend said she talked to him on the phone in his hotel. She said not only was he acting erratically, he also claimed someone was watching him from the window."

Sophie took out her cellphone and opened up a notebook app. "What's the girlfriend's name? I don't know if we have it."

"No, probably not. Their relationship, for obvious reasons, was a secret, but I trust your good judgment." I gave her Amanda's full name. "She was hesitant to confide in me, so please use as much discretion as possible when contacting her. The girl is a student at the university. She doesn't want it to get out that she and Nick were dating."

"I get it," said Sophie. "Dating your professor is a definite no-no. I will question her after the initial results of the autopsy come back. And I will be as discreet as possible."

"Well, he wasn't *her* professor, but it was still a student-professor relationship. Anyway, I'm glad to hear an autopsy is being performed."

"It's mandatory in suicide cases like these," said Sophie, putting away her phone. "We'll get a preliminary report of what was in his blood and urine this afternoon from the assistant at the morgue."

"When you hear, would it be too much trouble to contact me as well?" I stood.

She grabbed for her phone again. "Actually, I think I have your number," she said, smiling. "You know, Professor, you might have made a pretty good cop."

"Really?" I said. I tucked my purple scarf into my coat.

She nodded. "Really."

"Well, if I don't finish my book soon, I'll remember you said that. I might need a new profession."

Chapter Twenty-One

LATER THAT AFTERNOON, I walked to campus to talk to the registrar. Since spring break, I had been thinking about Olivia and her course with Molly Jaspers. Now another professor was dead, and although I didn't think Olivia knew Nick personally, my first instinct was to take a closer look at the students on the trip. She was the only other one who had a private connection to Molly: she had failed Molly's class last spring and been subsequently kicked out of her sorority. If anyone had a reason to seek revenge on her professor, it was Olivia Christenson.

Registrars hold important positions at universities: they are the guardians of grades and academic records. Fortunately for me, our registrar was a revolving-door position; the university could never keep anyone in the job longer than a year, which meant the person would know that much less about the rules. Not that it was difficult for a professor to find out a student's grade. There were awards, inductions, ceremonies—all sorts of things that required us to know a student's GPA or grade-point average. Still, Olivia had never been one of my students, and I knew little about her. What reason did I have for inquiring about her GPA? If there was anything I was good at, though, it was making up a story.

The registrar's office was in the basement of Pender, the hall where the beautiful Pender Auditorium was located. Walking down the narrow steps, I took my first right, pausing briefly as I passed a vending machine. I checked my pockets but had no loose change; my afternoon chocolate craving would have to wait. I kept moving toward the office with the glass door marked OFFICE OF THE REGISTRAR.

"Hello," I said to the girl at the front desk. She wore a ridiculous bang bun and sported our campus color: red. I tried to remember her face from the student newspaper but couldn't. She played either softball or volleyball or maybe both. I wasn't good at keeping up with the sports teams.

"Hey," she said.

"Is Vicki, the registrar, in? I need to talk to her about a student who… well, I just need to talk to her."

"Yeah, I think so. Do you want me to check?"

"No, no," I said. "I know where her office is. I'll just go back and take a peek."

The area was small, so I didn't have far to go. Vicki's door was open, but I knocked anyway. She dropped her pencil.

"I'm sorry. I didn't mean to startle you," I said.

"No, come in. Are you Maxwell?"

Do I look like a Maxwell? I wanted to say. "No, I'm Emmeline Prather. I teach English?"

"Oh my god, what was I thinking?" She rubbed her forehead. "Of course you're not. I've been doing audits on seniors all day. It's been crazy."

And it showed. Her eyeliner on one eye had disappeared completely, and her hair was twisted back with a pencil. The ends frayed out in all directions, making her face look like the center of a sunburst.

I smiled. "I understand completely. It's midterms, and that means a hefty amount of work for you. I'll only take a moment of your time."

"Hefty. That's the word. But you know, they told me that when I signed on. I just nodded and scribbled my name on the dotted line." As she spoke, she was digging through the drawer for something. "Anyway, what can I help you with?"

"Olivia Christenson. I need to know about her grades last year—Molly Jaspers' class specifically. It was something in History." I tried to think back to the conversation at the restaurant. "Western Civ."

She pulled out a pack of mints from the drawer and held it out. Never one to pass up candy, I took one.

"Is that with an 'e' or 'o'?"

" 'O,' I think."

"Why do you need to know?" she asked as she typed in the name.

"For her sorority. Sorority purposes."

She looked up at me. "I didn't know you worked with the Greek houses in town."

"I've dealt with them a time or two," I said, not completely lying. "As a … liaison." I liked the word and had always wanted to use it.

"Well, it doesn't look like she'll be in the sorority for long, not with a 2.8 GPA. I think most houses require at least a 3.0. Last spring she failed Jaspers' class, another class, and withdrew from a third. Luckily she added Photography and did well in that."

So it had been a difficult time for Olivia all around, which meant she didn't have a reason to retaliate against Molly Jaspers specifically. My suspect pool narrowed. Out of curiosity, I asked, "What was the other class she failed, besides Molly's?"

"Music Appreciation."

Tough semester indeed.

AFTER I LEFT Pender, I stopped at the stone bench in the quad just to take a breath. The day hadn't warmed much, but the wind was slight, especially in the quadrangle, which was surrounded by the pillars of the campus: Stanton Hall, Winsor, and Pender. I enjoyed a few minutes of reflective silence, trying to make sense of the information I had gathered on Molly's death. It was half past the hour, and everyone was in class, teachers and students alike. Had I never been part of campus life, I wouldn't believe that in forty-five minutes, the quad would burst into a bustle of bodies and bikes.

Spring semester was halfway over, and next fall's schedule was in the planning stages. Molly's death was sure to impact André's future university trips abroad and ergo, mine. The university was going through the busywork of filing insurance claims and refunding faculty and students' travel fees, and if Human Resources never saw the word "Paris" again, I was sure it would be too soon. I wanted to believe a French major was still possible, but even for a dreamer like me, it was impossible to think that the fiasco of spring break would soon be forgotten, especially with the death of Nick Dramsdor. Besides, fall semester had proven to be a disappointment on so many levels. Two students had failed their introductory French course and would not be progressing anytime soon. Without French majors, there would be no need for advanced French courses, such as the French literature course I was to teach. Fall enrollment would begin soon, and perhaps André could encourage parents and students to consider a foreign language during their exploratory visits to campus. But even André's charm had its limits. If mothers heard the words "criminal charges" in the same sentence as "French professor," it would mean curtains for André. I was imagining him taking a great stage bow of farewell when suddenly he appeared before me. I looked around to make sure I hadn't fallen asleep. With my constant insomnia, it was always a possibility.

"André!" I said. "I was just thinking of you."

"And I of you," he said, setting his satchel down on the ground. "I came by your office to give you this."

He pulled a bottle of wine out of his bag. The label read *Trois Frères*.

"It's a bottle of your family's wine," I said.

He nodded and sat on the bench beside me. "I have a bottle for Lenny, too. He expressed some interest."

I turned the bottle over in my hands, reading the back. The organic label was nowhere to be found. "It's not organic," I said, my belief in André's innocence confirmed.

His dark eyebrows furrowed. "Did you think so?"

I nodded with a smile. "I thought maybe it was, after hearing you talk about the winery. Your father's processes sounded very traditional."

He shook his head. "We are an old family and winery. We do not have the resources to worry about the certifications that these new fads require. They come and go. Our winery stays." He threw his hands in the air. "Who knows after this debacle? It might be back to the fields for me."

"And Freshman English for me?"

We shared a laugh.

"Which is worse?" I said.

He nudged my shoulder with his. "I needed a laugh. Thank you."

"How *is* Dean Richardson?" I asked.

"He is not happy, and I can't blame him. He has parents calling him, the grant committee, all sorts of misery."

"Did you talk to him any more about the French major?"

"I didn't breathe a word of it," he said. "Until the truth comes out about what happened to Molly, he will always wonder if I had something to do with it. And now the suicide of the cowboy?" He shook his head. "My academic reputation, I do believe, is ruined."

Head in his hands and shoulders slumped, he stared at the hard ground. It looked as if he hadn't shaven for a few days, and while a five o'clock shadow was attractive, a three-day-old beard was not. I wanted to figure out this murder, and soon, for him and the students. Travel to foreign countries was an important part of education. I hated to see an opportunity for them and myself disappear.

I put the wine into my bag. "Don't worry about your academic reputation for one minute, André. I am going to get to the truth of the matter; I promise you that. Then we can see what Dean Richardson says."

He smiled. "You are good at telling stories."

"Not telling stories, just trusting in my research abilities. As you said, I'm a keen researcher." I stood. "Thank you for the wine. I think we will need a glass before the week is over."

"The week? Em, I think we shall need a glass before the day is over."

After exchanging goodbyes with André, I walked to my house, wondering why Sophie hadn't called me yet. It was four o'clock, and she said the preliminary autopsy reports would be in this afternoon. As my bungalow came into sight, the answer became clear. A police car sat outside my house, and next to it stood not Sophie Barnes but Officer Beamer. He was next to Mrs. Gunderson, who took great delight in his presence. She was wrapped in her faux fur overcoat and spoke excitedly when I joined the conversation.

"Emmeline, you have an officer from the Copper Bluff Police Force here to see you." A smile touched the corners of her bright pink lips.

I held out my hand. "Officer Beamer, it's good to see you again."

"Ms. Prather," he said, shaking my hand. "I hear I missed a visit from you today at the precinct."

Mrs. Gunderson's eyes grew wide with curiosity.

"Why don't you come inside?" I said, motioning toward my house. "It's getting chilly out here."

"I have a nice hot dish in the oven that'll warm you up,

Officer," said Mrs. Gunderson. "It will be done in about thirty minutes."

"Thank you," said Beamer, "but I'm sure my wife has something on the stove. I'd better come home hungry if I want to stay in her good graces."

"Well, if you change your mind…" said Mrs. Gunderson. "And you, too, Emmeline."

"Thank you, Mrs. Gunderson," I called out as I walked up to my front porch. Beamer was right behind me.

Once in the house, I flicked on the lights. I wished the room were tidier. Three books, a coffee cup, and a stack of students' folders were on the coffee table in the living room, and the dining room was no better. When I'd noticed a wren in my *Arc de Triumph* birdhouse, spring fever took hold, and I brought my books to the dining table so I could watch it. They were the tiniest birds, wrens. And fascinating to watch. But now I wished I had kept the clutter contained to my office. I had to move stacks of stuff off the chairs so that Officer Beamer could sit.

"Coffee?" I said as I cleared the chair across from him.

"No thank you."

"I wish I could say I had a hot dish in the oven, but I don't," I said. "In fact, the entire notion of a hot dish is still a little bit of a mystery to me."

"That's the idea," said Officer Beamer, putting his gray coat on the back of the chair. "Nobody knows what goes into those things."

I laughed. It was good to see Officer Beamer again. I had met him last semester when a student of mine died unexpectedly. He was a careful man with a deep wrinkle between his eyes from thinking too hard about his cases. In his mid-sixties, he had hair graying just above his ears, which I thought might have been caused by the stress of the job. The rest of his hair was so dark as to almost be black, and his shoulders gave no indication of his age. They were solid and straight.

"Is this about Nick Dramsdor's autopsy results? Did they find… anything?" I asked.

Now it was his turn to smile. "You know, Ms. Prather, I think it's remarkable how much interest you take in my job. It would be flattering if it weren't so disturbing."

"Really? It's disturbing? I would think anyone would be concerned about the suicide of her colleague. I'm sure you've had numerous calls on the subject already."

He shook his head once. "No, I haven't. Not one. But I did have a call last week from one Jack Wood. He seemed to think you knew something about the death of Molly Jaspers. What was the word he used…. I remember. Suspect."

"What did you say?" The question gave me time to get over my surprise that Jack Wood had called me a suspect.

"He had you tied to this fellow André Duman, who he has pegged as a prime suspect, but I disabused him of that notion. I said you were an overly curious English professor who had read too many books. That you were very concerned with anything that had to do with your university."

"Thank you, Officer Beamer. I cannot tell you how much I appreciate that. Jack Wood is, well, he's just overworked. He's a big-city cop who's trying to put this case to rest as soon as he can so he can move on to the other hundreds of cases dumped into his lap every day. Now his partner, Ernest Jones, he was busy, too, but much more interested in getting to the bottom of the truth. He was very kind."

"Yes, I talked to Ernest Jones," said Beamer.

"What did you think of him?"

He folded his hands on the table. "I think he sounded like your long-lost brother. You weren't born in Minneapolis, were you?"

I shook my head. "No, Detroit."

"My point is, the FBI is overseeing the case, so I need to make sure everything is done by the book. Since you are an English professor, I bet you know what I mean."

"I do," I said.

"And I bet that means you know I can't have you asking questions or calling coroners or pathologists."

"Of course," I said. "I was thinking of doing no such thing."

"Or stopping by the precinct to pump an old student for information," he added.

"I wasn't 'pumping her for information'; I was *giving* her information," I replied, trying not to get excited.

"That's why I'm here," he said. "Your tip from the girlfriend put Nick Dramsdor's blood sample on my radar. When it came back, I noticed the amount of amitriptyline in his system. It was lethal."

"What's amitriptyline?" I asked.

"An antipsychotic. An antidepressant," he said.

"So he overdosed on his antidepressant and then shot himself with a gun? Don't you think that's overdoing it a bit?"

"That's the thing. He didn't have a prescription for an antidepressant that we could find in his hotel room. As far as we know, he wasn't on one."

I inhaled deeply. "Someone gave it to him? Is that what you're saying?"

"Let's not jump to conclusions yet, Ms. Prather. Let's leave that to the scientists on campus." He took a tiny notebook out of his front pocket. "Did you notice anyone arguing with Nick Dramsdor the night of his death? Sophie said you were at the visitation for Dr. Jaspers with him."

"No, but he got very upset there, and Amanda, his girlfriend, said he told her that someone was watching him from outside his hotel window."

"Sophie and I re-checked the scene with that scenario in mind but didn't find any corroborating evidence—no footprints. Could the girlfriend be lying? Did she have a motive for killing Mr. Dramsdor?"

"I know what you're suggesting," I said, "and maybe she *is* trying to deflect suspicion from herself, but I didn't get that feeling this morning. I felt she was grieving the loss of a loved one. In fact, she called Nick her 'true love.' " Of course, Amanda wouldn't have been the first woman to kill her true love to keep him for all time. Faulkner's "A Rose for Emily" was testimony to that phenomenon.

Beamer wrote something in his notebook and then shut it. "Well I don't think I can rule out the possibility that the girl made up the stalker outside Nick Dramsdor's window. The front-desk clerk saw no one enter or leave his room or any suspicious activity before the shooting."

"What about the antidepressant? Who from the original group is on antidepressants?" I said. "Could one person be responsible for both deaths?"

"We're not sure the deaths are connected. Heck, Minneapolis doesn't even have proof someone *is* responsible for Jaspers' death," Beamer said. "And plenty of people are on antidepressants. It's not as easy as you think to get warrants for peoples' medical records."

The two deaths were connected. I would stake my career on it. In fact, I was staking my career on it. Unless I could find the perpetrator, André's reputation would always be sullied by the fatal spring break, and the French major would remain a pipe dream.

He put his notebook back in his pocket. "If you think of anything, let me know. In the meantime, keep yourself safe—and your questions to yourself. If you've got any suspicions, bring them directly to me."

"I will," I promised. "And you'll keep me informed?"

He put on his hat. "Of course. I can't think of any other way to keep you out of my precinct," he said with a grin.

Chapter Twenty-Two

THE NIGHT HAD grown dark, and my house was lonely. I thought about taking Mrs. Gunderson up on her invitation to come over and eat hot dish but then reconsidered. I needed someone I could talk to about what Beamer had told me, someone sympathetic, someone like Lenny. I looked at the clock. It was six, and I wondered if Lenny had eaten. Then I wondered if I could bring food to his house without him teasing me about my dating situation. The truth was I wasn't scared of his jokes; I was scared I was growing closer to him than I liked to admit. In Minneapolis, I could have sworn we almost kissed. And while kissing was inconsequential with my other dates, with Lenny, it would change everything—from our relationship to our careers. And nothing had turned out well for me—or him—thus far in the romance department. Did I really want to put our friendship up against our shoddy dating records? I shook my head. With the looming problem of Nick's suicide on my mind, I didn't know and couldn't decide. It was dinner, nothing more. I was way overthinking it.

I grabbed my cellphone out of the bottom of my purse and sent him a noncommittal text. Was he up for takeout from

Vinny's? I needed to get out of the house. When he responded with a yes and his order of spaghetti Bolognese, I called Vinny's and then slipped out of my trousers and into my jeans. I pulled on an old blue sweatshirt as a clear signal I wasn't dressing for a date. After pulling my curls into a haphazard ponytail and feeding Dickinson, I was ready to go.

Thirty minutes later, I was at Lenny's door. I raised my finger to the doorbell and stopped. He was playing the loveliest piano song I had ever heard. I was still standing there, transfixed, when it stopped and Lenny pulled open the door.

"Hey, sorry. I just saw you," he said. He was dressed in a T-shirt and jeans, but his living room was the cleanest I'd ever seen it. His black couch was clear of clutter, and his glass coffee table looked as if it had just been dusted.

"I didn't ring the bell or knock," I explained. "What were you playing?"

He took the takeout bag from my hand. "Nothing, really. Just fooling around."

"It was beautiful," I said.

He placed the takeout bag on the coffee table and took a seat on the couch. I sat down beside him, leaving one cushion between us, and pulled out the bottle of wine André had given me.

"Compliments, food, wine? Are you trying to seduce me, Prath—" He stopped midsentence. "Is this the wine from André's winery?"

"We don't have to drink it," I said. "I mean, I brought it to show you it's not organic. He didn't kill Molly. He has a bottle for you, too."

He raised one eyebrow. "*We don't have to drink it?* What's the matter with you? I've never known you to leave a bottle of wine corked while eating Italian."

His teasing put me at ease, and I pulled a wine opener out of my bag.

"Ah, there's a girl after my own heart. She carries her own utensils. Let me get glasses."

He disappeared into the kitchen, and I opened the wine. He came back wiping two glasses with a towel. "They were a little dusty. I wasn't expecting fine dining on a Tuesday night."

He set them on the table, and I poured.

"So you were right about Scarf Man after all." He took the Styrofoam box marked spaghetti Bolognese. "He didn't kill Molly. Hey, do you need a plate?"

I shook my head. "No, I'm good."

"How's the wine?" he said, opening his spaghetti container.

"Excellent," I said. "I can see why André wants the winery to stay the way it is."

"So this is good news," he said, taking a drink. "It makes it official that André had nothing to do with Jaspers' death."

"We're convinced," I said, "but until we uncover the identity of the real culprit, he'll be under suspicion. Especially now that another murder has been committed."

He set down his wine glass with a clang on the table. "Not Nick Dramsdor. I saw on the news that it was a suicide."

I proceeded to tell him about my conversations with Amanda and Officer Beamer while he twirled spaghetti around his fork. I told him about the gunshot, the gun residue, and the amitriptyline. When I finished relaying the details, I took a bite of my ravioli, and we both chewed in silence for several minutes. Then Lenny said, "But André wasn't even at the visitation."

That was right. We never saw André once at the visitation; I didn't think he had attended. "True," I said, "but maybe the police will see that as the opportunity he needed to murder Nick in his hotel room."

"Nah," said Lenny, setting his container on the coffee table and grabbing his laptop from the floor. "That stuff has to have time to get into the blood stream. What's it called again?"

"Amitriptyline." I set my container on the table, too, and scooted closer to him to see the results of his search.

"See? Fifteen to forty minutes. 'A reaction occurs within fifteen to forty minutes upon lethal administration.' "

"It fits," I said. "The drug overdose could have accounted for his strange conduct at the visitation, too. It says here an overdose can cause 'manic' behavior." I pointed to the screen. "Manic. That's exactly how I would describe Nick that night. Wouldn't you agree?" I read several more facts, but Lenny was silent. Was he tuning me out? Why was he so reluctant to get involved when the evidence was right before our eyes? I looked up. He was staring at me in such a way that made it impossible for me to ask.

He reached over and touched my hair. "You know what I love? I love these little curls that fall over your ears. No matter how hard you try, they never stay back where they're supposed to."

"I . . . I know. They're absolutely hateful," I stuttered.

"Em, do you think when this is over, we could. . . ." He stopped and took a drink of his wine. "I don't know. Go out on a date?"

I couldn't answer; I could only blink.

"Oh god, please don't blush. You make this so damn hard. If you were any other girl, I wouldn't have thought twice about it. But somehow you got me into a way of thinking that is a hundred years old—maybe two."

"I'm sorry. Am I blushing?" I put my hands to my face; it felt hot. "I do. I would. I mean, we could try it."

He nodded. "We could try it. I know we both have shaky dating records, but maybe it could work."

"Hey, speak for yourself," I said. "I dated Ricky Anderson for nearly two months before I told him I thought it was asinine for a grown man to wear a high school letterman jacket."

"Cathy Carter? I went *three* months before saying anything about her Pokémon Go addiction. She was on that thing all the time." Lenny smiled. "But this will be different. This will be… us."

"This will be us," I repeated, and suddenly I felt less nervous.

He put his wine glass back on the coffee table. "So, the drug…. If it was administered at the visitation, who was there from the original thirteen?"

I thought for a moment. "Me, Nick, Amanda, Kat, Meg, Olivia, Bennett, Judith…. Arnold had to have been there because his painting was on that easel. Remember?"

Lenny nodded. "So that clears everybody else?"

"If we have *one* murderer," I said. "I suppose it's possible we have two and the second death is retaliation for the first, but I don't think so."

"Okay, so who out of those people, present company excluded, needs an antipsychotic?"

I smiled and took a drink of wine. "Here's one: Kat told me in my creative writing class that Amanda was acting very strangely. And then there's the story about the person outside the window, which Officer Beamer wasn't able to confirm. Maybe Amanda killed Molly because Molly found out about her affair with Nick and then killed Nick because he didn't propose? She's smart enough to get away with it; still, that's two passionate murders for one level-headed college girl."

"Maybe she was reacting badly to her meds? They make people do crazy things, I've heard." He took a big bite of his spaghetti and swallowed. "I knew a guy who shook like a leaf after taking his."

"It's a possibility," I said. "But they're suppose to control your psychosis, not set it off." I was silent for a moment while a thought hovered at the edge of my mind.

"What is it, Em? Did you remember something?"

I shook my head. "No, it was just a feeling I got. I can't remember exactly."

"Maybe it's the wine," he said, refilling our glasses. "Wine makes me forget a lot of things."

I agreed. "Tomorrow's my creative writing class, and Kat's in it. I'll ask her if Amanda is *on* anything. Discreetly, of course, through implication."

"Yeah, weave it in there between your lesson on hyperbole and personification."

"Good god, Lenny, we're way beyond that. It's a sophomore class."

Chapter Twenty-Three

THAT NIGHT, I had a hard time sleeping, which wasn't unusual, but the circumstances keeping me up were. Lenny had asked me out… on a *date*. As I tossed and turned in my Eiffel Tower pajamas, I wondered what a date with Lenny would look like. Where would we go we hadn't gone before? Would he drive, or would I? Would he be different? Would I?

After I readjusted my pillow for the seventh time, my cat, Dickinson, got fed up and jumped off the bed, leaving me more room to stretch my legs. It was during this short interval that I must have fallen asleep and dreamed the most wonderful dream about Lenny. We were in my yard, on a bench, surrounded by the wildflowers I had planted. They had grown into something only plausible in a historical romance novel. Complete with hedges and gates, my garden rivaled a distinguished manor's. It was so large, in fact, that my house was nowhere in sight. When I awoke, I was smiling, and I wished I could stay in bed for the entire day, surrounded by flowers, sunshine, and Lenny. But it was Wednesday, and my creative writing class met this morning. I hopped out of bed and into my slippers. It would take a healthy dose of caffeine to pull me out of fantasyland today.

When I walked out of the house an hour later, Mrs. Gunderson was only too happy to yank me back to the present, and all visions of flowers wilted with the sound of her sensible voice.

"Interesting visit you had from the police department last night," she said by way of greeting. She was standing outside with her white mutt, Darling, who was peeing on my tree. He yipped aggressively as I walked down the stairs.

"Good morning, Mrs. Gunderson. Hello, *Darling*," I said. That was the only thing I liked about him. His name. I liked saying it like a 1940s movie star.

"I hope you're not in trouble, dear," said Mrs. Gunderson. "It's never good for the neighborhood when police cars start showing up outside of houses. Next thing you know, you start hearing about drugs, drug addicts. That's how they found out about Mr. Winkle, you know. He had a terrible addiction to morphine. Nearly lost his business. Of course his wife was right to ship him off to that clinic in Minnesota. That's what saved him."

"Oh, nothing like that," I said. She did guess right about the drugs, though. Just the wrong one. "One of my colleagues committed suicide Monday night. Officer Beamer came to talk to me about that."

Darling scratched at the ground with his back paws. "Oh, how *awful*," said Mrs. Gunderson. "I'm so sorry. But you know those academic types." She tapped her forehead. "Some are a little . . . touched."

I opened my mouth but didn't know how to respond.

"Have a good day, dear," she said.

"Goodbye, Mrs. Gunderson," I said with a wave.

The street was quiet, except the occasional bang from a student rushing out a door. I loved the ten minutes before class, the absolute insistence of them. I picked up my pace. In the summer, the street would change. It would grow desolate as houses stood empty, waiting for the students' return. Lawns would go unkempt and porches be left unoccupied. Forgotten mail would pile up in the boxes, and summer would cover the street like a great creeping vine. And that was the best thing of all about Copper Bluff—the changing of the seasons. Days were collected like flowers in a garden, and when one died, another sprung to life; each made you feel new again. Each made you feel alive.

When I stopped at my office to grab my grade book, I noted Giles's door was already open. There wasn't another chair or professor who worked more hours than he did.

He hollered from his office, "Emmeline, is that you?"

Hollering of any kind was unusual for Giles, so I put my keys back in my book bag and went directly to his office. "Hi, Giles."

"Emmeline, what is this business with Nick Dramsdor. Is he dead?"

"I'm afraid so," I said. I debated whether to tell him about the antidepressant overdose and decided against it. I knew nothing yet for certain. Besides, he would only attribute it to my new affinity for crime. "He shot himself in the Happy Rest Hotel on Birch Street." I leaned on the chair next to the bookshelf, allowing my book bag to drop. "Well, not so happy for him."

He folded his hands on his lap. "Why? I was under the impression that he was an important scholar in the field of paleontology."

"Me, too. The story goes that he was grief-stricken over Molly's death and killed himself. Maybe a little too grief-stricken for just a friend?"

Giles surprised me by saying, "Oh, I don't think so. Molly was very much committed to her husband. He's a heck of an engineer. Did you know that? His company makes miniature robots that monitor everything from seismic waves in California to the oil rigs in Alaska. Fascinating man."

I leaned in closer. "Do you know him well?"

Giles took a drink of his coffee while he thought over the question. He was not a man to rush to an answer; everything he did was deliberate and methodical.

"I've met him three times at university events, so I cannot say I know him *well*. But he is well connected and have amassed a small fortune from his business. The university fundraisers are always glad to see him coming, if you know what I mean."

A detail from the visitation came back to me. "Nick said he was going to set up a fund in honor of Molly. Maybe a scholarship or something."

"Oh sure, I wouldn't doubt it," said Giles. "Molly would want students to continue to travel in her memory. She thought fieldwork was much more important than classwork. Of course, her work lent itself to that mindset." Giles smiled in a way that told me he disagreed completely. "Poor fellow," he continued. "It seems Bennett won't be off the hook, even with Molly gone."

Or would he? I asked myself. A memorial fund wouldn't be the first time he was asked to give money to a project for Molly's sake. Arnold Frasier said Molly had been quite an investor in the arts at one time. And with the meager salaries paid by the university, one didn't need to look far to see where she got her money. Maybe Bennett was weary of funding his wife while receiving none of the accolades.

"Whatever I said that put that look on your face, it was nothing, so you can just go ahead and forget it," said Giles. "You look a million miles away, and I'm pretty sure your creative writing class meets in the next building."

"My creative writing class!" I grabbed my bag from the floor. The gold clock on the wall struck the top of the hour, and I realized my grade book would have to be left behind. "See you later."

"Goodbye, Emmeline," said Giles with a shake of his head.

"No running in the halls," Allen Dunsbar called out with a laugh as I rushed by his office.

Thankfully, my class was waiting for me when I entered; it was just one minute past the hour. The university had a policy that stated if a professor was more than five minutes late, students were free to leave. The students took this policy quite seriously.

"Good morning," I said, a little out of breath. "Thank you for not leaving."

The class laughed.

"We knew you'd be here. We figured your bike had a flat tire or something," said Kat.

"No, I can't blame it on my bike. I didn't ride it today."

"If we have time, can I read a few new pages of my story?" asked Kat, holding up the pages in her hand. "I didn't have a chance to submit them."

"Of course," I said, pulling up our class drop box on the university's intranet, "but let's begin with Andrew and his bathtub. It seems to have gotten out of the bathroom and into the kitchen."

Andrew was interested in magical realism, a genre that didn't interest many in the classroom, but I thought his piece was terrifically original. It didn't generate a lot of discussion, however, so the class had time to consider it and three other works before we got to Kat's new pages. I suggested that she read them aloud slowly so we could follow along, making notes to ourselves.

As she read her murder mystery, I found my mind wandering back to Giles's office and to the real-life deaths of Molly and Nick. It was in Giles's office that I remembered Molly had funded Arnold Frasier's art exhibits. On the bus, Arnold had relayed his disdain for Molly's environmental zeal to me, and Nick had said something smart when Arnold challenged Molly's authenticity. What was it? As Kat read on, I remembered. Nick had said Molly discredited a theory of Arnold Frasier's in a journal article. Could it be that Arnold retaliated by murdering the critic? Artists were passionate creatures, especially when it came to their own work. And wasn't his painting prominently displayed at the visitation Monday night? Maybe its display was his idea of having the last word.

As Kat flipped to the last page of her story, Jason, the boy who sat next to her said, "Hey, it's just like we said on Monday. The murderer killed someone else."

I refocused my attention on the class. I wished I had paid more attention to Kat's story.

"It wasn't murder, it was suicide," said Claire.

"No, Jason's right," Kat said, shaking her head. "It might look like suicide, but that's not what happened."

"What? What could have happened? The guy shot himself in the head. Tell me that's not the textbook definition of suicide," said Claire.

Kat looked at me; I looked at the clock.

"We'll have to find out the answer to that question on Friday," I said. "We're out of time."

Chapter Twenty-Four

I WAS DETERMINED to see Arnold Frasier as soon as possible, so I decided to forgo lunch and head directly to the Fine Arts building after my creative writing class. I wanted to see him before my afternoon classes, which didn't leave me much time. Fine Arts was the only building set apart from the main campus and housed the Art and Music Departments as well as the theater. It was a place I knew well from last semester's play, *Les Misérables*. A student of mine had died on the set, and I had spent a good deal of time in the building finding out why.

I was walking briskly past the Student Center when I heard my name.

"Prather! Wait up."

I turned around to find Lenny coming out of the building with a cellophane-wrapped piece of pound cake.

"Hey, Lenny. I love that stuff," I said, pointing to his cake. "I suppose you don't have another piece in there?"

"Yeah." He took a second piece out of his brown paper sack. "You look like you are hell-bent on going somewhere. What's up?"

As I unwrapped the piece of spongy cake, I explained my

theory about Arnold Frasier. By the time I relayed the story of Arnold and Molly's argument on the bus, he had finished his piece.

"Ponytail Man?" he clarified.

I nodded and took a bite of my pound cake. Delicious. "He's in the Fine Arts building," I said, wiping the crumbs from my mouth. "That's where I was headed. Why don't you come along?"

"Oh sure, let's go down this rocky road again. Who knows? Maybe one of us will get knocked off in the theater. At least there will be a witness this time. Unless they get us both."

"No way," I said. "The Art Department is down the hall from the theater, and besides, the spring show is much lighter—a musical. *The Lion King*?"

"Last semester's was a musical too," grouched Lenny, but he started walking with me in the direction of the building.

"True, but hardly similar in content."

"So how was class?" Lenny said, making small talk as we crossed the street. I could see in the distance that the Fine Arts parking lot was full; something must be going on.

I told him about Kat and her mystery story. "I can't wait to see what she comes up with for Friday."

"Don't you think it's a little strange, Em, how she needed another murder to happen, and presto, another one did?"

I could feel my brow furrow at the suggestion. "Yes, I guess it is a little odd. But as they say, fiction often mirrors real life."

"Or the other way around...."

The Grant C. Hofer Center for the Fine Arts took up the entire block, if you counted the parking lot. It was a modern brick structure from the 1970s and looked quite different from the rest of the old buildings on campus. In front was a bronze sculpture that Lenny and I often speculated about. Was it the gavel of justice? Was it a hammer? We weren't sure. Today we passed it without comment as we entered the building.

Inside, noise was coming from the gallery that housed art exhibits year-round.

"I wonder what's going on in there? Do you know?" I asked Lenny.

He shook his head.

"Let's check it out," I said. We headed in that direction.

In a month or so, this room would display the works of graduating art majors, but today, the sign said there was a reception for artist-in-residence Jeremy Looks Twice, a Native American painter and sculptor who had several works prominently on display.

"Score! There's food," said Lenny, pointing to a table filled with snacks and refreshments.

"Hold on. Let's talk to Arnold first."

We walked around the perimeter of the room, glancing at some of the paintings. I loved them because they were painted with warm, bold colors. The fiery images seemed to jump off the canvas, so real and full of life.

"This guy is good," said Lenny.

I agreed.

A few steps later, I caught sight of Arnold's ponytail. He wore a dark suit jacket with a checked shirt underneath and looked the part of the thoughtful art professor as he observed a painting, nodding and agreeing with what the man beside him was saying.

"Arnold," I said when the two finished talking.

"Emmeline, I'm glad you could make it. Hey, Lenny," he said, shaking Lenny's hand. "There's a guy over there you might be interested in. He's a genuine drum keeper."

"Oh yeah?" said Lenny, looking toward a man setting up a drum in the corner. "I'll have to check it out."

"This is a fascinating exhibit. The artist is obviously very talented," I said.

"Jeremy's work is visionary. I'm sad that his residence is over, but I know his work will sell. Just look at this crowd."

"It's a wonderful turnout." I glanced around at the fifty-plus people in the room. "Arnold, I was wondering… did you hear about Nick Dramsdor's suicide?"

"Of course, I read about it in the paper. I can't say I'm surprised." He stuck his hands in his pockets. "The guy was obviously in love with Molly. I guess he couldn't move on."

"Did you go to the visitation?" I asked.

He blinked a few times. "I didn't. I suppose I should have, but I'd had enough of it all in Minneapolis. When Bennett asked if I wanted to contribute anything, I sent over one of her favorite paintings… or what used to be one of her favorite paintings. It was the best I could do."

"Hey, no one can blame you," said Lenny. "It's not like you guys were close anymore."

Arnold shook his head. "No, we weren't. But that didn't bother me. What bothered me was that she lashed out at anyone who didn't agree with her, even criticizing my article without supporting her comments with logic or research. That's not the way we do it in academia. There's room for difference—or should be."

"Did she really discredit your article?" I asked, leaning closer to him.

He smiled. "No, not *discredit*. Nick was exaggerating. She left a negative review on the website where the article was posted. It wasn't a big deal. I knew she was just mad that I had made a positive remark about the Midwest Connect pipeline earlier that week." He nodded at an attendee who said hello. "I mean, you just can't stick your head in the sand and deny that the times they are a changing, as Bob Dylan would say. Even with art." He motioned around the room. "Even our artist-in-residence is challenged to connect his art through technology and social media. I thought it was foolish that Molly couldn't acknowledge one positive outcome of the pipeline."

"What positive outcome?" asked Lenny. "I can't think of a single one."

"It would give lots of people in technology jobs, and I said so. In a meeting I had with other chairs, President Conner said that EROS Data Center had contacted the school about post-doctorial research opportunities. It seems that part of EROS's job includes monitoring and gauging the environmental impact of the pipeline. A job with EROS or one of their contractors would have kept more science grads in state, and you know we need to keep everyone we can to compete."

"EROS Data Center," I repeated. "They have over six hundred employees." EROS Data Center was a huge research facility for the U.S. Department of Geological Survey and housed one of the largest computer complexes in the U.S.

"I know. It's one of the best employers in the state, but Molly didn't bother to consider the practical view."

I contemplated this new information, wondering if anyone tied to the sciences agreed with Arnold and saw the pipeline as an economic benefit for the state. It didn't take long for me to remember Judith Spade. Although she taught for the School of Medicine, she was a champion of Health and Sciences all around and our new associate dean. Plus, she had attended the visitation.

A student approached. They exchanged a few words.

"We'd better let you go," I said. "We're taking you away from the exhibit."

"Don't forget to get some free food," said Arnold, turning back to the student.

"That's next on our list," said Lenny.

He and I began moving in the direction of the refreshment table. "Well, Arnold's out," Lenny said.

I looked back to see if Arnold overheard. Luckily he was engaged with the student. "Not so loud."

"We're in a room full of people," he said, taking four tea sandwiches and crowding them on his luncheon plate. "Jeez, what are we? Infants? Give me another plate."

I handed him one. "It's not an all-you-can-eat buffet."

"That's for damn sure," he said, scooping two pieces of cake on his second plate.

I took a sandwich and some grapes, leaving no room for cake on the tiny plate, and followed Lenny toward the corner with the drum keeper. We listened to him play the drum as we ate our sandwiches. When the drum quieted into a steady background beat, I asked Lenny what he thought of Arnold's information about EROS Data Center.

"I was surprised," he said. "I wouldn't have made that connection. But I see the logic. It's hard to keep graduates in a state where the median income is so low."

"You know what other connection it made me think of?"

"Bennett Jaspers?" he said, taking a bite of cake.

I put down my grape; that was a thought. "No… I was going to say Judith Spade."

"Hey Jude, our soon-to-be associate dean. That should be fun."

"I think she'll do fine," I said. "I like her."

"I like her, too, but she and Dean Richardson are polar opposites. I wouldn't want to be in that office during budget talks."

"As I understand, she will be the associate dean of administration, not academics," I said.

He shook his head. "I can't keep all the titles straight in my head, let alone what they actually do."

I looked at his second piece of cake. "Chances are, you'll never have to talk to her unless you run up against a nasty case of plagiarism. Then she'd probably sit in on the mediating committee."

"I think they just make up stuff to do so that they don't have to teach. Maybe I should look into becoming a dean."

"Yes… look into that."

"God, Prather. Hand me your plate already," he said. He scooped his extra piece of cake onto my plate and handed it back to me. "I suppose you need a fork."

"I took one just in case," I said with a smile. I had a terrible sweet tooth. "Thank you."

"So you think Judith could have killed Molly and Nick? She *is* a physician. I guess I can see why she'd target Molly—because of the job—but why Nick?"

I finished chewing and took a sip of my lemonade. "Nick was setting up a fund in Molly's memory. He said so at the visitation. Can you imagine Judith wanting Molly's work to continue? Nick would have made certain that the funds were put to their intended use, especially when it came to tenure, trips, or anything administrational."

Lenny shrugged. "Well, when you put it that way, I suppose it's possible, but I think I'd believe just about anything when it comes to your gift for web weaving. You really do read too many mysteries."

"And she was at the visitation," I said, pointing my fork at him.

"That's two. You need just one more thing to achieve a trifecta."

"What's that?"

"Her antidepressant prescription."

I DECIDED TO go to Winkle's Pharmacy and Drug after five o'clock because college kids worked there nights. I knew this because every time I went to get my melatonin supplements, the student workers were more than happy to answer questions. They liked trying out new words they had learned in class. The last time I'd endured a particularly grueling bout of insomnia, I'd grilled the kid behind the counter about melatonin's efficacy for a good twenty minutes. Had I gone during the day, old man Winkle would have told me to get a sleeping pill, and that would have been the end of the conversation. Plus, students were very good at forgetting a face. Mr. Winkle not so much.

My plan was to say that a doctor had recommended that my friend start taking amitriptyline, and I had questions about the drug. After all, it would be only natural for me to show concern for a friend, and I didn't want them thinking I had been prescribed the antidepressant, which they could easily look up on their computer database. It would be a way to gather credible research about the drug that had been used to kill Nick Dramsdor.

Satisfied with my strategy, I walked through Winkle's front door at six o'clock. When the bell jingled, a young female cashier wearing heavy eyeliner looked up and smiled at me. I smiled back. Although it was discreetly tucked under the plastic bag hanger, her math textbook jutted out below. She had been using the downtime for her nightly studies.

I looked around. The store itself was a hodgepodge of bric-a-brac. Postcards, thimbles, Christmas clearance—they were all jammed near the front of the store on three-tier shelves. The aisles, which numbered five or six, were lined with humidifiers, bandages, gift wrap, and food. The pharmacy, located at the back, was where the cold medicine, cough drops, supplements, and vapor rub were sold.

I meandered through the food aisles so as not to make a beeline for the pharmacy. There was a neat display of wines from a local winery. A wine made in South Dakota? This was something I had to taste to believe. I selected a bottle, surprised Winkle's qualified for the grocery store status to sell it. Then again, the store did have quite a few staples. Unable to pass up the buy-one-get-one-free sale, I picked up two chocolate bars as well. It was getting too close to dinner to be shopping in the snack aisle.

Now I moved on toward the pharmacy, where two young men stood behind the counter, one filling prescriptions and one running the cash register. I didn't know if they were the same men who had helped me with my melatonin questions. It had been too long ago to remember.

I approached the cashier. "Hello. My friend's doctor recently recommended a prescription, and I thought you might have some information on it. I don't think she has all the facts. I'm worried it might be dangerous."

"I think we can help you with that, can't we, Joe?"

Joe, the young man filling pill bottles, nodded without looking up.

"What's the name of the drug your *friend* was prescribed?" the cashier asked.

I ignored the implication. "Its name is amitriptyline. Do you know anything about it?"

The cashier looked to Joe, and Joe answered, "Sure, what do you want to know?"

I started with the basics. "What is it used for?"

"Mostly to treat depression," he said, shoving a bottle of pills into a white bag and zipping it closed. "Is your friend depressed?"

"No, not at all."

"Is she anxious?"

I thought about that one. "I don't think so. Why did you say 'mostly'?"

He hung up the bag and joined the cashier and me at the register. "What do you mean?"

"You said it's *mostly* used to treat depression."

"I meant there are other things it can be used for." He looked at the bottle of wine in my hand. "Like treating recovering alcoholics. It can help with sleep disturbances."

I blinked. Was this the man who had helped me with my melatonin? Now that he was closer, he did look familiar. "Oh, this information is for a friend."

The cashier snickered, but Joe had the good sense to elbow him in the side.

"For all the facts, your friend should get in touch with her doctor," said Joe.

My face growing warm and probably red, I excused myself as delicately as I could. What I really wanted to do was make a headlong dash out the store. "Well, thank you very much, gentlemen. You've been most helpful. I will tell her what I've learned."

I paid for my groceries at the front of the store and quickly walked to my car. Once I started my Mustang, I touched the Safari app on my phone. When Lenny and I had researched the drug, nothing came up about alcoholism, but the moment I added alcoholism to my search, the young man's words proved to be true. Indeed, the drug was used to treat withdrawal symptoms of alcoholism, including sleep disturbances.

Instead of going home, I went to my office. I needed to search the academic databases in light of this new information. The English Department was deserted, so I was able to go straight to my office without answering questions about what I was doing there after hours. A few faculty knew about my nighttime walks through campus when I couldn't sleep, though, so maybe I wouldn't need an excuse. Still, it was way too early for bed.

I logged on to our university's research databases. Munching on a candy bar as I scrolled through articles, I found out that amitriptyline could cause hallucinations in cases of over medication. In one case study, a nurse had given a patient the wrong dose, and the man had jumped out the window to his death.

I threw my candy wrapper in the trash bin and shut off my computer. According to this study, the person in the window whom Nick described to Amanda could have been a hallucination, a side effect of the drug. Nick was murdered at the visitation, and now I guessed by whom. I needed one more piece of evidence to confirm my theory.

Chapter Twenty-Five

The next day was Thursday, so I didn't have classes. I was thankful because I had to prepare for Student Fest, a daylong event that highlighted students' contributions to their academic fields. Their submissions were voluntary, and participants went to some trouble to create panels, find moderators, and conduct research for their projects. I myself was moderating for a group of literature students. The best and brightest scholars would receive awards for their efforts.

But before the event commenced, there was something I needed clarified, and fortunately I knew someone who taught earth science and might be able to help. Professor Owen Jorgenson taught in the Thompson-Carter Science Center, an orange brick building that housed several enormous lecture halls. As I stood inside, I took a few minutes to ready myself after what seemed like a long walk to campus this morning. While the sun was radiant against the cobalt-blue sky, the wind was blowing from the north, bringing with it a fresh arctic blast.

As I fiddled with my belt, tucking it back into the loops of my spring trench coat, students passed me en masse. It was fifteen minutes after the hour, and classes were being dismissed. Unlike most Monday, Wednesday, Friday classes, which were fifty minutes long, Tuesday/Thursday classes went seventy-five minutes. As I started walking against the wall of students, I saw Owen standing outside one of the lecture halls, talking with a student. One more was waiting in line. I stalled until he was finished with both, and by the time they left, the crowd had thinned considerably.

"Owen," I said as I approached him.

"Emmeline, it's been a while." Owen was an athletic man in his mid-forties. Just from looking at him, you could tell he exercised regularly.

"I know. I'm sorry. I meant to check in."

"That's okay. What's up? It's rare that I see an English prof over this way. What brings you here?"

"Is your office nearby?" I said, looking past him down the hall.

"It is, but I have another class in fifteen minutes. Do you want to come back?"

I shook my head. "That's all right. I've got to get over to Student Fest. This won't take long. I have a question about EROS Data Center, and I don't have time to research it before the event." I hoped he would think my question was academically related. In theory, it was. It related to a couple of academics on our campus. "What's the connection between EROS and the pipelines?"

Owen placed one of his hands in his suit-jacket pocket. "Well, EROS uses remote sensing to monitor land use. I assume they monitor the effects of pipelines on the environment."

No one associated with Molly Jaspers worked at EROS as far as I knew. "Okay. So EROS monitors the land surrounding the pipelines. How do the pipelines monitor themselves?"

Owen went into professor mode, speaking very patiently. "See, the pipelines place little sensors—they're like tiny computers—throughout the pipe. When a leak is detected, the manager can shut down that section of the pipe remotely so that the leak is contained to one area. It's smart in terms of stabilization. It ensures a leak doesn't pollute any more land than necessary. Someone told me the new pipeline, Midwest Connect, is planning to install technology that can detect lower oil flow rates, which will be a godsend. That was the trouble with the pipeline in North Dakota in 2013. No sensors were in place to detect the leak; a farmer ended up finding a six-inch spurt of oil in his field. Before they were able to fix it, over eight hundred thousand gallons of oil leaked into his wheat field."

I remembered hearing about it. This leak was one of the reasons the Native American tribes in our state were fighting the new pipeline so vigorously. They didn't want their sacred lands contaminated, and I didn't blame them. It wasn't worth the risk.

"So these new sensors, they could be a good thing for the business manufacturing them?"

"A good thing?" He laughed. The muscles in his neck showed. "They could be a *great* thing. Just by way of comparison, TransState plans on using sixteen thousand of them—if that line is ever completed." Although TransState passed through the Midwest, it did not run all the way through the Southern states as originally planned. After so many leaks and questions about the quality of pipes, the continuation of the line was on hold.

I was stunned. Of course the Midwest Connect pipeline would mean big business, just as Arnold Frasier had said. I thanked Owen for his time and ducked into an empty study alcove down the hall. It was time to talk to Officer Beamer and tell him my theory. I dug into my purse and found his card beneath a candy wrapper. On it, he had written his cellphone number, and I dialed it immediately. When he answered, I told him who I thought had killed Molly Jaspers and Nick Dramsdor. He agreed that it made sense but was waiting for a warrant on the prescription drug to confirm. He expected it to arrive any minute.

I told him to meet me at Student Fest as soon as he got the results. An award ceremony would take place at noon at the Student Center, highlighting the best submissions. The award winners would be printed in our campus newspaper as well as our annual student magazine. Students and finalists would be there as well as the professors sponsoring the projects and panels.

After I ended the call, I started off in the direction of the library. I was moderating a panel titled "Romance, Mystery, and Intrigue: The Genre Novel and Female Empowerment." Four of my literature students, three females and one male, had created the panel after our discussion of the domination of female writers in the cozy and romance genres. Despite their domination, however, critics still had plenty to say about women's fiction. Even readers, some quite famous, felt guilty for reading and enjoying these genres. It was the group's purpose to explore and dispel the myths surrounding the genres that led to guilt and shame, two emotions common to women reading books, rearing children, or ruling the workplace. I couldn't wait to hear them present.

As I entered the Herbert Hoover Library, a musty building with three book-laden floors, I noted the easel marked with the day's schedule. My students' panel would be presenting on the second floor. I walked up the metal staircase and turned left. It was twenty minutes before the presentation, and a student was at the table. A few attendees were scattered in the twenty-odd chairs set up for the presentation. One of them was Lenny, looking dapper in a camel jacket and jeans. When he saw me, he waved, and I motioned that I had something to tell him.

"Lenny! I'm so glad you're here," I said.

A few footsteps away, he said, "I couldn't miss it when I saw the title. What did you do? Bribe them into reading your research?"

I held up my hand. "I promise you, Lenny, they came to this idea all on their own when we were discussing *Rebecca* last month."

He raised one eyebrow. "*Rebecca,* by Daphne du Maurier? What did Giles think of that selection?"

"Giles doesn't question my selections. He thinks anything that will spur me on to finish my book is a good thing. And you know romance has been a creative outlet for lots of women writers, so it's not that much of a stretch. Besides, I bet he's read *Rebecca* more than once. You should have heard how engaged he was when we discussed it." I grabbed his hand. "I have to tell you something, though. Come on. I only have a minute."

I walked into the heart of the second-floor collection, where we were surrounded by towering bookcases. I could tell the aisle was rarely visited by the amount of dust particles wafting up from the shelves as we proceeded as far in as possible.

"It must be a hell of a tidbit," Lenny said behind me.

Satisfied that we would not be overheard, I turned to face him. "It's about Molly and Nick. I think I know who murdered them."

"Miss Scarlet in the library with a," he took out one of the dusty tomes, "a hefty book?"

"I'm serious, Lenny."

He put back the anthology. "Sorry. I'm listening."

I proceeded to tell him my theory and my plan for outing the murderer. As I relayed the details, my voice grew more animated. Saying it out loud, I thought it made perfect sense. I was waiting for Lenny to agree when he asked if I could prove it.

"Well, not court-of-law prove it, but I would say the evidence is pretty convincing. Wouldn't you? Besides, Beamer will be there. He will have confirmation."

"I would agree," he said, "but then again, I'm not exactly an unbiased observer." He relaxed against the bookshelf. "In fact, you had me when your lips started to do that thing they do when you're excited."

My hand moved to my mouth. "Are they doing something?" Claudia Swift had once said something about my lips twitching when I was excited.

"It's not unbecoming, Prather. In fact—how would one of your romance novels put it?—it's rather… fetching."

My heart was beating fast, and I didn't know anymore if it was the murders or Lenny that had my pulse racing. As he took a step closer, I knew it was Lenny.

His lips barely grazed my own, and I can't remember if I even closed my eyes. I only remember the moment being electric and unlike anything I had ever experienced. When he stepped back, I wondered if I had imagined it. But the tingle on my lips told me it was real.

"I guess I couldn't wait until after," he said.

"That's so like you."

We lingered a moment longer, paralyzed by our newfound feelings. Then I nodded in the direction of the presentations. "I'd better get back."

We returned to the program area, where an audience was now seated in five perfect rows, but I couldn't stop thinking about Lenny. Even as the first student started to present her essay, my mind drifted back to that moment. It was hardly anything, a brief passing of the lips, and yet it meant a great deal. It meant something was happening between us, something I couldn't define and didn't want to. It felt so right, so natural, as if everything before had been leading up to that moment. As I pondered the kiss itself, that fleeting interlude, a thought occurred to me, a radical thought that had nothing to do with Lenny and me. I sat up straighter in the chair, and my student at the podium turned at the noise.

I smiled. I knew exactly how Molly had come into contact with the mysterious peanut, and I was going to prove it.

Chapter Twenty-Six

After the presentations, I was detained by questions from the audience and students, and by the time I finished, the area was clear. Lenny had gone ahead to secure a spot at the reception, and while I knew my seat was saved because I was presenting an award, I rushed through the Tech Lab, which linked the library to the Student Center. I hoped to have a chance to talk to Officer Beamer, but the man was nowhere in sight as I hustled in the direction of the banquet halls. The dividers had been taken down to reveal one large room and in it at least a hundred people. Still, I couldn't find Beamer in the sea of faces. The professors presenting awards to students sat at a skirted table near the microphone. I noticed Bennett Jaspers at the table and was puzzled to see him seated next to Dr. Judith Spade and Arnold Frasier. Then I remembered: he was giving one of Molly's students an award in Molly's place. I thought it a little strange that someone else from the History Department couldn't bestow the award, but maybe Bennett had asked to do it in order to honor Molly. There was one empty seat, mine, and I moved toward it quickly. It was the farthest away from the podium, so I assumed I would be presenting last. I was giving an award to a student from Advanced Composition who had demonstrated extraordinary commitment to research in a mere 200-level course.

As I took my seat, I gazed out at the crowd and recognized several students from classes and from the trip to Paris. Amanda and Kat, Olivia and Meg, Aaron and Jace—all the old ghosts from the failed excursion were assembled here. Lenny sat next to André and Giles and a few other English professors, including Thomas Cook, his wife Lydia, and Jane Lemort.

I refocused on the crowd. Still no Officer Beamer. I was confident that he would attend, though; he wasn't a man to go back on his word. Judith Spade stepped up to the microphone and tapped on it, signaling the ceremony was about to begin, and I turned my attention to her. I admired Judith's easy, direct way. She didn't have to assert her authority; it was just there. She explained that she herself had read each of the conference proposals and the papers receiving awards. And while all the students who submitted work to Student Fest deserved praise for going beyond the classroom to exchange ideas with the larger academic community, the students we were recognizing this afternoon showed extraordinary merit. Then she introduced her own student, none other than Olivia Christenson's friend, Meg. After reading a snippet from the work, Judith summoned Meg to the podium, and the crowd clapped politely. Judith shook Meg's hand and posed for a picture for the campus newsletter, *Campus Views*.

Arnold Frasier was next to hand out an award, but I didn't know the student. Arnold waxed poetic for at least ten minutes about a painting that, by the time he finished, I was sure should be displayed in the Louvre. The student accepted the award and took the perfunctory picture.

Bennett was up next, and I leaned in curiously to hear what he would say.

"I'm sure most of you are surprised to see me here. My wife, Molly Jaspers, should be standing in the spot where I am now, but as you know, she passed away two weeks ago on a trip she was looking forward to a good deal. She died doing what she loved, and for that, we can be thankful.

"When the History Department told me one of her favorite students would be receiving an award, I knew she would want me to be here, to tell Amanda Walters how much she had come to mean to her over the last few years." He nodded in Amanda's direction; Amanda looked as if she were going to cry. "She wasn't one of those teachers who think of students as inferior. She considered them equals, and that really pushed students like Amanda to give it their all." He smiled at Amanda and the audience.

"I wish I could say something prophetic about Amanda's work, but we don't travel in the same worlds, I'm afraid. As a businessman, I can tell you that I know talent when I see it, and I see it in Amanda Walters. She's an incredibly gifted girl who has a terrific future ahead of her." The crowd applauded as Amanda, eyes brimming with tears, walked up the stairs to the makeshift stage to receive the award.

After they returned to their seats, it was my turn, and I reached the microphone in a few steps. As I scanned the crowd one last time, I noticed movement in the doorway. It was Officer Beamer with a white envelope in his hand. He gestured with it and nodded, and I knew my theory had been correct.

"First of all, I want to thank Bennett Jaspers for that moving speech," I began. The audience clapped. "Molly would be proud of us… or would she?" The clapping trailed off to one or two claps, and several people in the audience looked at each other. Giles glanced at Lenny for an explanation, but Lenny just stretched out his legs.

I lowered the microphone to accommodate my height. I really wished I had worn those matching red heels. Besides adding inches, they would have gone perfectly with my crimson shirt. "I raise the question because despite the outward display of grief for our dearly departed colleague, her death was no accident. It was murder, and how could she really be proud of any of us when we've allowed an assumption to go unchallenged?"

The room exploded in murmurs, and Officer Beamer approached the front of the stage and crossed his arms in a formal stance. "Please let the professor continue." All murmuring ceased with what was clearly a direct order.

"Thank you, Officer Beamer," I said with a nod of my head. "You see, I was with Molly Jaspers on our ill-fated Paris trip, and from the moment the headcount was revealed as thirteen, I worried about bad luck."

Judith Spade crossed her arms. Obviously, she was not superstitious.

"It seemed an unlucky break that Molly would die from anaphylactic shock when everyone on the plane knew she was deathly allergic to peanuts," I continued, "but it was no unlucky break. It was a carefully crafted murder."

I gestured to André Duman. "Suspicion was immediately cast upon my good friend and colleague, Professor Duman, because he had argued with Molly Jaspers minutes before her death. I knew that my friend and your professor couldn't have killed Molly over a difference of opinion, though." André nodded, and I continued, "When Nick Dramsdor died suddenly after Molly's visitation and André was not in attendance, I knew beyond a shadow of a doubt he hadn't killed Molly. I was certain that the same person who poisoned Molly Jaspers also killed Nick Dramsdor."

Amanda, who was seated in the front row in her straight skirt, let out a small cry. It was an involuntary reaction, one that students of her pedigree didn't make. I had mixed feelings about continuing, but the truth had to be revealed to everyone in the room. And nothing was valued at the university more than truth. We were individuals who had dedicated our lives to it, revered it, and did our best to instill it in the young minds we taught. Amanda would understand why I had to continue.

"So, who had the motive and means to kill both of these talented individuals?" I asked. "More people than you think. Eleven, aside from the victims, participated in our trip abroad, and it made sense to start with those individuals. Now, we all know there has been a time or two when you have wanted to murder your professor." I gestured to the students. This got a few laughs. "But there was only one student who really bore a grudge against Molly Jaspers, and that student is dead. Skylar Erickson committed suicide not long after being told by Professor Jaspers that he was not cut out for the field of history. The fact that his red-haired mother was at the airport and on the plane made me wonder if she didn't seek revenge on Molly for her cruel words. But it turned out that this red-haired woman was a red herring." I nodded at Kat, who sat behind Amanda. "For while she *was* on the plane, her plans to visit her sister in Paris were confirmed by the Minneapolis Police, and she was nowhere to be seen the night of Nick's death. So I turned to the students who were present, and that included Amanda, Kat, Meg, and Olivia."

The girls tensed in their seats. "Olivia, you were the obvious choice because Professor Jaspers gave you a grade that subsequently ended your stay in the sorority on Landon Avenue."

"I didn't have anything to do with her death!" Olivia protested. The opposite of Amanda, Olivia was not a student who kept her opinions to herself. "I got a lot of bad grades that semester. I was going through a horrible breakup."

Glad she had admitted to her low grade point average herself, which I was not at liberty to expose, I continued, "I didn't say you killed her; I said you were the obvious choice.

"That left Amanda and Kat, who were both close to the professors and who had only good things to say about them. Amanda, you alone talked to Nick before his death, and for some time, this was a concern, especially with your revelation about a person in the window whom the police could not identify." Amanda raised her hand in protest, but I motioned for her to put it back down.

"And Kat, while you were not as close to these two individuals as Amanda was, you were working on a story that seemed to be writing itself as each event unfolded. We all know creative writers often use real-life incidents to create fiction, but would they jeopardize someone's safety for the sake of a story?"

Kat's eyes widened in anticipation.

"I didn't think so. So that left the adults on the trip, the four of us on this stage." I looked at the three people to my right, and so did everybody else. "Arnold, you were at odds with Molly, and that was immediately apparent on the bus. You were angry that you could no longer count on her support of the arts. Everyone overheard your argument and wondered if your defensiveness might be blamed on resentment. She had even lashed out at you in writing when you made a comment in support of the pipeline. Her opposition to your article was a blow to your authority and perhaps your ego."

Arnold smoothed the sides of his head with his hands. "But you said the same person who killed Molly killed Nick, and I was not even at the visitation." Bennett gave him a stern glance, and Arnold added, "Sorry."

I leaned an elbow on the podium. "That's right. You were not at the visitation, and I was convinced the two deaths were connected, not coincidental. Nick began to act erratically before he even left the funeral parlor, so I knew the poisoning occurred there."

At the word *poisoning*, I turned to Officer Beamer, and he nodded, confirming what we both had guessed.

"So that leaves the rest of us. Judith, you're probably the smartest among us," I said, trying to smooth over what I was about to say with some flattery. "It would have been easy for you to orchestrate these murders, especially with your knowledge of the human body. And you and Molly were vying for the same job."

Bennett nodded in agreement.

Judith was as calm as I'd ever seen her. In fact, she seemed to be enjoying herself. "And what reason did I have for murdering Nick?"

"Nick was adamant that Molly's vision be realized, especially her qualifications for tenure requirements. Perhaps this worried you, especially with Bennett Jaspers' wealth and power behind it. You know how the university thrives on donations and goodwill. It could have been a force to reckon with if Bennett tied the money to modifications you didn't agree with."

"It's a wonderful story, Emmeline, but it's simply not true." She looked out at the crowd, still unperturbed. "I don't know what else I can say to clear myself."

"You don't have to say anything because I know you didn't kill Molly, and now I will prove it. There was one thing that bothered me from the beginning, and that was Bennett Jaspers' declaration that his wife was allergic to peanuts. Mr. Jaspers, you travel… a lot. You travel enough to know the airline that rules the Midwest routes serves peanuts on every flight."

He nodded. "Exactly. That's why I contacted them about the snack selection. They assured me it would be a peanut-free flight."

"Yes, you said that, and at first, I believed you. But on the ride home from Minneapolis, André said something that I hadn't considered: he bought the tickets—all of them. He alone had the reservation number and gave us the tickets at the airport."

The gray streak in Bennett's hair shone like steel as he turned his head toward me. "Oh sure, but I had the date and time. That's all I needed to contact the airline about my concerns. And I did. Like you said, I fly all the time."

"If that were true, why *wasn't* the flight peanut-free?" I continued before he could answer, "The airlines are happy to accommodate allergy requests and take them quite seriously. They even have rows of seats that are nut-free zones. So how did Molly come into contact with a peanut? This was what baffled the police in Minneapolis and prevented them from charging anyone, for while they confirmed traces of peanuts in her saliva, they couldn't confirm that they were in her snack or even near her. Although some of us ordered the peanuts, none of us got close enough to contaminate her—except you, a fact I remembered only an hour ago." I glanced at Lenny and continued, "You embraced Molly shortly after the flight took off. The kiss was spontaneous, romantic… and lethal. You yourself ate peanuts because you knew the allergen would stay in your saliva. Research suggests that not even brushing your teeth gets rid of the allergen, and you were aware of this because you knew Molly's allergy best."

"That's preposterous," Bennett said. He was trying to remain calm but couldn't completely conceal the ugliness in his tone. "I was the one who tried to save Molly. I injected her with the EpiPen."

"Yes, you did," I said. "But it was well past the time it would have needed to be administered to prevent a reaction severe enough to cause her death. That's why it didn't work. The peanuts had had plenty of time to get into her system."

He stood up from his chair. He looked much taller than I remembered. "I don't know why I bothered coming today."

Officer Beamer immediately moved to Bennett's side of the table to prevent him from leaving. There were four other officers stationed at the doors, and they readied themselves for Beamer's orders.

Bennett looked at me and then at Officer Beamer. "You can't tell me that you're taking a harebrained theory concocted by this… this crazy English teacher seriously?"

"Dead seriously," Officer Beamer said, holding up the white envelope in his hand.

I hid my smile. Officer Beamer had a humorous side I hadn't seen before, although it was true I didn't know him well. "Of course he is," I said, "because what he has there in his hand is evidence of your prescription drug amitriptyline, which is the drug that made Nick Dramsdor hallucinate and eventually kill himself in a fit of paranoia."

Bennett Jaspers sat back down in his chair, the weight of his large shoulders buckling him. The gray streak on the top of his head glowed white with the fluorescent lights bearing down on it.

"Amitriptyline is an antidepressant, and though this threw me off at first—you didn't seem depressed—I soon realized it is not only prescribed for depression, it is also prescribed to recovering alcoholics. You never ordered a drink at the French restaurant and your hands often shook—enough evidence to suggest this could be your prescription. So I asked myself how you went about poisoning Nick at the visitation, and it didn't take long to uncover your method.

"Nick's coffee was cold, and as a family member, you would have been the first to arrive at the visitation to ensure everything was arranged according to your wishes before allowing the public to enter. This gave you the means to poison Nick's coffee before you yourself handed it to him. It also accounts for the temperature and taste of the brew, into which you had dissolved several amitriptyline pills. You figured an overdose of the drug would kill him, and it might have, had he not killed himself in a fit of paranoia. That was a bonus, which made you so confident you didn't hesitate to come here today and play the grieving widower. Pathetic."

A noise came from the crowd, and I looked over at Kat. She was whispering something to Amanda. When she saw me looking at her, she said, "But why, Professor? What was the motive? It seemed like he loved his wife a lot."

I nodded. "It *seemed* that way, didn't it? But the truth was, Bennett Jaspers was sick of funding his wife's expeditions with other men. He was willing to tolerate it, though, until her actions were about to affect his bottom line. Then he decided to do what any good businessman of the diabolical variety would do: kill her midflight to collect on what insurance companies call *double indemnity*. The beneficiary receives twice the amount of the policy—double when the death is deemed an accident. Of course this looked like a tragic accident to everyone, even me. Until I discovered that Bennett's company was the one contracted with the Midwest Connect pipeline to make the sensors for the entire line. Her nixing of the pipeline, a stance many of us applauded, would have meant dramatic losses for his company and a direct bite out of the hand that fed her pet projects. Nick guessed at the company's involvement; I heard as much on the bus ride home. That's why he was adamant about setting up Molly's fund immediately after the visitation. In effect, he was calling Bennett's bluff, and now so are we."

All eyes were on Bennett, and he looked from me to Officer Beamer to the assembly. He circled the room with the motion of his hand. "Only here could something like this happen. If we were in a place of business," he pursed his lips and ground out, "never. It would never happen. You wouldn't dare to call me a murderer to my face in front of my employees. I'm the president of a company, a CEO. But you…." Here he looked directly at me. "That means nothing to you. To any of you. It's like you live in another world."

Officer Beamer winked at me. "They get that a lot."

I smiled, and Beamer approached Bennett with his handcuffs. The officers stationed at the door moved forward.

"I want a lawyer," said Bennett.

Epilogue

As Kat finished reading the last words of her story Friday morning, several students clapped, even though we never did that in class. But I didn't say anything to reprimand them. I'd enjoyed Kat's mystery, and if I weren't her professor, I would have applauded too. As it was, I didn't want to show unfair preference for her writing. Students could become incensed when they felt one piece was preferred over another, and the truth was, I had enjoyed all their stories this semester. They had opened up a brand-new chapter in my career.

"I read that nobody believes in heroes anymore, least of all women," said Claire. Her voice was tinged with irritation. "That's why books like *Gone Girl* are such big hits. Authors just kill people; they don't have some man with a gun come in at the end and save the day."

One of the girls sitting next to Kat said, "But this was a woman."

Another said, "And she didn't have a gun."

"Professor Prather, what do you think?" asked Kat. Her hazel eyes were gray and searching for reassurance.

I came out from behind the podium and sat down in one

of the chairs facing the students. "I've read the article in the *Atlantic*, too, Claire, and I understand why those books are popular."

And I did. Violence begets violence, and the world could be a cruel place, especially to women. Writers needed to express the anger that had been suppressed for so long, had been told wasn't natural, wasn't *feminine*. And maybe heroes *were* myths, throwbacks to fairytales and fables, like Olivia said. Or maybe they were as real as you and me. Who was I to say?

What I did say was, "There's room for all types of writing, books with heroes and books without. If Kat's truth includes a well-informed heroine and a hunch, then so be it. Her truth is to reassert order amid the chaos, and we can't begrudge her that."

The class was content with this answer.

"So what are you going to call it?" Jason asked Kat.

A couple of students called out suggestions.

Her eyes sparkled green. "I already have a title. I'm going to call it 'Thirteen for Murder.' "

I clapped. She really did have a future in mystery writing.

Julie Prairie Photography

MARY ANGELA IS the author of the Professor Prather Mystery series. She is also a teacher and has taught English and humanities at the University of South Dakota and the University of Sioux Falls. An active member of Sisters in Crime and Mystery Writers of America, she enjoys reading, traveling, and spending time with her family.

For more information about Mary or the series, go to www.MaryAngelaBooks.com.

From Mary Angela and Camel Press

Thank you for reading *Passport to Murder.* We are so grateful for you, our readers. If you enjoyed this book, there are some steps you can take that could help contribute to its success and the success of this series.

- Post a review on Amazon, BN.com, and/or GoodReads.
- Check out www.maryangelabooks.com and send Mary a comment or ask to be put on her mailing list.
- Spread the word on social media, especially Facebook, Twitter, and Pinterest.
- "Like" maryangelabooks and camelpressbooks on Facebook.
- Follow Mary (@maryangelabooks) and Camel Press (@camelpressbooks) on Twitter.
- Ask for Mary's books at your local library or request them on their online portal.

Good books and authors from small presses are often overlooked. Your comments and reviews can make an enormous difference.

When one of Professor Emmeline Prather's students dies while working on the fall musical, Em has reason to suspect foul play. She teams up with fellow English professor Lenny Jenkins to comb the campus and vicinity for clues, a venture that puts their reputations, their jobs, and even their lives at risk.

An Excerpt from

An Act of Murder

Prologue

DEATH TEACHES US humility. This is what I thought as I walked into the single-road graveyard, becoming more aware with each step the life it took to walk and talk and breathe. It was no easy task, to stay alive, and yet the majority of us managed to do so, and often into old age. But here was an exception, *a tragedy*, and I wondered at its meaning while I traversed the uneven ground. As an English professor, I would have told my students that tragedies were meant to teach us as much about good as evil. I tried to apply that philosophy now and failed.

The good was in life, the walking down this brown path surrounded by sturdy trees. I couldn't help but feel this way as my boots crunched the dead leaves that littered the dirt lane. Had he been alive, my student would have enjoyed this walk. He would have found beauty in its peace and remoteness. I smiled. He might even have found poetry.

The gravestone was small and freshly placed, and as I stood at the marker, a terrific wind came up in the trees. The branches swayed to and fro, making me dizzy with the sheer force of their movement. The wind continued to bend through the branches and bushes until it found me, reassuring like a childhood prayer. I knelt down, my slim book of verse in hand, and read the poem he had chosen for my class. It had always been one of my favorites.

Chapter 1

It was fall at the university, and the campus teemed with life—booksellers stocking tightly bound textbooks, professors copying last-minute syllabi, and freshmen hustling into the dorms with cheaply purchased furniture. The chokecherries and honeysuckle flourished, too, and soon I would watch the orange and red leaves fall from the maple trees to the trampled grass of this little-known Midwestern campus. With the opening of a window, gone were the laws of Newton and *Poetics* of Aristotle. Replacing them were the sights and sounds of earthy prairie life, never far beyond the classroom in this small college town.

Copper Bluff, situated in the eastern corner of South Dakota, gave way to a river and lush bottomland. Most of the town was surrounded by fields of soybean, alfalfa, and corn, though the neighboring state had the monopoly on corn. Or so I'd been told. With more moderate weather, they had nothing to do but spread the seeds and watch them grow, an old farmer once said. He didn't have to convince me. I couldn't get anything to grow in my garden except a rhubarb plant, which I had nothing to do with. Yet I never grew tired of trying, and this perseverance was as much a part of this place as anything else. Its spirit, its *sine qua non.*

My house was surrounded by shade, and although I knew little about growing things, I imagined sunshine was rather important to sustainable growth. The trees on Oxford Street were so large that only stray rays of sunlight penetrated the leafy foliage that formed a makeshift canopy over the road. Hostas grew copiously around the front rail of my porch, relishing the shade of the towering pine trees dividing my lot from my neighbor's. A nice-sized bungalow, my house was a block from the campus and a beautiful shade of yellow. I took pride in the fact that I was able to purchase a house and didn't have to rent one of the split-up places at the end of the block. I had lived in plenty of those as a student. Still, my 1917 home had required a good deal of hard work when I moved in a year ago. I had pruned bushes, painted rooms, and torn out carpet, all before giving my first lecture, but it was worth it. The location allowed me to walk to and from campus, a necessity since my only mode of transportation was a red '69 Mustang convertible, a car I'd bought cheap from an uncle who owned a body shop. When my dad scoffed at its impracticality, his brother simply responded with, "She hails from Detroit. Her car oughta have character." My dad relented more easily than I thought he would, probably because the car was inexpensive, but I still hoped to restore it when time and money permitted.